# THE FATALISTS

# THE FATALISTS

*A Novel*

## PATRICK BLENNERHASSETT

NON Canada

*Publisher's note: This book is a work of fiction. Names, characters, places and
incidents are either the product of the author's imagination or are used
fictitiously, and any resemblance to actual persons living or dead
is entirely coincidental.*

**Library and Archives Canada Cataloguing in Publication**

Blennerhassett, Patrick, 1982–, author
The fatalists / Patrick Blennerhassett.

ISBN 978-1-988098-20-3 (paperback)

I. Title.

PS8603.L46F38 2016          C813'.6          C2016-905031-9

Printed and bound in Canada on 100% recycled paper.

**Now Or Never Publishing**
#313, 1255 Seymour Street
Vancouver, British Columbia
Canada V6B 0H1

**nonpublishing.com**
*Fighting Words.*

We gratefully acknowledge the support of the Canada Council for the Arts
and the British Columbia Arts Council for our publishing program.

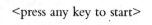
&lt;press any key to start&gt;

Quick.
Someone in your family will die.
Choose.
Five seconds.
No explanation.
One
Two
Three
    Four . . .

Stop.

I am about to drown.

Inside a mid-sized, silver, four-door sedan.

Twenty feet underwater, the car sinks like a penny in a wishing well. Weight of the vehicle falls with the river on a downstream curve. Pressure pulsing against glass, forcing it to ache and moan. Engine floods, metallic compartments fill with freshwater. We tilt, coins empty out of the ashtray; currency raining onto the seats and windows.

Touch down gently on the bottom, Mars Rover hovering to the surface. The internal contents shift downwards, settle like dust.

Wind knocked out of me. I squirm in pain.

Ears about to burst.

Lungs wrapped in stress.

Each breath labours out like a dying animal.

Liz knocked unconscious in the backseat. My leg, wrapped in a snake of a seatbelt, crushed against the passenger door. Bouquet of steel, aluminum and carbon fiber shards chomp through the bones and cartilage of my leg as I try to free myself.

The sedan lies on the riverbed like it's been parked. Murky, dusty brown outside.

Inside a universe of water.

We're going to *fucking* die.

I scream to my sister.

"Elizabeth!"

Slumped against the seat, blonde hair strewn across the interior.

Floor squishes as it fills with water. Pick my foot up like I'm scared to get wet. It fills to the seats, to the knees.

I'm going to drown to death.

I imagine what it will feel like to have my lungs burst.

Water fills the dashboard, flows out of the air conditioning vents. Seeps in through the windows.

Tears stream down.

Heart thumps 150 beats per minute. Lungs taking in over three gallons of oxygen—six times in nitrogen, every three seconds.

Dying to live.

Up to my chest. Grimy brown liquid swims through the open wound in my leg, stains the water plush red. I splash my hands around, trying to regain my hold against the dashboard and the window.

"*Fuck!*"

Half scream, half growl—all frustration.

Death has come for me, and I don't even have a weapon. Not how I wanted to go.

Not how I was supposed to go.

Panic.

Utter and complete panic.

Angry beehive of thoughts.

After everything that's happened in the past five days, this is how it ends?

Carbon dioxide poisoning my heart, forcing it to stop beating. Too much water, not enough oxygen, that's all it took.

I spit out what tastes like mud and motor oil and take in what I think is my last gasp of air ever.

The average person can hold their breath underwater for about a minute. I give myself two tops.

A figure appears outside the driver's side.

Swims down.

Ears fill up, world goes mute.

Vision blurs—corneas cease to focus.

Metal taps against the window trying to break it . . .

But I can't be sure if it's the front or the back.

yeah . . . almost done editing the seventh draft. meet you in the lunch room in 15 . . .

—*Sent from my BlackBerry—Virgin Mobile Network (June 10th, 2016)*
Tristan Schultz, Public Relations Officer, B.A.
DEPARTMENT OF PUBLIC ENGAGEMENT, MEDIA RELATIONS
PFIZER WEST COAST HEADQUARTERS (SEATTLE, WASHINGTON)

Pfizer is inspired by a single goal: Your health. Since 1848, Pfizer has been dedicated to developing innovative medications to prevent and treat diseases. But we believe to be truly healthy, it takes more than medication. That's why Pfizer is also committed to promoting the many small things we can do to stay healthy.

CONFIDENTIALITY NOTICE: This e-mail and any attachments are confidential and protected by legal privilege. If you are not the intended recipient, be aware that any disclosure, distribution copying, or use of this e-mail or any attachment is prohibited. If you have received this e-mail in error, please notify Pfizer immediately by replying to this e-mail and delete this message from your system. Fuck you, and have a nice day.

. . .

Six-by-seven foot cubicle. Tie as noose. Feet nailed to the floor. Eyes on the baby blue oval logo branded into everything. Crafting, track changing another template press release about potentially raised cholesterol levels due to a new brand of anti-depressants. Concentration: gone. Releasing on a Friday after-noon in hopes of washing the story into the weekend news cycle, and the Mariners' home stand with the Yankees: check.

Check Facebook, nothing. Twitter, nothing. Instagram, noth-ing. Google News, today's top stories according to unique visitors:

Obama Urges Congress to Pass Gun Bill; ISIS claims responsibility for Rome blast; Telecommunications Satellites Cause Information Glitches; Arctic Sea Ice Hits Record Low; Solar Flares Light up Night Skies; Lindsay Lohan Back in Jail, Again.

Swivel in my seat; stare out the window at the perfectly concave Bank of America tower. Float off into an endless stream of debilitating technobabble.

Wait.

Stop.

*Pause.*

Forced exhale. Happy place. Happy places. Back in time. Gorgeous girlfriend walks around our apartment on a Sunday morning in her underwear. Eating Froot Loops, lounging in the bed, hiding in the sheets. Long weekend trips to the Oregon coast. Being in love. Loving someone. Before it got complicated.

Give me air, an oasis, and a fifteen-year time out.

Send my entire life into the junk mail folder, so I have an excuse for deleting it. Run the Disk Defragmenter over my mind.

Back to my computer.

Slithering wires crawl into my mouth—the Ethernet, broadband, high speed, USB cords, telephone lines, power network cables, headphone jacks, modem adaptors. Barreling down the throat, into the stomach, into the pit of my existence. Attaching me, connecting me, to everything, regardless of consent.

Please cut/copy me out of this equation. Delete. Escape. Backspace. Power off.

Press release, done. Document, saved as. Emailed, CC'd and BCC'd to death.

I rub the palm of my hand across my face like a brushstroke erasing a mistake. Edit/Undo. Lean back in my uncomfortably ergonomic chair; and all I hear are fingers dancing across keyboards like clattering teeth. Chitter-chatter on the phone. A fax machine pukes out documents. Thousands of monkeys fight over one typewriter.

Wait . . . we still have a fax machine?

Org charts, templates, action items, inter-office etiquette, stakeholder relationships, corporate rhetoric and all-hands meetings. Double-blind studies, currency exchange forms, timesheet coding, operational items, paper jams, replace toner, check tray three. Resist urge to *Office Space* the printer.

Fifty milligrams, twice a day. May cause vomiting, drowsiness, dry mouth, fatigue, loss of wonder, sense of accomplishment, and personal identity. Keep out of reach of children, take with food, do not consume alcohol, operate heavy machinery, or ask questions outside the strategic plan for the current fiscal quarter.

If I don't respond to this email in thirty minutes, avenge my death.

Coffee breaks, beige coloured lunchrooms, water coolers, food trays. The same vending machines staring at me every morning as I try to wake up with pre-medicated 5-Hour ENERGY Shot heart attacks.

Red Bull night tremors.

Shaking like a fleshy tambourine.

</>

*The air so thick you could cut it with a knife.*

*Brianne sits on the couch, exhausted. I'm exhausted, too. Lean my body against the kitchen counter. It's well past midnight and we both have to work tomorrow. My throat sore from arguing.*

*Her curly blonde hair falls forward, hiding her face.*

*Two hours into a yelling match with someone I love. And it's going nowhere. I'm losing at life. Failing at living.*

*We had dinner earlier with Mike and Miranda at Wild Ginger. They have a one-year-old. Had to hire a babysitter to come out on a Thursday night. Moved out of Seattle and now Mike commutes an hour and a half to work every day. Miranda's on maternity leave dealing with postpartum depression; it's cut their income and made them home poor.*

*They look so tired. Exhausted. By the time the dessert menu came, Miranda was ready to pass out.*

*Two years ago, they'd just gotten engaged, were living in the same Capitol Hill area as us. We used to go out all the time on double dates. To the movies, out to clubs, drinking and dancing, catching shows at Benaroya Hall. We'd been on trips with them to Vegas, New York; the* ladies shopped and the guys went to football games and gambled. Awesome times, some of the best of my life.

Then they had to start planning their wedding. Miranda got stressed. Mike started coming over, wanting to get away from her, go for drinks with just me. It pissed her off even more. They got married and everyone was happy again, for a night. She got pregnant. Mike wanted a boy. They had a girl.

I asked him if he'd ever actually wanted to get married and have kids. He said he wasn't sure, but he was sure Miranda did, and he loved her.

I look at Brianne. Freckles dot her shoulders like constellations. Soft blue eyes. My South Carolina belle. I love everything about her.

Except this.

And 'this' is killing us.

"Seriously, were you at the same dinner I was?" I ask.

Looks at me.

"Yes, Tristan." My name heavy on her lips. "I was there."

Rolls her vowels out when she's frustrated, her Southern drawl thick and slow. My west coast ramblings much more fast-paced as they leave my tongue.

"Honestly, like seriously, honestly tell me you think they're happy."

She stands back up.

"Yes, they're tired, but they're starting a family. It's never easy when you start a family."

"When does it get easy?"

"It's not supposed to be easy."

"Why can't we just do easy?"

She takes a deep breath. I see the stress in her eyes, around the pupils.

"Just because you didn't have the same type of family I did . . ."

I cut her off.

"Don't go there. Why do you always go there?"

Her family in Greenville. Four siblings, half of them already two kids deep. Her parents, grandparents. Everyone living in the same town they grew up in. Every holiday a chance to go home and spend time with countless relatives—endless backyard barbecues and family reunions. A world away from my upbringing. Parallel opposites, at competing ends of a historical spectrum.

Tristan, I'm just saying: you didn't have that type of family. One where everyone loves everyone else, where they look after each other."

"What, are you saying my family doesn't love me? That I'm not going to look after you or something?"

"No, it's just that we've been dating for well over two years now, and I haven't even met your dad! I've only met your sister once, for dinner. We live together!"

Rub my forehead in displeasure.

"My family is my family."

"That's what I'm saying. You don't know what it's like to have family close to you."

Glare at her; she's attacking my upbringing now.

"I had a fucking family. Don't for a second think you know what I went through; I know what it fucking feels like to have a fucking family."

She knows I'm pissed because I'm swearing. She starts to speak, but I beat her to it.

"Look, I'm stuck at Pfizer. I mean, the only reason I got a job there out of school was dumb luck. I never asked for this career, I never chose this career. I took the job because I needed a job, that's what I was supposed to do after graduation. What if I want to do something else in a few years? Travel, change careers, get my Master's? How can I do that with a kid and a mortgage? We won't have the money. I'll be stuck at Pfizer updating their fucking Twitter account for the next ten years until all the baby boomers in management croak and they wheel them out in caskets."

Brianne slumps down onto the couch, head in her hands. Her shoulders droop.

"I think we want different things then. I can't convince you to do something you don't want to do. Maybe we don't love each other as much as I thought we did."

"Don't play that card with me, Bri. You know I love you. I've loved you from the moment I saw you in Chicago. I just don't want to be a fucking slave. I'm only now starting to make good money; the economy is only now starting to normalize. You said you want to do your Master's? You said you wanted to backpack through Europe. Why don't we do those things? If we both get raises next year, we could move to a high-rise on Pike with a huge deck. I mean, we'll be pulling in great money in a couple years. And we're going to waste that on a kid and a huge wedding?

*Why not Spain? Why not blow that money on a month in Spain sitting on beaches? I mean, fuck."*

*Brianne inhales again.*

*She stands, looking at me. Looking through me.*

*"I'm going to bed," she says.*

*And I'm sleeping on the futon, again.*

*She walks into our bedroom and closes the door.*

*I turn and head for the futon.*

*Stop and stare at it.*

*This fucking futon.*

*God, I hate this motherfucking futon.*

*"Fuck!"*

*The bedroom door opens.*

*Brianne stands in front of me, tears in her eyes.*

*"I'll move my stuff out this weekend."*

*My heart sinks. Drowns.*

*I'm hurt. So I do the only thing I know.*

*Retaliate. Point my finger accusingly as I speak.*

*"You're just scared of being alone, aren't you?"*

*She doesn't respond.*

*"Like if you don't start a family or find someone soon, you'll be past your prime, you'll have to settle for some half-ass guy down the line. Like if you don't have a kid and get married to me, I won't be tied down and just walk away for someone younger?"*

*Still no response.*

*A sound. Choked. She's crying. I start to speak again but restrain myself.*

*She speaks.*

*"You're a fucking asshole."*

*Closes the door.*

</>

"I'm telling you, it's the greatest thing I've ever done," says Bryce.

I smile, lean back in my chair in our white-walled department lunchroom. I'm picking at a day-old chicken salad, nursing a bottled water, decompressing from another mind-numbing press release; 250 words that took four days, seven signatures and 12 rewrites for approval. Bryce's suit smells of vapour smoke and bachelor Bounce sheets. His shirt wrinkled, white collar furling out like a withering flower.

"Seriously, man," he says, punching the numbers on the microwave for his burrito, "it's the most liberating feeling, you should try it."

I stab my salad with my fork, take a drink.

"Yeah I dunno, man, how would I keep in touch with people?"

Bryce sips from his coffee as he sits down, holds his pen like a retired smoker, tie dangles like a dog's tongue.

"Keep in touch with who? Really, are even a quarter of them actually like your friends? Not a chance."

I smile. He is speaking the truth.

"I'm telling you, my life is considerably less stressful, and I don't feel like I have any less friends or any of that shit. I mean the people I really want to keep in touch with, they can text me or call me, email me. The people you talk to on the phone are really the people you kind of actually hang out with."

"Well I would," I respond, "but I have family I want to stay in touch with."

"Whatever, either way, deleting my Facebook, Instagram and Twitter account was the greatest idea of my life. I feel so *fucking* liberated. I have so much more time to like, sing with the birds, and walk in front of tanks, and masturbate to internet porn."

We chuckle.

". . . wait, what about your LinkedIn profile?" I ask.

Bryce waves his hand at me.

"Shit, man, I need my job. Pfizer would fire me if I did that, right?"

Director of Public Relations sticks his head in before I can respond, makes a motion signalling it's time to head to the war room. Bryce and I wrap lunch chat lickity-split.

Corner office city skyline teleconference about our high cholesterol press release. I'm stuck against the wall in a chair beside Bryce, not even at the table.

I settle into reading my phone to pass the time.

Response.

After four hours my ex has finally texted me back. Decades in SMS time. Especially frustrating knowing how tied to her phone she is. I know she read my message right away. I'd only recently put her back in my contacts, only recently re-typing her in—Brianne. I left out her last name, as if I was trying to reinte-grate myself into her life slowly, one piece at a time. I'd been checking my phone all day, waiting, trying to be patient, trying to be a good man about this.

*okay maybe we can meet for dinner tomorrow night . . .*

It all got fucked up. Royally.

We broke up. She moved out. But we were still madly in love. She was all I thought about. I counted the seconds when I woke up until I first thought about her in the morning. Sometimes I'd dream about her, her blonde hair, her figure, images like a ghost when I'd wake. A nightmare stapled to me I just couldn't shake.

I'd finally found someone to re-open my heart. For so long, I'd gone without loving anything more than myself. Until her. She was all I needed. I dove in headfirst. Never took the time to think about whether it would actually work in a real-world set-ting. Long term, down the road, didn't matter. I was reckless.

Love was enough for me, but not for her.

*So . . .*

She dumped me.

Moved out.

Left me alone in our one-bedroom apartment.

I'd never been dumped by someone I was still in love with.

I went to counsellors. Tried to date other women. Drank enough alcohol that alcoholics started telling me I had a problem. The loneliness set in, the regret, the self-doubt.

I find myself going through the silly work emails we used to send back and forth. Flirting, joking, links to Trump toupee memes. Bathing in the past, trying to vault myself back there for a moment or two.

Two weeks ago, she finally got around to breaking up with me on Facebook. We had close to 100 mutual friends. It was like playing it out all over again. Texts from buddies asking if I was okay, her friends writing encouraging 'you don't need him' notes on her wall. Then she started popping up in tags all over downtown, Instagram nightlife selfies in low-cut dresses. Random guys writing on her wall—*had a blast last night Bri, hope to see you again soon!* My single friends showing me her Tinder profile, a photo I took of her in a dress I bought for her.

Swipe right across my throat with a knife.

I'm such a cliché Millennial.

So *fucking* embarrassing.

I went through the agonizing process of un-tagging myself in three-plus years of pictures. Then I just gave up and de-friended her and all of her friends and family.

Through it all, though, I couldn't get up the courage to change my status to single. I picked the coward's way out and hid it from my profile.

The thoughts kept coming: maybe I did want to get married? Maybe I did want kids?

I started calling. First she ignored me. Then showed signs of life. We met for coffee. I saw her in the flesh, told her I wanted her back, wanted to make it work.

Now she'd agreed to meet for dinner.

I was clinging onto this date for my life.

The meeting's dragged into the early evening. Watching the local news reports on the televisions to see if there's any coverage. Bryce beside me, scrolling through a company iPad for social media updates. Nothing. Bullet, dodged. Cholesterol, still raised. I'm leaning against the armrest in my chair, eyelids like 100-pound weights ready to drop to the floor.

Finally just before seven o'clock, I'm told I can go home. King 5, KCTS 9, KOMO and Q13 Fox News pundits a ramshackle of thoughts holding up my skull with sanity for ransom; news clipping package for upper management, one they'll haphazardly check before they head off for a San Juan Islands boating weekend on their cheekily named yachts.

I head down to the parking lot, push the remote car lock on the keys to my 2013 nondescript four-door sedan that looks like fifty per cent of every other car in the parkade. Inadvertently hit the Panic button.

I stop.

Horn blares, echoes through the empty lot. For some reason I feel like crying. Not for anyone in particular. I feel like crying for everything. But I don't.

Turn the siren off. Silence deafening.

The whole car ride home north along the veiny vehicular congestion of the I-5 I fight sleep as my boss talks to me on speakerphone. He wants another clippings package of all the media by end of Monday for the 4PM meeting, which means I'll be tracking news reports on my laptop and cell all weekend. Which means another Monday without a lunch break or a chance to breathe.

He starts to cut in and out.

'Your call has been lost,' says my car's female automated voice.

Particle wave of static washes over the airwaves.

The lights on the car's dashboard flicker like an arcade machine.

Slow the car down, as if it might be ready to crap out on me.

I stop at a stop light, turn the car off and back on again.

Wait for him to call back. Nothing.

Try calling him. Nothing.

Take a deep breath. I'm sure I'll get an email within the hour outlining all the work waiting for me. The highlight of my day? Not having to drive in rush hour because I got stuck at work so late.

Loft off I-5 in Capitol Hill. Space Needle forever off to the west lined by its less intrusive brothers. The lush parks I never seem to grace, full of college kids meandering home drunk, the hungover hipster brunch crowd lining up at the artisan eateries. Brick mortar buildings and the start of suburbia seeping its way into the downtown core like backwards urban sprawl.

I live in America, but I've never felt American. My late mother was born in Washington State but left for Canada years back. The dual citizenship always an ace up my sleeve. I could roam freely across the border from job to job. If I knew where I'd be in a year I'd tell you. But I'd been bouncing around the globe like my father. Vancouver, Southeast Asia, London, Portland, only settled again in Seattle for the time being. Nomadic. A wandering note set adrift from a symphony.

When I get to the door I see my father.

The sight of him stops me.

Sitting outside the complex on a steely, post-industrial bench lit by postmodern overhead lighting. Looks as if he's under illuminating interrogation. I got an email from him last week saying he was coming, but he never specified the date, and as always, never responded to my reply.

Much like his son he's tall and built, though I'm devoid of the thick cop moustache he still sports despite retirement. Looks like me in twenty-five years. My straight chin starting to sag. Thick eyebrows have lightened and found a grey tint. My broad shoulders hung down an inch or two. And my dead-eye, dark brown stare? Well, it's still there on him, no signs of fading.

Only difference in terms of physical appearance is that for some Godforsaken reason I came out platinum blonde like my mother.

There's a travel briefcase, a backpack, and what's left of a six-pack by his feet.

He stands up. "You don't answer your phone anymore?"

Apparently my father thinks people still use landlines. The only reason I have one is because it's tied to the building's intercom, paid for through strata fees.

"My house phone? I haven't been home since this morning."

Stop a few feet from each other. No handshake, no hug.

"Working late?" he says. I nod. I look at him. He looks at me.

"Where were you?" I ask.

"India. New Delhi mostly."

"Ah . . . ok," I say, expecting a more localized answer.

I pull my keys out, signalling we can head in together. My father gets his bags and follows me inside. Nothing's said until we get into the elevator and start up to the twenty-third floor.

"So I take it you're gonna crash here tonight? How long were you outside? Why didn't you just call my cellphone?"

My father looks at me, trying to figure out how to answer three questions with one response.

Poor guy's been left behind in the technological rat race. Takes weeks to respond to emails, has no cell, can barely navigate a computer to save his life. Still gets his photos developed at London Drugs. He's a proverbial 8-inch floppy disk.

But in the countries where he travelled with the insurance money from my mother's death and his healthy cop pension— he's a Swiss Army knife. Trained officer of the law—firearms, hand-to-hand combat, and proper navigational skills. Self-sufficient if lost in the woods, expert survival and tracking experience. Anything physically structured he's mastered. Fuck, the guy can even arc weld.

His travels are unknowns, and I deeply admired that. No postings of gratuitous beach shots or endless photos of him drinking umbrella-topped drinks—tagged here, checked in there. He'll show photos upon his return, ones he's developed and put in albums. Pictures of random people he befriended, weird locals and middle-aged travellers. Each shot a story, each picture carefully constructed—wild boar he killed with locals in the Sahara, ancient caves explored in Nepal, untranslatable Russian Vodka he drank with Tartars.

But in the summer of 2016, as Justin Bieber approaches his umpteenth Twitter follower, my dad's drifted away from his kids, his son and daughter. Disengaged from them as they continue to engage in the information revolution.

I stand beside him and we seem three generations apart.

Growing up he taught me rural skills of the trade. How to fire a weapon, repair, fix, and maintain machinery. How to make do if lost in the woods, how to track prey. But that all faded after my sister and I left for travelling and college and failed to return except on the intermittent statutory holiday.

My mother was, and would have been, the glue that kept the four of us together. Had her Master's in Public Administration from the University of Washington. Graduated summa cum laude. Trilingual, voracious reader. Already high up at the City of Portland, political aspirations on the way. Came up to Canada and met my father one night at a pub out of the blue, both out of their societal comfort zones. I'd never asked so I was always forced to fill in the blanks. I'm guessing she fell in love with his conviction for the law, his ability to draw a clear line in the sand. Right and wrong, legal and illegal. To do what needed to be done.

Either way she liked what she saw and moved. Found herself a career in government during a time when women were supposed to be in the kitchen or hanging laundry. She was the real killer of the family.

She would've had everything figured out if the tragedy didn't involve herself.

"I have to go meet someone tomorrow," he says.

"Who?"

"Someone."

Typical.

The only person I can think of that he would know in this area is Brad, Liz's ex, who's now a cop somewhere in Washington State. Him—and maybe a few leftover relatives of my mom's. The ones who stopped talking to us a few years after the fire. My dad gave up on trying to keep in touch with them and just let it drift.

"Okay then," I say, watching the floors tick up. "Good talk."

It's what passes for passing conversation. The two of us standing here, and we can't find a way to say a proper hello.

The son, wrapped in his Central Business District Club Monaco navy blue suit and Perry Ellis narrow-toed dress shoes, is more than an arm's length from the father's dark North Face jacket, basic polo shirt, tired jeans and New Balance hiking boots. Two competing ideologies, stylistically and, now more than ever, culturally. No amount of melting pots or mosaics could bring this cross-section of gene sequencing back from oil and water. The chemical change of father-son separation complete just in time for the patriarchal science fair.

We head inside my apartment. I barely own anything except some kitchen supplies, a bed, and a bunch of work clothes. Most of the furniture left with Brianne. What I've got is uniform—consumerist additives purchased one afternoon at IKEA.

Left the futon though.

That goddamn motherfucking futon.

The only good thing about the pad is the deck, facing downtown and Puget Sound. High up enough to see all the way along the coast. I spend more time on the deck smoking pot and drinking beer than I do in the house these days, precipitation permitting.

My dad puts his stuff on the couch, and the beers on the kitchen counter. I drop my keys and my cell beside them; they slide across the linoleum. Head into my room and slither out of my suit and tie into some fitted joggers and a Supersonics T-shirt.

By the time I get back to the living room he's already on the deck. I head out; he cracks a beer open with his forearm, hands it to me. Now that he has his jacket off I can see the viscous burn marks, the faded scars that litter his arms and neck. The guy is intimidating to the naked eye—always has been.

He's staring at the sky.

"What are you looking at?"

Holds his hand out, traces it across the horizon.

"The sky here, is it usually like this?"

I look out. Faint hint of purple tingles the ocular senses. Fault line of amber fire across the field of vision.

"Yeah, it does look strange."

He keeps staring, takes a pull from his beer, transfixed at the sight. It's as if someone was burning acres of kerosene lilacs in the middle of the ocean.

I pull from my beer, too, still looking. Bland purple smears, wafts at most. Dancing creatively through the stars. You think you can see them, but then again, you're not sure. Translucent aurora borealis.

I decide to do what I always do, make small talk. It's all we've done since my mother's passing.

"So, how was India?"

Nods before he begins to speak, as if in some kind of nonverbal understanding that he's also willing to do the small talk thing tonight.

"Was good, yeah, spent some time in Mumbai, Goa, Chennai, but mostly New Delhi. Got sick for about a solid week, dropped a good ten, fifteen pounds out my ass."

I chuckle. He continues.

"Funny thing about those people over there, they're not big on public displays of affection, but all the guys are holding hands all the time. And that bobblehead thing they do. I'm getting in an auto telling the guy fifty rupees and he's looking like he's shaking his head, but the guy is telling me it's all good."

"Bobblehead?"

My dad turns to me.

"They do this thing where they kind of shake their head, but it's more of a weird chin wag, and I guess it means yes, like everything is good to go. But hell does it look like they're shaking their head."

I smile. I'm imagining him staring down some gaunt Indian kid the way only a retired cop who's never read a *Lonely Planet* in his life can.

He's been travelling the world nonstop for the past few years since retirement but still carry-on lugs his centrist mentality everywhere he goes. I'm not sure if he's actually travelling or fleeing familiar scenery. Constantly putting himself in foreign lands hoping to stir up foreign thoughts. Something other than what he's known his whole life, literally a world away from what was taken from him—abruptly, without consent.

I head back into the kitchen, check my phone. No email from work, no more texts from Brianne, just the dinner acceptance. Hanging there. I text her back.

*Where and what time?*

Little X beside the response. Failed.

I type it again. Send it. X.

Rub my face in displeasure, let out a noise.

"Fuuuuuuuuuuuuuuuuuuck me."

I'll try again later.

My dad comes back in, puts the beer on the kitchen counter.

"You gonna sleep on the couch?" I ask.

He nods.

"Okay, I'm going to bed," I say. "I'll see you in the morning. How long are you gonna stay? There's spare keys on the holder by the wall."

"Okay," says my dad.

It's all he says, so I head into my room, taking my cell.

I don't brush my teeth. Just lie down, check my phone. No calls, emails or anything in the last few hours. Something must be wrong with my mobile network. I try rebooting, switch to airplane mode and back again. Chances are I inexplicably got water on it or dropped it on a hard surface. Probably means a trip to the mall kiosk tomorrow. I take a deep breath and drop my ball-and-chain on the night table. It's Friday night and all I want to do is sleep.

Exhale. Remember to exhale after inhale.

Temporary silence is mental morphine.

Even though I know it won't last.

Aches and tiredness suffocate me, relaxing my marrow for the first time in close to twelve hours. Drifting aimlessly through thoughts—father, ex-girlfriend, job, life.

But I'm too tired and nothing sticks.

Nothing ever seems to stick anymore.

</>

*Backed into the Bengal Lounge at the Empress in Victoria, British Columbia, downtown on the waterfront. Lounge decorated like Queen Victoria had a threesome with an Indian Prince and a bourgeois colonial banker. My father and I, and my sister who just received a full-ride scholarship to start pre-med at UVic.*

*Ethel Mackenzie Scholarship Award. Bursary given to one female student per year. She won it on her exam scores alone.*

*My father was proud; his daughter had the brains of her mother. I had something, yet to be determined, possibly requiring medication.*

*I'd been missing out on Liz's achievements for years. Returned like a lost cat from overseas debauchery at the back porch one day, covered in filthy unknowns.*

*He despised the way I split after the fire. The way I left town, then country after high school, using my cut of the insurance money to bum around Southeast Asia for half a decade. Leaving him and my sister in the ash of tragedy.*

*Only fragments of that night remain. A faded picture, torn, matted in the corners. The smell of tar, corrosive carpet glue burning. Paramedic wrapping me in a blanket and calling me brave. Images slowly drowned out by a second life—transient worker, North American free bird, nomadic public affairs staffer, IRS paperwork scapegoat, cubicle monkey, customs aficionado. My passport a worn back alley whore.*

*So far from that night it feels like another lifetime.*

*I had to go. Watching my father suffer through his own external silence made me sick. Back to work almost right away, a stubborn mule pulling an empty cart off the end of a field no one was harvesting anymore. His boss tried to make him take more time, but he wouldn't. He figured he could work through it somehow. Finally it came to a head—breaking up a coke party on a warrant search, he beat some drunken frat boy within an inch of his life after the guy spit in his face.*

*Luckily the kid had a knife in his pocket, and my dad's partner testified he pulled it, escaping with nothing more than a demotion to desker and some anger management sessions.*

*His lines started to show after that. Lost weight, picked up the bottle again, started reading self-help books in secret like a hidden drug habit. Dragged us all to counselling to talk about our feelings. Spent years trying to fix us, to keep us together.*

*After a while we were just running in circles, reliving something I wanted to move on from. Yeah, my mom died in a house fire. Yeah, it sucked—a lot. Do I want to continue talking to you about it for six more years at $100 an hour?*

*Fuck no.*

*I didn't ask permission to travel. I just did. I needed an entity between the incident and me, not seconds and hours of silence and awkward family moments. Travelling turned into school, which turned into jobs. Overseas, or across the border in university, I've been hiding from them for the past decade. After all the effort, all that trying to repair, to rebuild, I walked away.*

*It's my greatest regret.*

*My albatross.*

*Three of us sit in a verbal coma at the Empress, and it's like having dinner with strangers. My father, his dark polo shirt. Burn marks along his arms. My sister, blonde as blonde gets, pale Viking like her brother.*

*With our mother's eyes, soft and welcoming yet holding intense analytical skills bordering on outright skepticism.*

The last time I shared any extended amount of space with Liz, I was in high school. Unfamiliarity between us then and now. Never spent more than a few days in her presence, never enough to go below the surface and actually figure out this person I called my sibling.

Unlike Liz and I, my father and I were the same. But there was a hard friction there, a tension that'd been heating for years. We'd been going at each other for most of the day. What about, I'm not sure. Penis size. Who could throw rocks the farthest. Who could take the biggest shit. Super important male stuff.

I'd just returned from a public affairs internship in the UK. Borough Market, Southwark train, Spitalfields, cathedrals, jackhammers on the sidewalk, the waves of the Thames. Noise still deafening me from afar. On my way out I caught a Rangers-Celtic clash up in Scotland. Old Firm rivalry. Got hit in the face with a police billy club and ingested enough tear gas to take down a pack of elephants. Tucked my tail between my legs and headed back across the Atlantic vowing never to get sucked into The Big Smoke and her circus act again.

When I returned stateside, there was an email waiting from my dad. I'd missed Liz's high school graduation. Missing this too was unacceptable, now that I was on the same continent.

The three of us sit in silence, taking turns at the buffet, sipping curry and eating biscuits. I look up at my father, drinking a coffee.

"I have to get back to Portland tomorrow to start my training for Pfizer," I say, staring him down.

He looks at me, drops his spoon. It clinks on the glass table.

"You said you were going to stay until Monday. You told me you had the day off. I have us booked for some whale watching."

"I don't want to watch whales."

"It's not about the whales, it's about doing things as a family. This is a special time for your sister."

"I know that, but I've got so much stuff to do before I start on Tuesday . . . I don't want to get behind. I need to get back home."

My father inhales. Exhales. The three of us, crammed together in a tight triangle of uncomfortable silence. The temperature climbing on our argument, ready to boil over onto the oven coil.

*Before he can respond to me, my sister responds to us both.*

*"Holy shit, you two. You are the worst."*

*We look at her.*

*"This is my time right now, and you guys are bickering like you always do and leaving me to clean up the mess."*

*She points at us, one after the other.*

*"Tristan, shut up. Dad, shut up."*

*Silence. My mother speaking to us from the grave, channeling her womanly roar through her daughter. Being put in our place, as what usually happens when the two of us can't sort our shit out between our own X chromosomes.*

*"Tonight we are going to go see* Ratatouille, *not* 300. *Because I want to see* Ratatouille, *not* 300. *End of discussion. Tomorrow morning, we're going to swim in the hotel pool and go whale watching. Then Tristan can take the ferry home to Portland to start his new job."*

*My dad's about to speak, but he's cut off. My sister leans forward in her chair.*

*"Seriously, you guys think I didn't lose someone that night? You lost your wife, you lost your mother. But you have each other. Where's my mom? Huh?"*

*No response can be mustered.*

*"You think it's easy growing up with two lunkheads? Nobody to talk to about my period, about boys, about getting boobs. You think you two have it tougher than me?"*

*Again, a legitimate question.*

*"Who am I supposed to talk to when I need advice on relationships and junk like that? Tweedledum and Tweedledee here, who can't navigate a women's emotional construct to save their souls?"*

*"Excuse me, what?" I blurt out, taking it as a personal stab.*

*"Yeah, Tristan, you. I hate to be the one to say it, but you're in your late twenties and you haven't had a relationship that's lasted longer than a freakin' semester."*

*It stings even more because it's true.*

*"And you, dad . . ."*

*She sounds like she's going to speak again, but restrains herself. Starts to cry, chokes it back. My dad reaches over and rubs her shoulder. A bubble in my curry pops.*

*She's right. We're fucking lunkheads.*

*I sit like an idiot, watching them. Uncomfortably nailed to my chair. Wishing I knew where I fit in. Could find my place in this equation.*

*A figure appears behind me. I feel its presence.*

*I turn.*

*A cop. Full RCMP regalia.*

*Liz jumps up.*

"Brad!"

*In his arms in a nanosecond, leaving the two of us sitting there, still feeling stupid. Hands her a bouquet of vibrantly colored flowers. She gushes.*

*Brad spins her around, the yellow line on his pants twirling.*

"How's my super smart, soon-to-be-doctor girlfriend? So sorry I couldn't get off shift, babe."

"It's okay. I understand," she says.

*Puts her down. They face us; my dad and I stand.*

*Brad reaches out to my father.*

"Detective Schultz, always a pleasure."

*My father got Brad a job. He'd finished a tour in Afghanistan with the Canadian Armed Forces, went straight from high school into the military. Came home looking for something. Found my sister. My dad pulled some strings and got him onto the force, hoping to make a man out of his daughter's new squeeze.*

*Brad turns to me. We're eye level, weight level. It's like looking into a mirror, sans his jet black hair. A yin to a yang, Ryu and Ken; we could be brothers or best friends.*

*But I have no idea who this fucking guy is.*

"The ever elusive Tristan," *he says, shaking my hand.*

*He squeezes hard, hard enough that I start to squeeze back.*

"Nice grip. Mr. Schultz tells me you box too. Cruiserweight, light heavyweight?"

*Throws a shadow jab at my face out of nowhere. I flinch back, throw my hands up.*

*Brad smiles, laughs boisterously like it's completely preposterous that an on-duty cop would do such a thing.*

*I flash my dad a 'did that fuckhead just do what I think he did?' look.*

*"Ah shit, man. I'm just fucking with you, Tristan," he says, slapping the side of my shoulder.*

*Grabs my hand and pulls me into an awkward man hug.*

*I officially want to push his head through a glass wall.*

*He wraps his arm around Liz, dwarfing her just like the two of us do.*

*"Okay, so how amazing is this little lady?"*

*"She's pretty amazing," my dad says.*

*"Full ride scholarship, pretty cool." Brad leans down to kiss her on the forehead. I watch Liz. She looks like she's in the arms of a loving animal, safe, but alert of its physical power over her.*

*"So how's work going, Brad?" says my dad.*

*The only real intel I've gotten is that Brad came back from Afghanistan like every other soldier—with baggage. PTSD, the usual laundry list of mental problems. Guess he watched his battalion get lit up by an ambush or something. He was like the start of every Hollywood movie about the wars in the Middle East.*

*He'd already been given a hand slap on the job for punching a clubber outside Steamworks who wouldn't pour out his beer. Once again my dad made some calls, and all Brad got was anger management classes.*

*The irony of it. The similarities of the three men standing around Liz. It's like she was seeking a younger version of her father to dive into. I mean, who was I kidding? We are all stereotypes of archetypal tragic love stories.*

*Caricatures in an elaborate play.*

*"Okay babe, really sorry, but I'm still on shift—I've got to run," Brad says, resting his hand on his gun holster.*

*"Detective Schultz. Tristan, a pleasure to meet you."*

*Squeezing my hand again. I wanna pull his wrist in and introduce him to the topside of my forehead.*

*Is this what being a big brother feels like?*

*Foreign emotions.*

*He kisses his girlfriend, turns, and leaves.*

*I watch Liz turn back to us.*

*She senses the look on our faces.*

*"What? Oh fuck . . . don't you two start with me."*

</>

Bones and skin labour in bed. Squirming, tossing, turning in night sweats. Egg beater mix of sheets and pillows. Sleep without medication a challenging conundrum. Since Brianne left, I've painted myself into an over-the-counter corner of multi-coloured pills. My body tried to wean itself each time, with little success.

Window shades usually let in the dank glow of the street-lights—lines of yellowing prison bars. But not tonight. I squint, look more closely, but too dazed to register this change in scenery with anything more than a passing thought.

A stressful yet commonplace feeling surrounds me. Usually my phone goes off during the night, Google Alerts set to track the company as the Eastern seaboard wakes and takes notice of our late-day activities. I periodically check them as I sleep in fits and spurts anyway.

But nothing this time, so I sit up.

7:02PM. No service. Squinting in the dark, lit only by a Blackberry backlight, small moon of technology. I look over at my alarm clock—8:15AM.

I sit up in bed; look at my cell more closely. No service. No emails, no Wi-Fi.

A knock on my door.

"Come in," I cough through my rusty larynx.

My father opens the door, light sneaks in. I'm suddenly more alert, almost blinded.

"Something's going on," he says.

I stand up, stagger out of the bedroom like a zombie, shielding my eyes. Make my way into the living room where my dad is. Biological clock telling me it's morning but I'm more trusting of my Berry—go figure.

"Look at this," he says. Turns on the TV. Starts flicking. All of the channels have no signal. Nothing.

Turns back to me, but doesn't say anything.

I head over to the landline on the wall. Dial tone.

Who do I call?

Brianne, our dinner, but I can't remember her number. I look it up in my BBM contacts. Call her.

Just a hard tone.

And still the same X beside the last text I sent her.

I try sending it again.

X.

*Fuck.*

I head over, sit at my laptop. Pop-up, no network found, no connectivity. I feel like I'm on a dial-up modem in the late 90s. I try restarting. Nothing. Email, nothing. Lean back in my chair. This is usually the point where I call IT.

"*What the . . .*"

"That's not all," says my dad. Nods towards the deck.

I look out, notice something. Something different.

We head onto the deck.

Eyes instantly widen.

White sky.

Not cloud white, but *white*. Dusty, hazy, bone discoloration.

I squint for a second. As if an exposure issue with my display brightness—cranked up to maximum, ghostly white.

Faint outlines of clouds the vision can barely recognize. If this was winter I might be more inclined to buy this new backdrop, but it's pushing 75. It's the white that makes its way to the ocean that's most out of place. Even if it's overcast the blue overtakes the sky before it becomes parallel with the sea. But not today. It's white, then dark blue, a straight line dividing the two, disturbing my depth perception.

I look at my father—short crop bed head, dusty five o'clock shadow and disconcerting look. He's staring at the horizon. Faint sirens cry a terrifyingly muted lullaby. Horns honk, off by the waterfront a small plume of creamy black smoke lifts up from a building behind a high rise.

I look back at the sky, rub my eyes. Just white. Paper white as high as the eye can see. I shake my head.

"*What the . . .*" I say again.

Landscape with no memory, wiped clean in a debug gone wrong.

New Document.

"I'm gonna head down to Starbucks and see if they have Wi-Fi."

He stares at me. I remember the HAM radio he had in our garage growing up, the mechanical pitch and squeal as it searched for life on the other end.

Head back into my room, throw on a dark blue H&M hoodie and some fitted jeans.

Out into the street. Everything appears normal. However surprisingly devoid of people. A guy zips by on a bicycle, first sign of life.

Slight de-elevation of heart rate.

I head into the Starbucks. No laptops open. Before I can even get to the counter the barista answers my question.

"No wireless," he says in his condescending *I work at Starbucks but somehow I'm better than you* voice. "Also we can only take cash; debit machine is down."

A coffee grinder starts up and my response is muted. I look around. People sit, reading the paper; a girl checks her phone. She looks distressed, like someone's trying to ever so slowly end her life.

Head back outside, check my.phone. No signal. Hold it up in the air, hoping to entice a bar or two. Nothing.

I turn my phone off. Take the battery out, restart it.

Nothing.

I'm not sure what to do. My manual ends at this page.

Back to my apartment. My dad's making scrambled eggs. Obviously this lack of connectivity and blatant white sky isn't affecting him to the same degree. Also, looks like the gas is still on.

I take a breath in. Check my phone again. Local network must be down.

I walk around my apartment, starting to pace. The eggs cooking on the frying pan, crackling with cholesterol.

He looks up at me.

"Would you stop pacing around."

I hold up my phone.

"I'm not getting any service."

Looks at me like I just told him the capital of Uzbekistan.

"Sit down, relax, it's Saturday."

Tashkent . . .

Weekends do not apply in the world of Public Relations. I'm worried about the coverage on our release. I don't know why I care so much. Just another mindless drone indoctrinated into thinking my job was more important than my livelihood.

I sit on the couch, turn the TV on again. Nothing. Frantic flicking. Numbers ascend on the side of the screen.

"Well, that's shitty," he says. "I was hoping to watch the Mariners game."

After a while I stop flicking and head to my computer. I have a massive cache of downloaded TV shows: HBO, some AMC. I throw as much as will fit on a flash drive and plug it into the TV.

My dad cooks breakfast and we eat in silence on my futon. Shovelling eggs into our mouths from the coffee table while we watch *Game of Thrones*. They seem to be rustling up the usual drama and deceit without iPads or Reddit.

Head back to my room, shower, and try to digest the slow pace I'm forced to proceed at. Someone's been telling me to run my entire life, and whenever I feel the obligation to slow and save sanity, it racks me with more stress. I run on fumes and caffeinated blood cells. Nobody told me to stop. Nobody told me there was any kind of roses to smell.

I'm supposed to be going for dinner with my ex tonight. Now I can't even get hold of her. Lack of connectivity stressing every corner of my physical make-up. I can't imagine what she's thinking after I went radio silent.

Back into my room, lie down on my bed. As soon as head hits fabric, I start to drift off. I've been catching up on sleep during the weekends for years, so I've trained myself to dive into slumber during any free block of time.

Body knocks the brain out with an uppercut of relaxation.

Asleep within a few minutes, sheets wrapping around the frame, asphyxiating me like a boa constrictor.

</>

Eyes flutter, sputtering wings. I roll over, light from the shades. Float a few minutes in a slumberous state of awake, yet still asleep. Dreams, thoughts, characters run around, compete for my complacent attention.

Ex-girlfriend screams at me. At the top of her lungs. I roll over, sit up, blonde hair a mess. Snort like a pig in the mud.

Ok, *I'm up*. Fuck.

Throw on my joggers and hoodie, head out into the apartment. I check my phone.

No signal.

Check my laptop.

No internet.

TV.

Nothing.

I notice a yellow sticky on my fridge.

'Back for dinner. Dad'

He just texted me à la 1989.

I check out the window. Dusk, white sky tinting acutely towards a dark shield of grey. Check my phone. Still no service, no texts. Dinner with the ex, obviously not happening. Fate has decided.

Must've been out for a few hours. I dread falling asleep again after killing most of the day in a beautiful nap.

Then I remember my stash of Ativan.

Grab some cheese, crackers, and beer from the fridge and decide to try and enjoy the solitude. I'm sure everything will be sorted out soon enough—or there will at least be an explanation on the way.

The silence is deafening. Also enticing.

I settle in for a few hours of *The Leftovers, Mad Men* and *The Walking Dead*.

A sense of blank bliss drips over my head through a small sieve.

This is how Saturdays used to be, I think to myself.

Before I got plugged into the global consciousness. Before everyone had everything to say.

Before I needed my news 24/7. Before I needed to know as soon as everyone else knew. Before buffering. Before torrents. Before streaming.

Before we all took the blue pill.

</>

My dad resurfaces a few hours later, two pizzas under his arm.

"Had to pay cash."

I loathe cash and rarely carry it. The only thing I pay for in cash these days is pot and poker games.

"Everything still down?"

"Yeah, seems that way. A few blocks up by Madison Park have no power."

"You talk to anyone about the phones, the internet?"

"No, but people asked me. Sounds like no one knows. I'm sure it will get sorted out."

Half-ass nod in compliance with his statement.

I figure whatever the solution is will not involve me. The best thing to do is enjoy the momentary lapse in connection. The temporary blissful hum of static. Revel in a few moments of airplane mode.

He puts the pizzas on the counter and heads to the freezer. Grabs an ice pack and puts it over his hand.

"What did you do to your hand?"

Grabs a beer from the fridge and pops the top with his thumbnail. He's not going to answer.

"Dad, your hand?"

"It's fine."

"You get into a fucking fist fight on the street or something?"

No response, again. No scars or black eye, either. I'm guessing he won.

"Good talk, again."

We eat pizza and watch *The Wire*. My dad talks to the show, debunking its validity in some one-sided conversation. 'No, get the warrant first. Perps would never take that. No judge would see that case. DA isn't that stupid. They'd never get up on those phones. McNulty's an idiot, fucking Irish drunk.'

End up killing half the first season on my futon, legs up on the glass coffee table, sufficient space between us. Before I know it, it's almost midnight.

I try calling Brianne again. Nothing. Hard tone.

I check my laptop. Nothing. Still nothing on the TV.

Fuck it. I read old *Vanity Fair* issues in bed until the Ativan kicks in and I doze off. The silence, she's screaming in my ear.

SHUT THE FUCK UP!

</>

Huff.

Sweat, poorly digested oxygen.

Sleep apnea sits on my windpipe.

Middle of the night. Roll over, check my phone, still nothing. Roll back, drift off. Another set of incomprehensible dreams.

Ativan sweats from my pores, onto my bed sheets—prescription mess of stress-related pills.

Pfizer's mission is to discover and develop innovative medicines and other products to improve the quality of life of people around the world. Our company is one of the largest contributors to health research in the United States.

Our diversified health care portfolio includes medicines and vaccines, as well as nutritional products and many of the world's best-known consumer products. Every day, Pfizer employees work to advance wellness, prevention, treatments and cures that challenge the most feared diseases of our time. We apply our global resources and science to improve the health and well-being of you as a profit margin, not a person.

Body temperature, sleep patterns affected by technology. I'm a wireless router of emotions. Solid green light. Blinking green light. Turn me off. Unplug me. Plug me back in again.

</>

Wake to the smell of depression and anxiety.

Body aches.

Moaning from too much sleep. I've reached the doorstep of hibernation. I cough, roll over and up.

Check my phone. No service. Says it's still Friday evening.

If this is a dream and I'm Bill Murray in Groundhog Day for the rest of my life on a lazy Saturday, DO NOT FUCKING WAKE ME!

I walk out into the living room. My dad reading books on the futon.

"What day is it? My phone's all fucked up."

He looks up, pointing to the clock on the stove. 12:34PM.

"Sunday?"

*God's day.*

Plop down at my laptop. Says Friday evening. No internet, nothing. Again.

I lean over, look out at the deck.

White.

Stand up.

"Man, did I ever sleep in. Why didn't you wake me?"

My dad looks over again from the book.

"Figured you were sleeping something off."

True.

Drops the book on the table. Stands up. Looks out at our environmental predicament. Two lost souls trapped in a tight ball of togetherness. No modern remedies to pass the silent awkwardness between us anymore.

"You wanna go hit the bag? I see your gym membership there." He's pointing to my card on the fridge. Family members are free.

Air in and out of my nostrils. Some pugilism might be the ticket right now.

I'm so out of shape my stomach feels like cookie dough shoved in a plastic bag. The best I could muster in the past few weeks was a couple nights on the treadmill while I watched other fighters spar.

"Ok."

Down the block to Rodney's Gym.

Underground basement venue, full ring, couple thousand square feet. Rodney was still there. Crapped out at the Olympics in Barcelona. Missed the podium by two points; lost to a Venezuelan boxer who was probably fighting for his literal life.

Ample photos of him with the requisites—Ali, Foreman, Mayweather, Stallone, even Mitt Romney.

Ruby red and black chipped paint everywhere. The usual suspects: lifer boxers who never made it out of state. Five hundred, at best, veteran fighters who couldn't remember what locker they left their gym bag in.

Rodney greets everyone that comes in. Runs a tightly rustic ship.

"Tristan! You motherfucker, you better not be sitting your ass on my treadmills again for an hour. Such a waste of fucking talent."

Rodney notices my dad.

"Who's your guest?"

"Rodney, this is my dad. Dad, Rodney."

"Nice to meet you, sir. I'd say I'd heard a lot about you, but Tristan's not much of a talker down here. Just abuses my cardio machines and punishes my cruiserweights when he feels so moved."

Rodney's face looks like it was abused through childhood by a meat grinder.

"FYI guys, heater is out, bit cold down here. Also my debit and credit machines are down so if you need something from the store, give me cash or put it on your tab."

We nod. Rodney's doing just fine with the disconnect.

Change in the dressing room. Third degree burn marks run down my dad's back like wind tunnel lines. He's still cut from stone. No PX90-Hydroxycut bullshit, starving himself of calories and iron. Full, protein rich muscles of someone who's been hitting the weights a night or two a week for the past four decades.

Stretching.

Ten minutes of light cardio.

Enough burpees, pull-ups and kettle bells to make any man throw up.

Crossfit till we're sweating like pigs.

Speedbag, some bodybag work.

"Tristan!" yells Rodney, across the gym. "You want in the rotation with your old man? You guys look like a decent enough catchweight."

He's holding up gloves and helmets.

My dad looks at me. I have a good ten-fifteen on him, but he's probably in game shape. I'm in recliner shape.

"Yeah sure, why not," says my dad.

Fuck me.

We get taped up. The bell rings before I can think this poor decision through.

Flashes of red mittens bludgeon my vision.

Rodney's yelling at me. Mostly swearwords. A few physical directions.

I'm getting pummelled by a guy who gets a discount if he rides the bus.

Kidneys scream like little girls.

Abdomen blacking out.

Chest pleads for mercy.

The sides of my face being gang-beaten from all directions.

Remember to breath. Push the air out with each punch.

Old fuck has been working out.

Ding!

Rodney's laughing from the pit of his stomach.

"Ah fucking good times, good times. My old man used to punish me after he hit the bottle, too. Sometimes you just have to eat shit, kid."

Second round I try to hold the center of the ring, push him into the ropes. His hands start to drop an inch or two, exposing his chin.

Dirty boxing, my favourite. I can feel his breath on my shoulder as he tries to push me back. Vitality kicking in against the geezer.

"Oh, the kid's woken up! Somebody pulled his ass out of bed!"

I start swinging my hands around, combo up to the face, left hook to the mid-section. Duck, step sideways, right block, left jab. Always landing the last punch of the exchange.

"There's the Tristan I know and love! Somebody wiped the lavender oil off his bottom!"

Ding!

Guys clap around the gym.

We've got ourselves a fight.

I'm back in my corner; Rodney yanks my mouth guard out, squirts water into my mouth without asking.

"This one time, I was boxing this Irish guy in England. Whole stadium was chanting 'Potato, potato.' Thought they had a nickname for me already. I mean, my head does kind of look like a beautiful potato. Oh how wrong I was."

Rodney's mid-round pep talks are more confusing than doing right side up algebra while hanging upside down.

I'm relying on pinker lungs. My dad's relying on experience. He's coiled back into the corner, strikes when I open, cobra waiting for his moment. He catches me off the right side of the face, sends me to one knee. Hoots and hollers from the gym rats.

Motherfucker.

I'm back, just swinging. Two decades of boxing training out the window and I'm throwing haymakers. Beautiful. I haven't sent a text in two days and I'm swinging my fists like I live in a cave, eat nothing but red meat and shit in the bushes.

Temporary oasis of pain and exhaustion.

Ding!

Uproarious cheers and clapping.

Three rounds of expertise. Two bodies collide for the sake of colliding.

Rodney's in the ring with us.

"Now that was a beautiful thing."

My dad taps me on the head a few times, mumbles something I can't make out through his mouth guard. Doesn't matter.

We shower up. I feel great. That fulfilling sense of soreness after a workout.

Rodney shakes our hands on the way out, chats about the fight. About the internet being down, no power at his place in Lake Union. Whatever, he's sure everything will be up and running tomorrow for Monday.

We walk home, change, and head out to try and find a place to eat a steak or two.

Most of the storefront restaurants are closed, so we cab to Pike Market. Chomp on steak and fries, looking out at Puget Sound, fulsome grey sky staring us down.

I keep catching conversations about what's going on. Nobody seems to know anything. Half the shops closed up, the other on full alert for potential shoplifters. People complain about the lack of credit machines when they go to pay for their chai tea and beaded necklaces.

My dad's worried about Liz. I want to tell him she's a Schultz, and a female one at that. If anything, she should be worried about us, two lost boys stuck in a freeze frame of disconnect, unable to locate our father-son compass.

But I know: if this blackout carries on, my father will have one, and only one, priority. His daughter.

Me, all I can think about is where Brianne might be. Do I go to her, even though we're no longer together? Is it still my place to try and look out for her? Protect her?

Our waiter comes back, says he has no idea what's going on, but the restaurant's closing early. Apparently the police are dealing with major robberies and break-ins at Denny Triangle and Belltown.

We walk back to East Madison Street, have a hell of a time trying to catch a cab in the dark. No buses, the metro down plus the transit tunnel's ominously blocked. Cop car comes barreling down the street, lights on, screeching around the corner, blasting sirens in our faces. We have to jump up onto the sidewalk. I look inside, officer in the driver's side checking the shells in his pump-action shotgun.

Something is going on.

Something is becoming very wrong.

Finally a gruff old guy picks us up in his Orange cab. He knows as much as we do—nothing, but tells us all about it.

We watch a few episodes of *Mr. Robot*, and then I lie in bed listening to the sirens of first responder vehicles.

Bellowing cries. Bellwethers.

Of what?

Brianne floats into my head. I can't stand the negative thoughts, replaying our fights and arguments over and over.

I force my mind back to better days. Back to the start of it.
To the start of us.
Before it all got so fucked up.

&lt;/&gt;

*I tap the microphone. Hold it to my mouth. "Hello? Is this on?"*

*Feedback. Everyone in the bar stops chatting, turns to face me on the stage. Eyes set their sights. Heart rate rises, thumping hard against the chest cavity.*

*"Hi," I say to the crowd, holding up my hand. A few throw 'Hi's' back.*

*"I just want to thank everyone for coming. Especially Brianne's friends and family, all the way from beautiful South Carolina. You guys are awesome for doing this."*

*Brianne's first birthday in Seattle. She loved parties, but was too modest to ask for anything elaborate. So I spent two months moving heaven and earth to get all her friends and family here, tonight, to The Alibi Room, a tiny spot buried in the brick, mortar, and cobblestone of Post Alley. Stained oak and wooden chairs that creaked when you sat down. Brick oven pizzas and flight trays shaped like oars.*

*To rent the bar on a Friday, I had to shell out a small fortune and call in some favours. Benefits of working PR for Pfizer. I was able to get the owner in the Annual Pfizer Charity Aldarra Golf Tournament. The Grand Prix of executive opulence.*

*It's worth it. The Alibi Room is Brianne's favourite spot. She fell in love with the place because of its name, joked that we needed an alibi to go to it. Before heading out, we'd make up silly stories about where we'd be that night:*

*"I'm hanging with Kato Kaelin. We're going for frozen yogurt."*

*"Between 7:30 and 9 o'clock, I'll be with the cast of the Muppets drinking hard liquor in an alley, plotting a gang war against Sesame Street."*

*I'd brought her best friend from Carolina in on the surprise. Jeremy, the most fabulous gay you'll ever meet. Cross-dressing singer; owned a salon; ran a non-profit supporting at-risk LGBT youth in the inner city. The funniest, most charismatic man I knew. Brianne thought he was the* only one who'd come to town for a visit, that the three of us were meeting for post-work drinks.

Instead, I'd amassed close to sixty people. Even found her best friend from elementary school. I mean, it was her 30$^{th}$. If anyone deserved it, it was her.

"Okay, so Jeremy says Brianne is going to be here in five minutes. We're gonna kill the lights, and then when she comes in, could everyone help me out and yell happy birthday?"

People chuckle, happily agree.

"Okay, awesome."

I pass the microphone back to the DJ. Head down and shake more hands, mingle with Brianne's family.

Jeremy texts me.

'We're outside kill the ligggghtsssssss!!!!! Lol. U the best boyfriend eva Tristan fyi!!!!!!!!'

Jeremy has a habit of ending each text with a blitzkrieg of emoticons and exclamation points.

I yell out, "Kill the lights, please!"

The bar goes dark. Quiet. People whisper. We hear the front doors open.

Two sets of footsteps. Soft female voice.

"Why is it so dark in here? Did the power go out?"

Lights blast the room with colour.

"HAPPY BIRTHDAY!"

Brianne covers her mouth with her hands. Tears stream. Jeremy puts his arm around her shoulder, walks her through the crowd. People clap and holler.

She hugs me. Tears on my dress shirt.

"Oh baby, you're so amazing."

Her parents and grandparents surround her. All her sisters and brothers, each with multiple kids under the age of ten running around on refined sugar highs.

Brianne's on hug overload. Smiles and laughter. Comes back to me when she's finished greeting everyone. Wraps her arms around my waist. Looks up.

"Kiss please, my sexy man."

I oblige.

*"Um, can I just say I know someone who's getting laid tonight."*

*She taps my butt. I love her frisky attitude. Even in public.*

*I smile.*

*"I can't believe you did this!" she says, looking around. "How did you get everyone out? This is, like, everyone I've ever known in my whole life."*

*Herding cats. Nailing Jell-O to the wall. Getting a tweener to put down their iPhone. I could think of harder things to do.*

*"No worries, babe. It was nothing."*

*She smiles.*

*We serve a cake shaped like a globe. Brianne moved to Seattle to take a marketing gig with an NGO. I asked everyone who came to donate money to a charity instead of buying a present, and to make sure to tell her which organization they chose.*

*I step back onstage. Tap the microphone.*

*Brianne front and centre with her parents.*

*"Hello again. One more round of thanks to all Brianne's South Carolina friends and family for braving this thing we on the West Coast call rain."*

*Chuckles.*

*"So I'd like to thank everyone for their donations, as per my birthday present request."*

*I look down at Brianne.*

*"Brianne, just to let you know, my donation went to a private company, so I apologize."*

*I pause. She frowns theatrically.*

*"But I think you'd be okay with my choice, given we did six months of long distance to start our relationship."*

*Someone yells out, "Skype!" I nod. Laughter all around.*

*"Okay, I'm going to hand the mic off, but first I want to say a few things about the birthday girl."*

*Brianne smiles at me. Her curly blonde hair falls over her shoulders. Limestone skin cut from stone. She's never looked anything but smashing.*

*"So for those of you who don't know, Brianne and I met more than a year ago in Chicago. I think 'unusual circumstances' would be a good description."*

*The audience chuckles. Jeremy lets out an uproarious, "Ha!"*

"Let's just say she made an excellent character witness."

More laughter.

"On a more serious note, Bri, I want to say a few things I love about you."

I reach into my suit pocket. I borrowed a paper roll from the bar's debit machine. I drop the wheel and the paper spools out across the stage, down onto the floor, rolls a good fifteen feet into the crowd. Everyone laughs. I start to pretend-read from my scroll.

"What I like about my girlfriend: her South Carolina sweetness and twangy accent, which gets stronger when she's flustered."

Carolina crowd hoots and hollers.

"Volunteers at a homeless shelter once a week. In marketing but only works for NGOs. Coaches a girl's soccer team . . . Her beautiful blonde hair and the freckles on her shoulders—stars to line my way. Those legs, that back, her toes, her ears . . . um, I'd say more about her physical appearance, but I didn't bring earmuffs for Brianne's parents."

Laughter. I continue, listing them off.

All the reasons.

"Sexy. Unapologetic. Expert communicator. Stubborn. Tomboy athleticism. Vivacious. Beautiful. Smart. Funny. Silly. Serious. Driven. Did I say sexy?"

The crowd laughs. Someone yells, "Hubba hubba!"

I stop. Look at her. Her hands over her mouth, fighting tears. I'm slicing open my heart. Something new for me. As a kid, I hid my feelings deep in the basement of my life. Now this beautiful Southern beauty's here, bringing it all up with natural ease.

"Brianne, you are my sun. I rise and set with you. Today is a celebration for everyone in this room—because we are the luckiest souls on the planet to have you in our lives. To have your beaming energy keeping us warm and giving us light. Helping us grow. You are our greatest gift."

I'm tearing up. Levees of emotions. Words from the pit of my soul. I am so fucking done.

"So I'd like everyone to raise their glasses and toast this beautiful lady."

The crowd obliges.

"Thank you."

Applause. I step down and kiss my woman.

*"Who is this man in front of me?" she asks. She's half-smiling, half-crying. It's like I'm physically watching someone fall in love with me. "That was the most heartfelt thing I've ever heard you say."*

*I hold Brianne, kiss her on the forehead.*

*"It's you," I say. "It's all you."*

No alarm clock.

Phone is useless.

I wake to the light. To a blank sky.

Strung into a tight density of unknown intensity. I'm off the grid, but not in a paid vacation sipping Coronas on an all-inclusive manmade tropical beach kind of way. Throw on the suit I wore Friday, trying to get as much mileage out of it as possible.

Still the same no damn signal on everything.

My dad is up, reading magazines on the futon. He doesn't know how to access the flash drive plugged into the TV I'm guessing.

The time on my phone says Friday evening.

It's Monday morning. If anyone knows what fucking Monday morning feels like, I do. I can smell that motherfucker in the air.

"I'm heading to work," I say, gathering my keys and slipping on my shoes.

I look outside. White sky, devoid of shadows. No sun to cast its shade, cut in through the buildings, or bounce off the endless panes of window glass above my head.

I just want to get to work and figure this shit out. I'm guessing dinner with Brianne is never going to happen.

Mind replaying over like a loop.

Fuck*fuck*fuck*fuck*fuck.

"I'll come along for the ride," he says.

"Okay, you wanna bum around downtown or something?"

He looks at me like I just tried to install PC software on his Mac.

"I don't think there's going to be any bumming around this morning."

I squint at him.

Down into the carport and out the front gate, up onto the street.

A car zooms by, nearly clips us.

I slam the brakes; my dad instinctively throws his hand in front of my chest as we heave forward into the dashboard.

Car's out of sight before I even know the model.

"Motherfucker."

"I'd keep an eye on the road today."

"I'm fine."

Onto I-5, white sky cuts the buildings off with a sharp tone. We're in an unfinished drawing—abandoned cityscape painting.

GPS in my car isn't working. One hand on the wheel, the other pushing buttons. Satellite radio. Nothing. Flip to FM, nothing. AM, static.

Highway's a littered mess of scattered cars disobeying traffic laws. Nascar on the beltway, everyone jockeying for position. Drivers abusing their signal lights, shoulder checking like quarterbacks dropping back into the pocket.

Seattle's population out walking cautiously as we cut onto 4th Ave, talking in small groups on the sidewalks. Some guy runs across the middle of the street and into an alley like he's being chased by death itself.

Fire truck rumbles by, blaring sirens as it runs a flashing red.

Drivers parked in their cars, fiddling with their cellphones or thumbing away at their radios. We make our way down 4th to Cherry St.

My office high-rise. Staring me down as it always does.

Park on P1, almost deserted. If only it was Monday morning and I was late, looking for the closest spot to the elevator.

Wait a second . . .

No security guards on the ground floor as we switch elevators. A lifelike tomb. Our feet pitter-patter and echo across the granite in the lobby.

Eighteenth floor.

Horizontal baby blue oval. Head down the long entrance hallway to the open concept portion lined with grey-walled cubicles and glass partitions about six feet high. A small group of coworkers huddled around desks like a proverbial campfire.

Lady from Human Resources looks back. I can't remember her name even though I've seen her almost every day for the past few years.

"Nobody knows anything," she says.

A couple others look at me.

"Is this it?"

"Yeah," she says.

Stress level elevating. Core temperature bubbling with precipitation of anxious tendencies. Cocktail of known ignorance to the present no longer suffices. Need something stiffer to numb the perplexity of the situation.

"Let's go," says my dad.

I stand, hands on my head. Walk a few paces forward to my boss's office. Nothing. Bryce, gone. Nobody from PR is here. Entire department MIA. I guess I missed the memo.

I nod in some odd form of self-acceptance of the situation.

Back out, down the elevator, into the parkade. Towards the car.

Lone man dressed in a tattered tracksuit comes into view. He's asking for help, mumbling and rambling like we're already mid-conversation.

We just stand there. As he closes in, we see he's the type of guy who might cry wolf instead.

Keeps coming.

My dad tells him to stop. He pulls out a switchblade.

"Give me your wallets! Now!"

My dad pulls out a G34 Gen 4 Glock that glimmers under the light.

All three of us freeze.

"Whoa *whoa*!" says the wolf, like he didn't consent to this level of weaponry.

"Get in the car," my dad says to me.

I'm still frozen.

"Now!"

We move towards the car, gun still on the wolf.

I get in; we drive away, chasing him off the path like a pigeon on the road. Wolf leaps out of the way, theatrically rolling into the side of a car in the process. Thud! I turn and watch his body flail off a concrete column and onto the ground.

Idiot brought a knife to a gunfight.

Guess *he* missed the memo.

We screech up out of the parkade.

Brianne. If it's all going to hell, I need to know: where is she?

"I need to see if Brianne's okay. I need to find her."

My dad doesn't answer; he keeps driving, pulls a hard left into a parking lot beside a downtown gas station. We pull up; he locks the doors, pulls his gun out and puts it on his lap, checking the magazine.

"What are you doing?"

Takes a breath in.

"Okay, we need a game plan," he says.

"A game plan? I want to go find Brianne."

"No."

"No? Who the fuck do you think you are?"

He motions with his hands, *calm down*.

"You fucking calm down! I haven't seen you in three years, you show up at my fucking door Friday like a lost dog, and now the whole fucking city is offline. What the fuck is going on?"

"Tristan, look, all that shit, all the shit between us, we can't discuss that right now. As you can see, something is terribly, terribly wrong."

I roll my eyes.

"Yeah, no shit. You must've been a detective or something."

Silence again.

Our Band-Aid bond breaking. Cracking under the stress of the situation.

We were never close. Two lost souls stuck in a room together, occasionally bouncing off one another. It hurt, because I had memories of life before the fire, when we were close. When we were father and son. Now he's some guy I see once in a while and have awkward conversations with.

I look around. He's right. The Shell station, one of the busiest in the city, is deserted. I'm too flustered and off-key to let anything cement in my mind; I'm in mental shock, and I know it,

which suspends me in more mental shock. My keyboard convert-
ed to another language, communication now stuck on standstill.

"Okay . . . *so* . . . what's going on?"

"I'm not sure. From what I can see, the sky is very different."

Eyes rolling like lottery balls.

"Tristan, listen. Something is very, very wrong. The white
means something in the atmosphere has changed. We know satellite service is down completely, and it's been over three days."

"What, like all over the world?"

"Judging by what we've seen so far, it's safe to say this isn't
localized. No satellite TV or radio means this probably extends
outside of the Pacific Northwest."

"I don't get it."

"I'm guessing Friday, the sky had something to do with it.
But let's look at the hard facts."

He starts listing them off on his fingers like errands to run.

"No satellite service, no cellular service. No GPS, no TV, no
radio. The military and police rely heavily on satellite and radio
so this is another thing to take into account as they're usually
the first to restore order in situations like this. They probably
would've shown up after seventy-two hours or so in a disaster
situation."

Seventy-two hours. I've heard that number before. Be prepared to be self-sufficient for seventy-two hours. After that?
That's when Red Cross and FEMA arrive with relief tents, food
rations, and celebrity telethon fundraisers.

It's pretty clear nobody's showing up anytime soon.

"Situation?"

He puts his Glock up on the dashboard like a cup of coffee.

"Right now we, and the rest of this city, don't know what's
going on, and it's fair to assume we should not be counting on
any government or police force for help right now. We need to
be on high alert. This is an emergency situation."

Brain's starting to crash. Hard drive reaching maximum
capacity. Part of me is scared. But for some reason, the other part
is excited.

Society might be gone. An overheating CPU.

My insulated life, so trapped I stopped pacing the cage and learned to love the bars across my view. Stockholm Syndrome. Tricked myself into acceptance, let my soul suffer and die beneath a stream of hollowly adorned status updates and hashtagged Instagram reveries.

Now someone's opened the fucking cage.

Do I even know what to do?

Too many questions enter my server. My consciousness starts swimming, then ups and fucking drowns.

"Fuck."

We sit in confused silence, stare at frozen screens of thought. I'm trying to focus on the tangible. Where is Brianne? Where is my sister? Is this the apocalypse? It doesn't feel like it does in the movies. It feels surreal, sublime, almost normal. The air still breathable, heart still rip-roaring through my circuitry.

My father rubs his hands over his face.

"Can we go look for Brianne?"

We've broken up, but I need to seek her out. I can re-build us. I can make us whole again—I'm sure of it.

"Okay," my father says slowly, "where does she live?"

"Mercer Island."

He sighs.

Brianne has never met my father, and I realize this will be a weird first encounter. But the thought passes as I stare up into the white sky, looking for planes or helicopters.

I'm not totally sure how to get to Mercer Island without my GPS. Brianne moved into a basement suite with friends after we broke up, and I've only been there once to pick her up for coffee.

We'd been hanging onto the leftovers of our relationship. I missed her company, I wanted to go back to the night we met. Our first encounter. The instant I fell in love with her.

But the present serves as a vicious reminder of how far gone the past really is.

"I think we need a map."

My dad looks over at me.

"A map?"

"Yeah, I've only been there once. She just moved."

"You can't remember how to get there?"

"Well, I think so, but I use the GPS in the car."

I tap my finger on the blank screen to signal my reliance on this technology.

"Okay," he says. He chambers a round, gets out of the car, and heads over to the gas station. I stay in the car, watching intently. Up to the door, but it's locked. I see him looking inside for people.

A map is the least of our worries. I can't hold a thought together. This is a different kind of stress, one I've never encountered before. One I can't numb with prescription medication, hard alcohol, and PVR'd HBO. One I can't plow through with blinders on. This one requires my full attention, something I rarely give anything anymore.

Kicks the glass door as hard as he can.

No luck.

Kicks it again.

Glass shatters under the weight of his foot.

He goes inside the store, comes out in a few seconds with what I'm only guessing is a map.

Gets back in the car. I stare at him, looking for an explanation.

None; just drops it on my lap.

Behind us, a car zooms down the street.

We look at each other.

"Time to go," my dad says, putting his seatbelt on and shifting into reverse.

"Yes," I say. "Yes it is."

I hold onto the dashboard with both hands as we screech around a corner away from the scene.

</>

*Chi-town. Public Relations Association of America Annual Conference. Crown Plaza Chicago Metro. The whitest towels known to man. I'd been soaking in the hot tub, dress suit and nametag lying on the double bed inside my fifteenth-floor room. Mini-bar, attacked. Per diem,* maxed. Two months in and I was off to a conference for a training/networking blitzkrieg. Brand spanking new Pfizer spin-doctor ready for Issues Notes and focus groups.

After I'd taken in and sweated out a sufficient amount of mid-priced strip loin steak and import beer, I hit the streets looking for a liquor store. Off on Halsted, north to the end of the block to West Madison. Dominick's Pharmacy, quite fitting. I head inside looking for the alcoholic beverages section, but the best I can do is Dayquil. Hotel lounge beer it will have to be.

Couple other staffers got us the green light for a VIP party at Excalibur. Downtown new-age club in a prohibition era Chicago banker building. Just east across the river into the heart of the nightlife district.

Seventeen guys, seventeen suits, seventeen loosened ties. I only knew a few of their names, but it didn't matter. Nobody cared who I was, and I was fine with that. We came in around the back just after midnight, greasing the doorman with bills I never saw.

Pulsating house techno. Multiple levels and layers of shiny iron ledges glistening in the strobe lights. Seated and served drinks by waitresses with fake boobs and sparklers held over their heads. Someone drops a company card, looking to max out a line of credit on overpriced panty remover.

After a few hours I'm drunk, and decide to call it a night. Too many sausages, too much testosterone and cocaine-fuelled rants about whether Obama is handling the economic recovery properly.

Wander off to West Ohio Street. Two people on the corner, waiting for cabs. I look at the girl: blonde, natural beauty, soft eyes—just my type. I consider initiating conversation but she's with another guy.

Then he turns and spouts out in a high-octane valve from the top of his throat.

"Oh my God I am not walking my ass back to the Marriott so help me God, girl."

Gayer than a three dollar bill.

I see an opening. Turn to her.

"No luck with cabs?"

She looks at me, smiles. Sign of interest.

"Yeah, we're just trying to get to the Marriott. I don't want to walk that far in heels and the L is down."

"*Ah, I see,*" I say, standing upright, trying to look as cool as I can in my two-piece suit and glassy eyes.

"*Where are you going?*" she asks, turning to me, leaving her friend to wave theatrically at passing cars—"*Hello, little help here! Beautiful man with bunions needs a lift!*"

"*I'm staying at the Crown Plaza. Here for a conference.*"

"*Oh yeah, cool. I'm here for a conference too. Marketing, at the Marriott. We're here from Virginia.*"

"*Cool.*"

She smiles again, turns to check on her fabulous friend, now almost stopping traffic with his perfectly manicured hands.

"*Motherfuckers gonna stop or I'm gonna throw down like nobody's business!*"

"*Sorry, he's a bit drunk,*" she says to me.

I smile. No problem here. Gays are gays, couldn't care less.

I see two guys walking down the street. Bears baseball caps and hooded sweaters.

"*Hey faggot, get off the street!*" yells one.

Both of us turn. Alert. I step a few paces forward.

"*Excuse me?*" Jeremy says, turning back onto the sidewalk.

"*Yeah, get the fuck out of here, you fucking queerbag.*"

This does not look good.

I'm closing in on the guys, now standing on the edge of the sidewalk, looking ready to take their homophobic aggression out on this Jeremy character.

Before anyone responds, I decide the best thing to do is channel their anger. At least this is what the alcohol inside me decides.

"*Hey shitheads! There's a black man in the White House and you're still playing the gay card? How gay are you two?*"

They look at me.

Jeremy lets out an uproarious "*Ha!*"

One of them tries to shove the wind out of my chest.

The other one not far behind.

When you dodge a left hook coming from a southpaw, the idea is not to move your shoulder, but to let your knees buckle until your head's out of the fist's striking path. It's all thigh strength. This way your stance stays correct, shoulders square, setting you up to return with an uppercut.

Jaw-breaking, base knuckles push the mandible up so far the lateral and central incisor teeth crack. Shockwaves pulsate up through the angle of the face, forcing the mind to black out, sending the body to the ground in a crumpled mess.

A right jab coming straight through is best blocked by the underside of the forearms. Bone first, two hands come together parallel facing the sky, deflecting the jab off to the right side of the shoulder. From there both hands wrap around the back of the skull, pulling down hard. Simultaneously the right knee comes up, searching for the nose bone. The two meet in violent symmetry, sending the body back up and off its feet.

Temporary loss of vision. Shattered nasal passage. Two down. Over four hundred pounds of drunken testosterone on the concrete.

They look at me.

"Ohmyfuckinggod Jean-Claude Van Damme here to the rescue!"

The whites of their eyes.

My knuckles still sting.

They're looking at me like only a verbal response will do.

"Used to box . . . well, I still do. My dad is a cop, I mean. I just train. Haven't fought in a while."

Still no response. The girl looks at me.

Police sirens.

Flashing lights.

Cop car screeches up onto the pavement. I back up.

Chicago's finest, out of their patrol car.

I'm confused and drunk. The scene does not bode well for me and my bloody hands.

When your head is slammed off the front hood of a police car, it tends to force a moment of reflection.

How did I get to this exact point in my life? one might say.

I decide the best thing to do is keep my mouth shut.

Thank God for dual citizenship and passing on the coke at Excalibur.

Three hours and a mountain of paperwork later I'm let out of holding at the CPD South Loop dispatch centre.

No charges. Only eye witnesses stating I acted in self-defense.

Jeremy and the beautiful blonde saved my ass.

*Back at the hotel, I head up to my room. I'm banking on two hours sleep and an icepack getting me through seven hours of Public Affairs presentations. I'm asking for miracles even God can't deliver.*

*There's an envelope on the floor when I open the door.*

To the hero of West Ohio Street
Dear Tristan,
Thank you so much for saving me and my friend Jeremy. Glad we could help out at the station after too. Sorry, I wanted to wait to thank you in person but had to go to bed. Can you take me out to dinner tomorrow?

Brianne
Marriott, Room 413

</>

South on Interstate 5, then onto the I-90 towards the Lacey V Murrow Bridge.

Glued to the window. Cars abandoned.

Groups of people stand around talking feverously, or heading somewhere quickly. First responder vehicles dart around, lights and sirens scream endlessly. When one leaves earshot, another enters.

No one out biking, no one out walking. Traffic so thin I feel as if we're in a different city. I'm not used to seeing so much unobstructed pavement.

We get onto the bridge and head across.

Check the map, reading out directions, tracing a finger along the roads.

Look over the bridge as we pass. Debris litters the water, more than usual for this tributary. As soon as we see homes on Mercer Island, it's clear there is no power. Usually the skies are littered with planes from SeaTac, but today there's nothing.

Mercer Island, a soggy jungle of flourishing evergreens and desolate buildings. An eerie, anarchistic feeling only heightened by a cop car chasing a Dodge Ram pickup off the island.

We follow the map through the Park on the Lid to 72nd.

A man hangs from a noose in a tree on a front yard.

A Bible on the ground below his feet.

His body an exclamation point on a growing fear. We have passed a point of no return. We have entered what his mind believes are the End Times. What was once anxiety is now cooking at a temperature to produce all-out panic. My father offers his first advice at a scene I will surely remember for the rest of my life.

"Turn your head forward."

I turn my head straight forward.

Eco-friendly garbage can on fire in the middle of the street, slowly burning away, melting—thick gooey green drips onto the asphalt with each lick of flame.

People watch us from their windows, hiding behind the drapes.

Brianne's place, the basement suite. My dad pulls the car up into the driveway, pulls out his Glock.

"You stay close to me, okay?"

I nod in acknowledgment. Check my phone again. I'm addicted to checking my phone. I haven't had service in more than three days but I still feel an insatiable need to check it.

Turn my ringer off in some misguided attempt to focus on the present.

But that just brings flashes of the Christian hanging by a rope above his lawn.

Shake my skull, physically and mentally.

Up to the front door. Locked.

Explosion off in the distance. It stops us; we look at each other.

Continue hesitantly to the back.

Door to the basement suite unlocked.

My dad pulls his gun up; I feel naked with nothing to protect me.

Into the cover of the suite. He leads with his firearm. It's quiet, with that air of abandonment an unfilled place has. I've never seen the apartment with no lights on.

Looks like she left in a hurry: drawers open, dishes stacked in the sink, a coat in the middle of the living room floor.

"Brianne?!" I say.

My dad stops, looks angry, like we blew our cover or something. I'm not into playing cop right now.

Walk past him through the living room and into the bedroom. Nothing. Women's clothing vomited everywhere. She packed and left in a hurry.

Stand there for a few seconds. Information seeps into my brain.

My dad comes around the corner.

"Anything?"

"No, she's gone."

Just gone. Disappeared.

I walk back out into the living room. Sit down on her couch, which used to be our couch. Lean back, put my hands on my head.

My father comes over and sits down on the love seat across from me.

Is this it? Not with a bang, but a whimper. The love of my life, off into the sky like a helium filled balloon cut loose. Left to try and wean myself off her, alone with my memories and thoughts.

He takes a breath in through his nose.

If we knew each other better, he might say something consoling. Instead he poses a question, trying to figure out who this ghost was his son was so adamant to get to.

"You loved her, hey?"

All I can respond with is a nod.

I'm vaulted back to the night my mother died.

Fire broke out while we slept upstairs. Sitting here with the physical spirit of my father, I can't remember the man he was before he lost his wife. It hit him hard, harder than I think anyone would have fathomed.

The cops never figured out where the blaze actually started. It was the 1980s, there was no CSI; they just took down my dad's story that he went downstairs and saw flames. He was a local hero, saved two people in the line of duty. Freak accident, end of story. Collect insurance payout.

Smoke inhalation is a sense like no other.

"We need to get your sister," he says.

I nod.

My sister. Liz. So clouded I forgot the most important thing. Family. Here I am, clinging to a sunken relationship, while my own blood sits scared in her dorm room in Victoria. Shame enters my brain.

"We need three things," he continues. "Then we cross the border, get my boat at White Rock and go over the Strait, and we go to your sister."

Not totally coherent or present, I nod again.

"Three things," he says again. He lists them off on his fingers.

"Survival supplies, food, water, medical supplies. Cash. Weapons."

Sounds like six or seven. Whatever.

Supposed apocalypse. Coworkers, gone. Brianne, gone. Attempted mugging, dead Christian in a tree, all before noon. I kind of wish I'd eaten breakfast.

"How are we gonna find Liz? We can't contact her. It's not like we can send her an email and tell her to stay put. What if she comes looking for us?"

Our reliance on virtual communication exposed like a fresh wound. For some reason, I'm thinking about the carrier ravens in *Game of Thrones*. I wonder if any of them ever got a bounce back. Return to sender. Delivery has failed to these recipients or distribution lists. The recipient's email address was not found in the recipient's email system.

He shakes his head.

"We have to rely on our own knowledge, and what the circumstances have given us. Chances are we should assume she thinks we're coming for her, and she will stay put."

He's right; it's all we've got.

My sister spent last Christmas with Brad. Trying to sneak into a new unit, one not fit for a depressing dramatic movie about downtrodden families.

A deep breath. I start for the door.

"Let's get the fuck out of here."

My dad follows, but he stops me outside in the backyard.

Looks me in the eyes.

"You gonna be okay?"

I look at him.

"Yeah, I think so."

I continue walking.

The car starts up. My dad peers around.

"We'll head back across the bridge. Let's go to your place and grab our stuff."

Back down the street, garbage can flickers away. I get caught in its dance of chemical change. Cars creeping around corners, leaping through four-way stops.

We pass the guy hanging from the tree in his front yard.

All I can think about is Brianne. My heart literally aches. It feels so cliché, but it fucking hurts. I'm running our conversations in my mind. Lines, looks, memories. Endless loops replay over and over. Scenes spool out in recurring fashion. The last time we had sex. The last time I saw her smile.

Shock. Hysteria. I place my hands on my head.

Defective hardware.

Software infected with a virus.

Overloading the processing capabilities of the system.

My father looks like he's about to say something.

But he doesn't.

I watch the body hanging in the tree through the rearview mirror.

*I just want her back so badly.*

We head across the bridge, passing cars zooming the other way. Slow up halfway across. Clouds of smoke billow out just after the bridge on Lakeside Avenue. Plush red fire—must be twenty feet high.

A car pulls up beside. I look over, a guy in the other vehicle staring forward at the smoke.

The thick grey clouds lift into the sky like a danger sign.

Do *Not* Enter.

The guy gets out of his car, walks over to us. Shaken. Like he hasn't slept in weeks. Signals to roll down the window. My dad doesn't oblige. He speaks through the glass, voice muffled. Pupils crazy.

"This. This, the white sky. It's God's way of punishing us for our sins. The white sky is our punishment."

My dad takes the Glock and taps it against the window. Metal clinks against glass.

"Fuck off," he says.

Crazy eyes stares at the gun, nods to himself, heads back to his car, and drives off.

"Goddamn religious nuts. You'd think they were waiting for this day," my dad says.

Turn around, head back into the darkness that is Mercer Island. He drives. I sit, encased in debilitating meditation. Scenes whip by the window, nothing registers.

Error code.

Enumerated messages.

Faulty software application.

Abort program.

</>

Back to my place, along the I-5. Turn the corner onto the high rise lined cul-de-sac.

Flash of another car enters our path.

We collide.

Twisting metal sheets, crinkled like paper, crashing alloy waves.

Wind pushed instantaneously from my stomach by my seat-belt.

Forehead jerks forward. Airbag flips the universe blank with a chalky taste in a fraction of a split second.

I bite my lip.

Hard.

Flesh tears between teeth.

Antonym of physical consent. Car comes up off its front tires, comes down just as quickly. Accessories fling into the abyss, side view mirrors, parts of the front grill.

Head bounces off the window, hard thump echoing into my skull as I squint in response.

Stars.

Blotched vision.

Brain cell massacre.

Thoughts scatter like cockroaches from a shining light.

Horn starts on the other vehicle. Loud, endless. Sound of sudden distress. Like a smoke detector, it's insistently calling to be turned off.

Flutters out. Off pitch, a terrible squeal, pig being slaughtered.

Silence, hissing of engine coolant, leaked valves.

The taste of blood in my mouth, tangy salt. My dad's taking his seatbelt off, turns to me. Fog encompasses my left eye, blotch of haze on the bottom right.

"You okay?"

Stomach's trying to turn itself back over, turtle stuck on its shell.

"Yeah . . . I think so."

He gets out, I follow.

Washington State police cruiser. Front end busted to shit.

A tall, dark haired figure appears on the driver's side, holding his neck.

Brad?

Motherfucking Brad.

"Brad?!" I say to both my dad and him.

Brad looks at us.

"Holy fuck, I'm sorry, guys. I was trying to find your place, Tristan."

He's sporting a shiner like a fucking black hole.

The mystery of my dad's busted hand: solved.

"Fuck, what are the chances I would hit you two guys?"

Still trying to sort out the fact that Liz's ex just clipped us in a police cruiser. I hadn't seen him since dinner in Vancouver with Liz and Brianne years ago. When he dumped his soul out to me while we stood in front of the restaurant sharing a flavoured cigar.

"Detective Schultz, I'm so sorry."

My dad looks unimpressed.

"What the fuck are you doing here, Brad?"

"I was looking for you guys. I was thinking you'd probably be heading for Liz. I was thinking we could go together, the three of us."

"Did I not make myself clear yesterday? You are not a part of this family anymore. You have been harassing my daughter to the point of no return. Maybe in a few years, if you keep your shit together and show us you can be a decent father figure, we can talk. Maybe."

Wait.

What the—

Frustration starts to colour Brad's face.

"It's my fucking kid! I have more rights to it than you do!"

I butt in verbally.

"Wait, what the fuck is going on?" I say. "Father?"

Brad pulls out his police billy club.

My dad takes off his jacket.

Shit's going down in the middle of the street.

*Wait, my fucking sister is pregnant?*

"All my life I've wanted to be a father!" screams Brad. "You're not going to take this away from me! From what happened to me!"

Dialogue, over. Violence, commenced.

Brad's club comes over his head like a tomahawk.

My dad sends it sideways with his forearm.

Punch to the gut, right in the breadbasket. Air leaves Brad's mouth like a pocket of aerosol pushed free into the atmosphere.

*Umpfffff!*

Elbow. Jab. Side forearm block.

Tossing punches at each other.

Brad whacks my dad across the shoulder with the club.

*Hard.*

Bear growl.

I step forward to intervene.

Brad sends the club again, but this time my dad grabs it mid-swing, twists it around in an instant, dislodging it from his grip.

Whacks it over Brad's back. I squint in pain as I hear it collide with his spine.

Brad lets out a howl.

Again, same spot.

Another wail of pain.

Again.

Motherfucker is getting tuned up. Feels like some police instructional video on how to take a guy down, hard. CompuBox scoring this one for my old man.

Three more whacks and Brad's on his hands and knees. Steel toe boot to the stomach for good measure; ribs crack like twigs.

The two of us stand there.

I don't know where to begin. I knew Brad moved to Washington State after he got kicked off the force in Vancouver. Liz dumped him, once again, or so her Facebook status implied.

*It's complicated.*

Yes, yes it is.

I look at my dad. Brad gasps in pain, hunched over. Spits blood from his mouth.

"Dad, explain. Now."

He just looks at me.

I walk over and grab him around the scruff of his shoulders.

"How the fuck does Liz's ex know where I live, and why the fuck are you going all Rodney *fucking* King on his ass? And he's a father?! Of what?!"

He looks into my eyes. Still breathing heavy.

"Speak for fuck's sake!" I scream into his face.

"Liz, she's pregnant, Tristan. Liz is pregnant, due any day now. Brad's the father. I met him yesterday. It didn't go well."

My mind vaults away. Unable to push into the future, all I can do is exist in the past. The present, lapsed.

Blood drips onto my tie. I wipe my lip. Hold my hand out. Blood pools in my palm. Drips down, runs through the lines in my fingers.

My eyes widen. Heart slams on the brakes.

"What?" I say, even though I clearly heard him. I've just been standing here, staring at my hand.

"Yeah, she's supposed to go into the hospital tomorrow to give birth."

"Motherfucker."

He nods.

"That's why you came to see me? To tell me?"

"Yeah, I was on my way to see her; I cancelled the rest of my trip when I found out. She told me Brad was the father. I came to see him, too. On Saturday."

Another big gulp of air. Things starting to make sense. My father's urgency resonates with clarity rather than delirium.

"I told her I wanted to help with the pregnancy. You know, however I could."

I nod, not sure what to say.

I'm going to be an uncle. My dad, a grandfather.

The thought had literally never crossed my mind.

Here I am, avoiding kids like the plague, and my sister pumps one out like a mid-term paper. Who gets pregnant like that? Especially Liz, the most levelheaded Schultz of all—the one about to start medical school. The one who walked two men away from the abyss of tragedy into a feasible life.

A kid. Brianne and I exhausted our vocal cords for the better part of three years screaming about the issue, and now my sister's going to make me an uncle in the blink of an eye.

*Nothing makes sense.*

I wonder if she knows the sex. If I'll end up with a niece or nephew. *Uncle Tristan . . .*

"Okay," I say.

Silence. Telling silence.

My thoughts flood to Liz, to how my pregnant sister is coping with this madness. This unprecedented mess. Is she okay?

Brad starts to stand up. Holding his ribs like they might spill out of his stomach.

"Wait. How the fuck do you know where I live, Brad?"

My dad looks at me.

"He's a cop, Tristan. We know where everyone lives."

Brad wipes the blood from his face. Smears it across the hood of his car. Staggers to eye level.

Holds his hands up in boxing stance like that opponent that just won't quit.

"Go home, Brad," says my dad. He sounds tired.

"It's my fucking kid, too!"

"You're a fucking mess. You don't deserve to be a father. You need to leave my daughter alone, once and for all."

He comes towards my dad.

The billy club stops him.

The realization that my father's assaulting a police officer in the middle of the street crosses my mind. I look around. Nobody's watching.

Brad leans against the hood of his cruiser. Blood dots the white painted metal.

"You think I won't go to her? You think you can stop me?"

I can see my father's chest heaving. He walks right up to Brad and grabs him, shoves him back against the car. He shoves him so hard he rolls off the hood and back onto the ground in a half somersault.

"You come within a hundred meters of my daughter again, and I will fucking end you, kid."

Turns to me, drops the billy club.

"Let's go, now."

</>

Holds her hand below the curve of the stomach, like the contents may spill out onto the floor if she isn't careful. Palm wrapped below the belly button. Swollen, containing the life that kicks inside, keeping her awake. The baby is restless.

Mother is restless. She moves back out of the bathroom, walks with a wide stance to the bed. Resorted to peeing in the tub when the toilet stopped working. She's embarrassed, even though no one's around.

Picks up her iPhone in the dark. Candles flicker light into the corners of the room. Muggy heat, beaded sweat along the brow, dark shadows. Sounds of chaos outside—just faint enough to perk the ears.

Sits on the sheets, thumbs through her phone. No signal. She hasn't seen anyone in hours. Locked herself in her one-room apartment. No friends appear at the door. No dad or brother; no word from anyone, not even the father of her unborn baby.

No power, no comfort.

She has never felt this alone.

Tries her laptop, searching for wireless. Antenna icon pulses out in little green waves. Nothing. Network connection problems. Closes the screen in a huff, tears stream down her cheeks. Somehow she'll see this through. She's survived worse, she thinks to herself. She's walked through storms, waded in murky water.

Walked through fire.

Will they come? Will someone come to help her give birth? Lifts her feet onto the bed, props the pillow behind her head. Lets her belly rest on her back. The thoughts tire her; she tries to let them drift off into the beats of the baby's heart.

Contractions have started. Sporadic. The stress of the situation. They physically wake her. Hormones fly around her insides. Backaches, shortness of breath, heartburn, swelling. The miracle of life, she scoffs at this now: get this freakin' kid out of me. She's done with the vaginal discharge, the bathroom trips, the all around discomfort. Pregnancy, as unplanned as this one was, has lost its allure. She's lost her glow.

Campus police came by Friday night, told her to stay inside, not to leave until she heard otherwise. They gave her a number to call, but her phone's not working.

Immobilized by fear, hampered by twenty-five pounds of extra weight, cautious and careful, she waits for the storm to pass. For someone to come to her. Her father, her brother.

She knows they're on their way. She's sure of it.

Because they are family.

The baby kicks against her stomach.

</>

Over the E Channel Bridge. Through an unmanned tollbooth and into the suburban sprawl of Bellevue. Mad dash for the 405.

Erratic power on both sides of the highway. Cars either speeding, driving too slow, abandoned, or crashed. Nobody daily commuting.

Check my phone. Nothing. Turn it off; put it in the glove compartment.

Faint clouds build stencil shade lines around the white. The plain paper above starting to cry, ready to disgorge onto us.

I'm trying to sort everything in my head.

Uncle. Daughter. Pregnant. Brad.

Liz.

We're in a race against time, a race against another cop. Not just a cop. A PTSD-stricken war vet with a gun, a badge, and a police cruiser who knocked up my lil' sis.

"We keep a steady pace," he says. "We move too fast, we're gonna end up running ourselves off the road. We move at the speed of this *thing*, whatever this is."

I watch my father drive as he speaks.

"Guns, ammo, cash. Then the border. He's got nothing on us. They won't let a uniformed cop from the States cross into Canada any easier than a civilian. And with his face and demeanour, we've got a leg up already."

Blood pumping through a vein on his neck like a garden hose.

A few days ago I was trying to stay awake during another Strategic Planning PowerPoint session. Wondering if my ex would ever take me back so we could split the rent on my apartment again.

Now I'm racing to reach my pregnant sister and watching two cops go all motherfucking Rambo on each other.

Whatever made sense has been thrown out the window. We have entered the surreal, the unexplainable. The entire planet did a hairpin U-turn going a hundred miles an hour and I didn't even have my seatbelt on.

Pull over by a textbook shopping mall—massive Wal-Mart in the middle of a concrete wasteland, sitting like a consumerist deity, cornerstone of the capitalist dream.

From half a block away, we watch the chaos.

People scatter, dart around. Congestion, bottleneck of confusion. I've seen it in the movies so many times, now I'm having the actual real world experience. Life imitating art. Predictable species we are. We are not intricate, unique, individual carbon-based life forms. The lowest common denominator always wins. We'd rather mimic and fall in line than break rank, even in the face of societal meltdown.

Three days.

Seventy-two plus hours of disconnect and we're freely looting. Part of me wants to be amazed at how quickly things deteriorated. The other half thinks three days without cell coverage, internet and emergency service communications is ample time for a population of mammals to break free from society once exposed half-baked fallacies propped up by nothing more than lies, deceit and Uber emerge.

Five-finger discount shoppers rush out of the store, carts full of bulk items. Some walk, most run. Flurries of activity, blizzards of confusion. Like watching an ant hill, you can only focus if you pick one and follow it.

Muffled blast, what could be a gunshot. People scatter. Some fall to the ground. Faint screams.

Flash of fire from the hood of a vehicle, then it drives out of the lot into a divider. White smoke spouts upwards. Car stops and a lone male gets out, staggers around, looking for something, possibly calling for someone.

"We need to find an ATM. I bet there's one in there that's portable."

I look at my dad. "An ATM?"

"Yeah, food, supplies, there are thousands of stores and Wal-Marts. What we need is hard currency."

"I don't get it. For what?"

"I want to purchase more guns, a hunting knife, survival gear. I know those stores; they'll probably take cash for the next few days before they get wise and close up shop."

What is this? Survival of the fittest? Are we about to head into the wild for six months trying to find the Sasquatch with Survivorman?

A middle-aged couple frantically pushes a cart full of bottled water out of the front entrance.

My dad drives into the parking lot.

"What are you doing? What are *we* doing?"

Apparently we voted. It was 1-0.

"We're going to steal the ATM from the Wal-Mart. I'm guessing it's the best option. It's full because people get cash back at the till but it's probably stocked well because it's at a Wal-Mart. We might get somewhere in the neighbourhood of five grand."

He's taken down guys who've taken down ATMs, so he has a general idea of how much money they contain. So yeah, apparently we're going to jack an ATM from a Wal-Mart. I place the item on my Bucket List for the pleasure of removing it.

Pull up to the edge of the lot. Chaos subwoofer surround-sound. People looting like crazy, in and out of the store. Cars drive up, unload, drive off. Then more cars, again and again. Conveyor belt of shoplifting.

"Okay, we're gonna go inside. Keep to a slow jog. Stay close to me."

Pulls out the Glock, chambers a round. We leave the car and jog to the entrance, weaving in and around people. Massive neon white lights flicker inside, spastic-bizarro techno rave of consumerist misrule. Anarchy, a bastardized version of Supermarket Sweep.

Left, down the checkout aisle, understandably underused. I haven't seen a blue vest yet.

There it is, right in front of the McDonald's: an ATM.

He walks up to it, slips his gun in his belt. Swivels the ATM around. Thing's not even bolted to the wall.

Grunts; it's heavy.

"Come over here, we'll furniture lift it."

Signals me to take the lighter top end.

People stare at us. It's mind-boggling, like stealing goods is fucking fine right now, but stealing cold hard cash—that's a no-no.

We pass the registers, a line of shopping carts, and rows of celebrity gossip magazines. Wait, Kim Kardashian is pregnant again? Arms start to burn.

Make our way outside, across the lot. People watch, but they sure as hell don't stop us. My dad drops his end. Opens up the back door as we cumbersomely navigate the ATM in.

"I'm gonna need some tools to open this. You stay here."

He's holding the gun up towards me, barrel pointed back at him.

I'm a kid again, at the shooting ranges. Massive neon orange trimmed ear muffs draped over my head. Check your background. Breathe. Both eyes open. Squeeze. Reload a magazine. Gun always pointed away, leg stance sideways, left hand over right. Safety check.

"You remember?"

I remember the hot shells burning holes in my jeans.

He jogs back into the store, abandoning me in the lot like an unwanted child. I stand there—idiot with a gun in a designer suit, bleeding from my lip, outside a car with a stolen ATM in the backseat.

My father. A retired cop. Just stole an ATM.

We will now cease to return to regularly scheduled programming.

People load their vehicles. Kids inside, looking wide-eyed and bushytailed—alert dogs not quite sure what's going on.

One family grabs my attention. Stressed father loads food and water into the back of a van, literally shoving his wife out of the way at one point, probably because she isn't loading fast enough. Her face swollen and red from what looks like hours of crying.

He closes the doors and gets into the van. Fuckhead almost drives away without her; she has to pull herself into the car as it's already out of park.

Bad marriages aren't made for the apocalypse.

Young guy in a Seahawks jersey comes out of the store with a case of water. Bumps into someone else on his way in. Water bottles drop to the ground and burst all over the concrete. They crackle and roll, break away in half circle escape routes.

All I'm thinking is—*Seahawks jersey, today? Really?*

He bends down to pick up as many as he can. It's futile. Kneels there, looking for someone to help Number 24 Marshawn

Lynch, but all he gets is passersby brush-offs and errant runners grabbing bottles, snatching up candy that's fallen from a piñata.

Clouds forming—colourless backdrop still an apparent illusion. Air particles cooling, sensory build-up before precipitation. You can feel the electricity in the air. This time it soaks in differently, a pulsating wave freefalling from the sky, matrix lines of code descend upon the earth like the final curtain of technology.

Magnetized entity hovering above—omnipotent. Surrounded by electric swells of gravity. I feel ten pounds heavier. Baker's dozen of paperweights inside my stomach.

As the chaos unfolds, the reality of what's going on tries to burrow deeper into my skin. What is this? What happened? Was there a nuclear war, and now we're living in the dust of nuclear winds? Is this some type of weird electrical storm? Who else has been hit by this? Is it the whole world?

What.

The.

*Fuck.*

No cohesive effort executed by my thoughts—none of them on the same page. So foreign, this idea society is completely unhinged, let loose to float in a raging storm. No scripted law, no moral responsibility pinned by the oversight of proper discourse.

A feeling's developing inside me. Excitement? Couldn't be. But it is. For some reason the end of the world appears to be dawning on us, and I feel invigorated, refreshed. Old thoughts dying in the corners of my mind. Ironclad fabric of the society that was telling me to get a job and start a family washed away. A stain cleansed in a shower of anarchy.

Was this what I wanted? What I needed? I'd cringed at the thought of watching my life tick away in some two-bedroom suburban home, of driving my kids to soccer practice while I worked an unfulfilling 50-hour week to support it all.

That life, the one Brianne wanted, it might not exist anymore. Society could be gone. Everything could be gone. The pressure I felt, from the ads, the movies, the couples on the streets pushing baby strollers and dragging dogs on leashes. The trips to

IKEA, the mortgage payments, the life we're all supposed to live because our parents did. Gone.

The idea, the notion entices me. A different life, a different world.

An answered prayer.

#thankgodfortheapocalypse

I think of the people who'd still be online during this shitstorm of a rat's nest. Checking in here, burning buildings there, tagging dead bodies, unable to stop the social media steam train even in the wake of the end of the goddamn motherfucking planet.

*What is this world coming to?* they would tweet, and retweet, and Like, and Share, and comment on, and post.

But if that were really happening, none of this would be happening, which is what *is* happening. We manufactured the gun, thinking the most probable outcome wouldn't involve it firing back. We created a world reliant on technology, and everything turned off. The apocalypse has commenced, and so far I've had my tail between my legs. I've done nothing but be pedestrian. An observer.

The time for inaction is not now.

Female scream.

Some guy drags a girl out of a car by her hair.

Enough of the sidelines.

Run over as he gets into the driver's seat and push the gun into his cheek. Veins pump with antagonized anger.

"Get out of the car," I tell him.

The guy and his neatly trimmed facial hair keep staring forward. He looks unimpressed.

"What, are you gonna shoot me, man? You're gonna shoot me for stealing a car? You wanna go to jail for the rest of your life?"

His introspective retort stuns me.

The brown-stained stock end of a brand new shotgun flies into his face with serious ferocity. Very distinct whacking sound. One of crushed flesh, shattered bones and ripped cartilage. The guy's limp across the front seat before I can blink.

My dad opens the car door and drags the guy out by his feet onto the pavement. Looks at me, looks at the girl, her hair a complete mess.

"Liz. Not this shit. We're not here to play hero, okay?"

I nod.

"We keep pace. Got it?"

Behind him, a white trimmed black hockey bag full of guns and ammunition.

The woman looks at us.

"Thank you so much."

"Yeah. Sure," says my dad.

I look at the girl. She looks at me.

"Anyways . . ."

We're away. Back passengers a bag full of weapons and a stolen ATM. Front hood like crumpled paper. If we get pulled over, I figure the best thing to do is tell the truth, because, well, fuck.

North on the I-5. Gas station corners and billboard signs. Modern ghost town, once lit store signs now darkened. Everything a muted colour, the vibrancy of neon gone from the world. I feel abandoned; the situation looks abandoned. I'm shaking my head. Also, I'm starving.

"We're heading for Liz, but we had time to stop and steal an ATM?"

No response.

"Any thoughts on what the *fuck is going on?*" I add, decibel increasing with each syllable.

No answer. We keep driving. Pass an accident scene. People walk around a car; inside, a person lies against the window, unconscious.

I point at the accident.

"Like that! What the fuck is that? That's not normal. Is that normal?"

The wreckage leaves my sight. I turn back for an explanation, like he's an adult and I'm a kid, and as society goes, he should be able to explain what's going on.

He rubs his face.

"We need to get to your sister as fast as possible, Tristan. That's all I know."

Sporadic power, cars whizzing around, people off the highway looking as lost as lost gets.

The best thing is to continue looking forward.
Just continue.

\</>

*For the better part of the day, I couldn't figure out why I was nervous.
Then it hit me.*

*I was nervous to have my sister meet my girlfriend.*

*Brianne and I planned a trip to Vancouver for the weekend, and Liz
was in town with friends on reading break. My father was chasing boars
somewhere off the Trans-Siberian Railway. Probably couldn't make it to
Flying Pig in Yaletown for a bite to eat.*

*I fidget, follow Brianne around H&M in Pacific Centre. She keeps
holding up dresses, looking at me like I have a say in the matter.*

*"This might be nice for tonight."*

*"Sure."*

*She turns to the mirror. I nod as she models a beautiful yellow sun
dress in the tri-part glass.*

*Crush of women on iPhones. Clogging the lanes, forcing me to lean
against brightly coloured clothing racks as shoppers plow through, bags in
hand. Overhead speakers bombing indie-hipster tunes into my ears. It's a
beautiful spring Saturday. Why the hell am I here?*

*I just want to run back to the hotel with Brianne, lounge by the pool.
Vancouver's like Seattle with more rain and fewer highways. All I wanted
was to get to dinner with Liz, sit down, let the two of them meet. The
anticipation made me want to grab a pair of twenty-dollar loafers and hurl
them at the checkout counter.*

*Why was I nervous? Brianne and I were living together; we were
cemented as a couple. And here was my distant sister.*

*Nerves at the thought of the two most prominent women in my life
meeting eating me alive.*

*I breathe out. Loud enough that Brianne hears.*

*"You okay?" she says, turning to me.*

*"Yeah," I say, rubbing my head, back and forth, front to back.*

*"What's wrong?"*

*She puts her Starbucks hot chocolate on a display, comes in close,
wraps her arms around my waist, and looks at me with those eyes. The*

*ones that smash through any emotional barrier I try to throw up. She always knows when I need to be touched.*

*"It'll be fine. I'm sure your sister and I will get along great."*

*Nuzzles her nose into my chest like she's trying to burrow into me. Speaks in a silly tone.*

*"My big tall boxer boyfriend afraid of two little women meeting."*

*I smile, look down at her.*

*"You suck," I say.*

*She tilts her head up, puckers her lips, asking for a kiss.*

*I oblige.*

*"Ten more minutes, then we'll head back to the hotel and sit by the pool. I promise."*

*Holds her pinky up.*

*"Pinky swear."*

*Pinkies lock in unison.*

*I let out a sigh of relief as Brianne holds my hands in hers.*

*"Tristan," she says quietly. "This is important. We're here to find a present for Liz, not just for me to shop, okay? I need to get to know your sister. Family is important. I mean, she could be my sister-in-law one day. This stuff matters."*

*I want to tell her I don't even know my sister. But this is not the time.*

*Blackberry rings in my pocket. I take it out. It's Liz.*

*Brianne grabs the phone.*

*"Hey!" I say.*

*She steps back, turns around.*

*"Oh, hey, Liz, it's Brianne . . . yeah hey! So we're at H&M . . . really? You're kidding. What section?"*

*Brianne starts walking, looking for a certain area of the store. I stand there like I just got robbed. She's still talking.*

*"Yeah, I know, he's funny, isn't he? . . . Oh, totally. Yeah no, I found a few dresses but I couldn't find any bathing suits that fit . . . Yeah, what's the deal with that? What, am I supposed to be starving rail thin?"*

*She continues walking, chatting on the phone like she and Liz are old friends. She turns the corner.*

*Out of sight, I hear her laugh.*

*I stand. Not sure what to do. Another guy in the store looks at me. He's following his girlfriend, carrying multiple shopping bags. He nods.*

*I nod back, and continue to stand, waiting.*

*Lost amidst the clothing, the fashion of it all.*

*Two hours later, I get a text from Liz:*

Brad is coming to dinner. I know I said we broke up. Don't ask.

*I don't.*

*The four of us meet at the Flying Pig. Liz hugs me tight. Again, Brad tries to crush my fingers with his handshake. I just squeeze back.*

*We sit against the brick-lined wall, facing the bar. Yaletown sensibilities, high end sales couples and upper class indie hipsters dining on skirt steaks and funky side dishes. Crispy brussels sprouts; bread dip with Evoo and balsamic vinegar.*

*I pick at an artisan meat and cheese board.*

*Order a Kronenbourg Blanc.*

*Brad drops his drink menu in frustration.*

"I'll have the same."

*Brianne asks Liz about medical school, what type of doctor she wants to be.*

*Maybe a GP. Possibly emergency room surgeon.*

*Brianne makes me smile. Showing genuine interest in my lil' sis.*

*I think about my younger sister becoming a doctor.*

*I'd be proud.*

"You watch the St. Pierre fight?" *Brad says, butting in, looking at me hard.*

*I listen as Brianne starts up another conversation with Liz.*

"Ah, no. I missed it."

"You see Hardy's arm? He almost fucking snapped it back."

*I was a boxing pureblood, and I hadn't taken to UFC. Would rather watch a classic Ali fight or one of the Ward-Gatti tilts then some Affliction meathead with cauliflower ears mud wrestle his doppelganger. But I try to keep the conversation afloat.*

"St. Pierre, you like him? He's a good fighter, hey?"

"Yeah," *he responds,* "good Canadian boy. Even though he's French."

*I chuckle. Brad smiles.*

*Later, I head outside onto Hamilton Street for a cherry Prime Time cigar. Liz and Brianne deep in chatter and their second bottle of wine, like* old friends catching up on years of gossip. The two women in my life finding a way to bond with no help whatsoever from me. Makes me smile.

Brad emerges out of the door, nods to me.

"Ah shit, man, can I have one of those?"

I hold the pack up.

"Lighter?"

He lights his.

"Cherry? Man, love these."

I nod, stare off at the restaurant across the street. I'm still not sure I want to invest any energy in Liz's on-again, off-again boyfriend. After all the ups and downs, I don't trust the guy. But I'm stuck being polite so that my sister and girlfriend can make up for lost time.

Brad comes around the side and faces me, takes a puff from his cigar.

"Hey man, I just wanted to say I've heard a lot of good things about you."

"Thanks, man."

"And I know—I mean, I'm sure Liz has told you that we've had our problems. I mean, I'm sure you and Brianne have had yours."

I grin. It's as if this twenty-something character in front of me is a thirty-something when it comes to relationship experience.

Truth is, Liz's Facebook is my best source of information about her and Brad. Like a flashcard rollercoaster ride.

In a relationship.

Single.

It's complicated.

Profile pics of them together.

Profile pics of her alone.

"Anyways, man, I just wanted to say that I respect you, and I love Liz. I would never hurt her."

I don't know what the fuck this guy is doing. Is this a normal thing for big brothers? A conversation we usually have?

"Cool, okay man," I say, looking at him.

He nods. Looks away. Doesn't want to get too mushy in front of another guy, maybe.

"Anyway, yeah, your dad is good shit. Got me into the force, I'll forever be in his debt. Man, I went fishing with him on his boat in White Rock. Fucking good times."

*Part of me is angry now. I imagine Brad in the boat with Liz and my dad, and it's like he's replaced me. Like my dad's found a son-in-law in the absence of a real one.*

*The memories I could've had if I hadn't left the continent.*

"Cool," is all I can muster.

"Yo, yeah, and he also showed me some of your boxing trophies. Your bronze at nationals for bantamweight. Impressive, man. You still spar, right? We should hit the bag next time you're up in Van."

*Now we're talking. A few rounds with this half-grown man-boy; some body work; a baker's dozen of combos. I could send his ego back a few years for a conditioning stint in the minors.*

"Yeah, man, that sounds like a plan," I say with a grin.

*He shakes my hand again for some odd reason, this time not as hard. In that moment, I see what Liz likes about this kid. He's affable in a childishly endearing way. You wanna help his handsome self get his GED or something. Like a project, a fixer-upper home with a decent starting frame on a corner lot.*

*Was this the type of guy Liz chased? Someone to fix? Was it because of dad and me? Because of Mom?*

"So I dunno if Liz told you, but I kind of went through something similar to what you guys went through."

*Not sure what's he's talking about. Liz and I don't talk, and we certainly don't talk about Brad, so I have no idea where this is going. But if he starts in on my mom in the wrong way, this foodie-wine night might have to incorporate a trip to the ER.*

"Yeah, my dad, he's American, was in Vietnam."

*I want to say the c-word, but Brad beats me to it.*

"I know, man, fucking cliché shit. Father in Vietnam, son in Afghanistan. Like a movie, right? Anyway, my dad, he drank a lot. We grew up on the Sunshine Coast. One night he just fucking walked into the woods. We never even found his body."

*A lone man trailing off into a forest, bottle in hand. A young boy standing on the steps of a cottage, watching as his father disappears.*

*What would my life have been like if my father had passed away, not my mother? What would I be searching for in place of her? An entire existence flashes through my bones and skin, one I cannot begin to comprehend with any real truth.*

*"Fuck. I'm sorry," I say.*

*I'd never met anyone who lost a parent like we did. Was this why Liz bonded with him so easily? I'm trying to find words to help me express the thoughts rushing through my head, but Brad speaks first.*

*"It's cool, man. I just—I know what it's like. I know how you guys feel. It fucking sucks, and people want to talk to you about it, but all you want to do is not talk about it, ever. And somehow it still ends up defining your whole fucking life."*

*I nod. It's all I can do. This kid is speaking truth.*

*"I just hope some day I can have a kid of my own so I can erase the mistakes of my family."*

*Words trail off into the night sky.*

*The sins of our fathers. The next generation always has the chance to break the cycle. Paint anew; awash the canvas and rewrite.*

*"Let's head back inside," I say. "Have another couple drinks, catch up to the ladies."*

*I tap him on the shoulder twice, fist closed.*

*Brad smiles.*

*We start to head inside. A gruff homeless guy stops us at the door.*

*"Excuse me, sir, could you spare some change?"*

*Holds his hand out to Brad.*

*Brad whips it aside.*

*"I'm an off-duty cop, you know? You know I could write you up for aggressive panhandling. Get the fuck out of here."*

*Brad shoves him off the sidewalk into the street.*

*I stand there, watching the homeless man stumble around.*

*I look at Brad with concern.*

*"Sorry, man, just fucking hate bums, they just leech off everyone, get a fucking job for Christ's sake."*

*I want to start something, but now is not the time, or the place.*

*Instead I walk by Brad back into the restaurant.*

*Liz and Brianne laughing, sitting on the same side of the table, holding wobbly glasses of Pinot Noir. Two beautiful blondes. Brianne looks at me.*

*"Hey, Diamond!"*

*They laugh. Liz blows wine out of her mouth accidentally. Which leads to more laughter.*

*My boxing nickname growing up. Tristan "Diamond" Schultz. After prohibition mobster Dutch Schultz. I never took to it. But I smile; it's all in good fun.*

"Diamond?" says Brad, like the very word itself is confusing.

*Liz and Brianne laugh together, lean in close.*

*Brad looks at me, as confused as a dog who's lost sight of a ball someone threw for him.*

"Don't ask."

*I motion to our waiter, hold up my empty beer bottle.*

*Brad holds up two fingers, mouths the word 'two'.*

</>

*North.*

An hour and a bit from the border. An hour from there to my dad's boat at White Rock. Two-hour boat ride to Vancouver Island and another half hour to the University of Victoria campus.

My father had no sympathy. He wasn't winning any awards for being forgiving or understanding. His daughter his only thought. I agreed. But I felt for the guy, too. Brad had lost his father; he'd always wanted a kid. Someone gave this to him, and then they took it away. I'd be fucking pissed off, too.

In that state of mind, we don't know what he's capable of. A father racing to his pregnant daughter is one thing, but a dad racing to the mother of his unborn child is a whole other story. Two cops, both of whom had killed in the line of duty. Both lost family close to them. Take out law and order, insert apocalyptic chaos. Stir, serve.

Shit mix of lunacy and mania, hold the ice.

I check my phone. Curse myself for checking my phone. Put it away.

Continue along the 405 to connect back up to the 5. Snow white sky devoid of flakes encases everything in an eerie standstill. Sky to fog, hanging overhead, as if God lowered his cloud to have a closer look at us during this devastating time.

I have an uncontrollable urge to get online. Check my Gmail, Facebook, Instagram, maybe Reddit. I remember the first thing I did after the Seattle earthquake was check my Twitter feed. Now I'm stuck with internal hearsay and circumstantial evidence.

Pull my cellphone out of the glove box. Still no service, that little X in the top right corner giving me the finger.

I put it on the dashboard in the faint hope of a signal.

We exit in Woodinville, winery town where the affluent escape from the sprawl in their updated period homes. Pull off after a few streets, take a couple lefts, my dad's head on a swivel. He's looking for something, but I feel like conversation might only be a stressor. He has a plan, might as well stick to it.

I'm wondering where Brianne is. Flashes of her whisk by like cars going in the other direction on the road. I'm trying to remember the good times, but for some reason I keep going back to the bad. Our last fight, when I said mean things, cut her down the way only someone who knew all of her deepest insecurities could.

I may never get the chance to apologize to her in person, or in any form whatsoever.

We pull into the back of a shopping mall. The usual customers, people flooding the grocery store and entranceway. Everyone's on Homeland Security Level Severe, leisurely not part of the regular vocabulary. Soccer moms on crystal meth, white picket fence families with the taste of blood on their tongues and the smell of fear in their nostrils. The ravenous animals of the working middle class doing what they do best: surviving. Now the context is different. The rules have changed. The game? Still the same. Eat or be eaten. No societal cushion anymore; primal beasts once again. Whoever told us our fitted pants and nail salons would make a difference lied to our faces. Now everyone's pissed, thinking they weren't sufficiently warned when the writing was on the wall all along.

Around the deserted back cargo bays of the mall, a huge line of evergreens guard the peripheral vision. We pull up around a line of industrial garbage cans and stop. I sit in the passenger's seat, flash flooding with thoughts.

He stares forward, then swivels, checks his blind spots. Gets out of the car, opens up the back door. I get out of the car too; have a look around like an idiot.

ATM crashes and rumbles onto the ground. Skids it across the slick black pavement with his foot. Goes into the trunk and grabs the hockey bag. Out comes a crowbar. Off come the corners of the plastic casing. They snap away, revealing a metallic box. He dives the crowbar into that box, but with little luck.

I'm half-watching, half checking for possible witnesses.

Swear words start to leave my dad's mouth.

Pries with the crowbar, trying to crack the safe open like a walnut shell. But it's not getting him anywhere.

Heads back to the bag and pulls out the sleek shotgun that recently fractured some guy's jaw and probably left him with a grade three concussion.

"Stand behind the car."

I stand behind the car.

Put the handgun into my belt by my ass.

He leans over the side of the hood to block his body from the shot. Cocks the shotgun, entering a shell into the chamber, and I decide to duck down entirely and turn around behind one of the wheels.

KERPLOWWWW!

Noise bounces off the building and comes back at us, a bombastic interval echo. Ears scream at the sound bombardment. I put my hands over them like I have the ability to go back two seconds in time.

Stand up slowly.

ATM's metallic bits cut open and jagged like a non-perishable food item that decided to fight back against the can opener. It's about ten feet from where it was previously, on its side.

However, it still looks intact.

I watch from behind the safety of the car as if he might fire off an unexpected round.

Rolls it over with his foot. Swears. Turns and looks at me, as if he's asking for my opinion. I hold up my hands.

"I dunno."

Turns back to the metal box, stands for a few seconds in contemplation.

Out of nowhere, a local cop car comes into view.

Flashing lights, blip of siren intended to get our attention. My father and I stand, red handed, as the cop creeps up about twenty feet away. Lone officer in the driver's seat.

Brad? Not possible. Not so fast.

He steps out of the car, gun pointed at my father.

"Drop the gun!"

As he nears, I realize it isn't him.

And somehow my stress level lowers.

My father obliges, shotgun rattles onto the pavement. Holds his hands up like he just washed for dinner. I wonder if he feels a sense of surrealism—having been a cop for so long, and having been on the other side of this encounter thousands of times.

Cop comes out, gun still raised.

"Come out from behind the car, hands up," he says to me.

I put my hands up and oblige.

Eyes me as I emerge into full view, then looks back at my dad.

After a few seconds of uncomfortable silence, he lowers his gun, slowly.

Examines the ATM on the ground.

"What are you guys doing?" he says in his rural Washington State drawl.

"I forgot my pin," I say, trying to break the ice.

No laughter. My father shoots me that look of disdain he's been shooting me for decades.

The cop looks like he might shoot me just for the comment.

"I'm a retired Royal Canadian Mounted Police officer, sir," says my dad.

Cop looks back at my dad.

"What are you guys trying to do?"

"We're trying to open this ATM locker."

Comes closer. My dad lowers his hands. I stand right where I am.

Cop looks down at the metallic box. Looks up at my father.

"Having a bit of trouble, I see?"

I interject.

"Officer, I was wondering if you could tell me what's going on? Have you heard anything, like, at the station?"

He looks over at me.

"The station is on fire."

I nod.

"Oh."

Looks back at my dad. Walks closer, kicks the shotgun across the pavement. Rattles like a shopping cart.

Holds the gun back up to my dad and tells him to step back. He obliges.

Then he bends over and picks up the metal box by one of its shredded corners. Starts to head back to his car.

Motherfucking police is robbing us.

"Oh hell no," I say in my best black lady accent, then pull my gun out from my belt and point it at him.

He turns and aims at me.

"Drop the gun!" he yells.

"Fuck you," I say.

He's taken back by my anti-authoritarian response.

"Drop the fucking gun right now!"

"Lick my balls."

Once again, perplexed. Doesn't seem ready to shoot.

 A self-contained cartridge loads into a firing chamber.

We both look over at my dad. He's pointing the shotgun at the cop.

"Drop your weapons!" he barks at both of us, trying to figure out which one he should point his piece at.

My dad speaks calmly.

"Sir, I know state troopers carry portable Jaws of Life in their trunks. We're more than willing to split whatever's inside that box with you."

Cop looks at my dad, points his gun at him. Then back at me.

The three of us stand there. I feel like I'm in a Clint Eastwood mise-en-scène. I've never pointed a gun at someone. Now I've done it twice in one day. My heart pumps blood, an overachieving organ. I get an urge to squeeze my trigger and be done with it.

But I don't.

Cop downloads the comment, processing it. I watch the percentage bar frenetically jump across his face from left to right.

Download complete.

Install successful.

Nods.

Lowers his weapon.

Drops the box on the ground.

He pulls his car keys out and his trunk opens with that distinct clicking sound. My dad and I lower our weapons, slowly.

"We're cool?" I ask, watching the cop pull the Jaws of Life out of the trunk.

He brings it back, looking at us.

"Yeah, we're cool. I've seen enough shit for one day."

What has this guy seen?

He's young, barely middle-aged. Asks my father to hold one end of the box as he fires up the hydraulic pump. I feel like I've been washed from the shore of reason into Cop Land.

The jaws close down on the box with slow ferocity. I imagine that thing on my leg and wince.

It closes all the way, exposing some cash. Cop goes back on the other corner. My dad continues to hold.

When it's done the second time you can see the bills. My dad picks up the box and turns it upside down. Currency spills out onto the concrete. Making it rain.

Cop holsters his gun. My dad gathers up the twenties. Puts them on the back hood and starts to sort them into piles. I look over at the cop, who's watching with guarded optimism.

"What's going on?"

Looks at me, shakes his head like he's covered in filthy memories.

"I don't have a clue. I was on shift Friday. About seven everything started to turn off. My tracking, cell, laptop in the car, the radio. Nothing. So I come into the station and nobody knows a thing."

He pauses. We both watch my dad sort and count.

"Shift change comes, and half the guys don't show up. Other half are like us, they have no idea. Today there's a fire in the basement, lights up the whole station. We think it was an electrical heater on a timer or something."

"Fuck."

"Yeah. So guys start leaving with cars, going home to their families. I mean I'm divorced, kid's in Portland. I'm thinking of heading there."

"Motherfucker."

He nods at my 'motherfucker.'

"You haven't heard anything from anyone?"

"No, nothing. A few of the guys in the office think it's got something to do with solar flares. Something burnt up everything in the sky, you know, that's why it looks like this and there's no radio or internet. Just hard lines. I mean, we have nothing, no dispatch, no EOC, emergency response, FEMA, military guard, nothing. We're on our own."

I nod.

"Seattle is chaos," I tell him.

He nods.

"Five thousand," says my dad.

Split into two stacks.

The cop picks up his half.

"Sorry, guys, I apologize. Been a tough morning." He puts his share under his bulletproof vest.

"You're telling us," I reply.

The cop looks at my dad.

"RCMP?"

"Yeah. MCU. Drug task force. Vancouver PD for a while, Staff Sergeant."

The cop nods again.

"Good luck. My advice would be stay low, don't fire weapons in back parking lots. Don't draw attention."

We both nod.

"We're trying to head north, cross the border," says my dad.

"Canada?"

"Yeah."

"I'm guessing the border might be under the National Guard. There's a base close by. If you were thinking of crossing,

I'd head for Aldergrove. Peace Arch and Sumas are probably a gong show."

With those words, he does a half-assed salute and heads back to his car with his money and Jaws of Life.

We stand, watching him leave. My dad pulls out another wad from his jacket pocket, what looks like a few hundred dollars.

"You fucking snake," I say with a chuckle.

"American cops, think they're superstars. He deserves it."

Adds the rest of the crumpled cash to the pile. Gives it a pat.

"About three thousand."

"I'm fucking starving," I say, like we should go buy a three thousand dollar meal.

He nods.

"You think he's right? The solar flares?"

Mulls the question.

"Yeah, it's possible."

I nod like it's an acceptable answer. He's right. When in doubt, stick to what you know. Guns, ammo, and cash. White sky, no cell coverage. Pockets of lunacy. Suicide. Random interface fires.

I've never lived in a world where all I know is what's in front of my face. I'm ill equipped in the Age of Disconnect. Do not have sufficient training or the proper upgrades to run this program.

I'm a VHS tape. My father is now Blu-Ray. High speed streaming. Top of the line. Apple iPhone version 5 million. Cutting edge, latest update. Standing outside Best Buy all night to get him.

Stick a pen in my headwheel to rewind me.

</>

*I can't figure out why their pants are so baggy at the top. Black coloured, yellow stripes down the sides, shiny brown boots. I look up and over at my father, standing there in full regalia, red serge in immaculate shape. I only learned yesterday that RCMP stood for Royal Canadian Mounted Police. I have no idea what mounted means, either.*

*I can't stop fidgeting. Someone made the grave mistake of letting my 10-year-old sensibilities loose in a green room full of sugared cookies. I'd stuffed probably fifty million into my mouth when my mother came over and gave me the look she always gives me. The one of disappointment, not anger. She tells me to sit quietly in a chair and try to name all the capitals of Canada. I start west and go east.*

*"Victoria, Edmonton, Winnipeg, Regina, Toronto, Quebec City . . ."*

*A man enters the room dressed in a suit.*

*"Dave, they're ready for you."*

*We all stand; my mother, sister, and I follow my father out of the room and into a frenetic flickering of lenses, flashes and distorting lights from the TV cameras. My mother holds my hand.*

*"What's the capital of Prince Edward Island?" she says.*

*"Charlottetown," I respond, eyes mesmerized by the scene.*

*We make our way to the stage. I look at Liz, barely able to walk as she adjusts the lining of her dress. My suit riding up into my crotch. I've never worn a suit before. The tie feels constraining, suspenders dig into my shoulders.*

*My father the centre of attention. He pushes out a forced smile. Stands as erect as a fence post drilled a hundred feet into the ground. People shake a lot of hands.*

*Commissioner's Commendation for Bravery. I have no idea what this means, except the word bravery, which has been thrown around in conversations above my head a lot lately. Some guy named a commissioner wearing more bells and whistles than a street clown makes his way up to the podium. Lines of chairs and faces, recorders and photographers. Everyone pointing everything at us.*

*"It is my honor to present the Commissioner's Commendation for Bravery to Constable Dave Schultz for his remarkable resilience in the line of duty."*

*Every time someone calls my father Dave I'm not sure how to take it. The name sounds so foreign to me. Shouldn't they call him 'Dad'?*

*"His courage and bravery under what can only be described as a remarkably stressful situation shows us all how proud we should be of our officers who answer the call to protect us, day in and day out."*

*My mother holds her hand on my shoulder. She's looking at my father, eyes locked on him, a genuine smile warming her face.*

"The events that transpired that night required a massive amount of courage. Courage Constable Schultz exhibited. His perseverance and quick-thinking saved the lives of two young civilians and one of his fellow officers."

I wasn't sure what a civilian was. Or the word "perseverance". Sounded like a fancy French purse. All I knew is what I'd heard, pieced together from various conversations. And the fact that my dad had been promoted to detective.

My father and his partner had gotten word that some 'drug' people had taken a young boy hostage. My father killed two, chasing a third down the street. The guy tried to take a passerby hostage. I didn't know how it played out, even though I tried to map it in my head. All I knew was that everyone was telling me my father was a hero. Except Jimmy from school, who said my father 'critically wounded' an underage teenager who pulled a gun on him in the firefight.

I was as confused by the situation as I was in awe of my father. A real life superhero, standing there in his uniform. Medal pinned to him. Bright red. I kept looking for the 'S' across his chest.

The only thing I was sure of was that he'd started smoking again since that day. And drinking. My mother didn't like this. They spoke, then yelled. He would leave and drive off for a few hours. Words like 'psychiatrist' and 'post-traumatic stress disorder' sounded through the floorboards of our home. He would brush her off.

In the morning I'd find him on the couch as I was getting ready for school, passed out on the sofa. He'd wake when he saw me, stand up and shake the gruff off, lug his bear frame down the hall and into bed.

My mother would come by later and pick up the bottle of alcohol and the ashtray he'd leave by the couch. She'd tell me he was stressed, that his job was tough, that although what he did was extremely brave, he was having a tough time with it.

Jimmy from school says that when you kill someone you take over their soul. He pokes me in the chest where my heart is, telling me that's where my soul is. He laughs. I shove him into the dirt as hard as I can. He falls awkwardly, scuffing his elbow in the process. He sees blood and starts crying, runs away holding his arm. It's the last time he ever picks on me.

Two souls?

Does my father now own two souls?

</>

I'm thinking back to Friday. The last day I knew what was going on in the world.

ISIS had claimed responsibility for a blast that went off outside a café in Rome, killing four people and the attacker. The suicide bomber, who of course shouted "Allahu Akbar!" before detonating was the latest in a string of retaliations between ISIS and a U.S. and French-led coalition. ISIS was claiming this would be the first in a series of multiple attacks across Western Europe in retaliation for the latest Syrian push. However, now with complete radio silence, I, like everyone around me, have no idea what's going on, and cannot fuel this infotainment fire.

I wonder if the terrorists have any idea what's going on. I wonder how effective Jihadism is now without mass communication, and if maybe they perpetuated another blast since then, but since there's no CNN, no Twitter and no *New York Times*, that their praise be Allah is getting lost in the shuffle. I wonder what this disconnect is doing in areas of the world where there was mass instability to begin with.

If this thing's global, I can't imagine the shit going down right now where civility was hard to come by to begin with. Hashtag firstworldapocalypticproblems.

And here I am outside an IGA on the glossy good life outskirts of Woodinville. Neatly manicured shrubbery lines the parking lots.

People loot the store in a weirdly pedestrian manner, like they're running errands in the apocalypse. Groceries, check. Dry cleaning, check. Semi-automatic rifle, check. Pepper spray and Febreeze, check.

My stomach grumbles like a grumpy old man.

"Keep your gun out of sight," my father says as he opens his door. "We get food, then we're back on the road. Steady pace."

We're in a race, and we can't do the one thing my father wants to do so badly.

Open up the throttle.

In this mess, it will surely get us killed.

Anxiety fuels us. Fills us with kerosene. The thought of reaching Liz too late, when Brad's taken her away, gotten them lost in this mess of a detachment.

This is our one chance.

Our *only* chance.

There will be no second place.

Up towards the IGA. A lady passes, shoving a shopping cart overflowing with canned foods. White clouds draw lines across the sky, elegant shading. Low flying cumulus nimbus, ready to burst at the seams like sliced pillowcases.

We enter the store. No clerks, shopping carts everywhere. Fruit rolls around on the ground. The lights in the bakery department spastically flicker on and off. There's a guy in the vegetable aisle eating strawberries at an alarming rate.

My dad grabs a cart. We're going shopping together. Awkward father-son excursion.

We start loading up. Nothing I throw in stays. I'm like a fucking kid. I try to put in a bunch of steaks; they get tossed out.

"What's the deal?"

"We need food that doesn't spoil."

Cops. Emergency Management training. My father was prepped with the skills to handle a disaster like this. He was on duty for both the riots in downtown Vancouver. I asked him what it was like during the anarchy, when the world ripped apart into a momentary cave-in of chaos.

People only respect one thing, he said.

*Violence.*

The thought of this conversation lodges itself in my psyche.

As long as this carries on, my father will use force to save us. Intimidation backed up. "Words?" he says with a shake of his head. "Dialogue? None of that works when it all falls apart."

Brute force is the universal language now.

Violence will keep us safe. Violence will get us to my sister, will reunite him with his daughter.

And her child.

I watch him push the cart. No list, but he knows exactly what needs to go in. By the time we're done, we've got jams, honey, garlic, bottled drinks, potatoes, canned fruit, beans, tuna, jerky, peanut butter, chips and trail mix.

The one thing he does let me put in are three 26-ounce plastic bottles of Polar Ice Vodka and a carton of flavoured cigarettes. He quit smoking years ago, but this might be as good a time as any to start back up again.

Eye contact with other shoppers kept to a minimum. As if thievery is okay if the shame level's cranked up. A can of lima beans rolls down the aisle and stops by a little girl holding her mom's leg. She looks down at it, then at me in my suit, white shirt and bloodstained tie, and hides from view. A moment later she peeks around to look at me.

I stick my tongue out at her. She smiles sheepishly.

We raid what's left of the pharmacy. Boost, packaged energy bars, supplements, Advil, decongestants, cough syrup, ibuprofen. Our haul starts to look like a shopping list for a meth cook.

This is fun.

This is fucking fun. We're robbing a grocery store. *Everyone* is robbing a grocery store. I'm not timesheet coding overtime hours or sitting through extended teleconference sessions on media messaging for FDA approval checks.

No, I'm stealing food to survive.

Anarchy.

Fresh cut anarchy like the lettuce in the vegetable section.

Some guy's cart spills all over the ground by the checkout. No 'clean-up in aisle six' notification over the loudspeaker.

Young punk snatches a bunch of his food on the way by. The guy starts to chase, but the kid darts off.

We head back into the white abyss and now we're almost moving in that weirdly leisurely manner too. Sound of shopping carts rattling across pavement like chattering teeth.

Food in with the hockey bag full of firearms. I spot a rifle with a scope, magazines of ammo, and what looks like a Colt pistol. I look over at my dad.

"Is that a fucking Colt pistol?"

He looks at me as he loads food.

"Old revolving pistols don't jam."

I know he just spotted that fucking thing and couldn't resist.
We get back in the car.

"Where are we going?"

"Let's go eat somewhere quiet, then head north. I'm not sure of the closest town."

"Everett," I say. "About half an hour on the freeway."

"Okay, we'll eat, then try to make Everett for gas. I want to scope out the border before dark. I dunno which crossing Brad might head for."

I nod, like I have any inkling of what the plan might be.

Liz. My sister. Pregnant. What the fuck happened?

The woman who held everything together when all we were trying to do was tear it apart. My own blood, alien to me.

Now the *only* end.

</>

*The weather decidedly West Coast Canadian. Rain, more rain, and then some rain thrown in for good measure.*

*I'm sprawled out along the couch in an ugly portrait pose, teenage legs dangling off into the air. Boxing special on TV, Oscar De La Hoya about to fight Félix Trinidad. It's Saturday, and I know what time it is, but I've planted myself on the couch in a lackadaisical form of protest I know will escalate into a scene. Youth and rebellion don't mix well with lingering tragedy.*

*My sister comes down the stairs, dressed in a coat and jeans. I'm still in my joggers and tank top.*

*"Tristan?!" is all she says.*

*I look over.*

*"What?"*

*"We have to go. We're going to be late."*

*"I'm not going."*

*She breaths in, first slowly, then quickly.*

*"Dad's going to be pissed."*

*"So?"*

*She stands there, staring at me. Looks up the stairs, then back.*

*"What's going on with you?"*

*Cynicism covers me like a blanket.*

"What's wrong with me? What's wrong with you?"

"Me? Nothing's wrong with me. But you're acting like an asshole."

*I smirk. I've only heard Liz swear a handful of times. Her pre-teen vocabulary just starting to sprout with expletives.*

"Whatever. I'm not going to fucking counselling. It's fucking stupid."

*My two swear words indicate I'm willing to raise the stakes.*

*No response. She stands there.*

*Footsteps down the stairs. My heart rate elevates. His bear frame comes into view.*

*He notices the TV first.*

"The Golden Boy, eh? Trinidad is doomed, I say."

*Holds his hands up, throws a few shadow jabs. Looks back down at me.*

"Okay, Tristan, get dressed. We have to go."

*I lay there, frozen in protest. The clock ticks a few seconds, and the tension starts to escalate exponentially.*

"Tristan?"

*Liz leaves the room, heads outside. The car door slams.*

"Tristan. Get dressed. We're leaving."

*I look over.*

"I'm not going."

"Tristan, I'm not asking."

*He steps a few paces forward, in front of the TV, blocking my view. My heart rate is escalating but I'm trying to remain as calm as possible.*

*He looks down at me across the couch.*

*I look up at him, and we lock eyes.*

*Silence. Thick, ugly silence.*

"Tristan, I'd like you to please get up and get dressed. We have our weekly counselling appointment, which we do as a family as part of our healing process."

*He's re-hashing lines learned at counselling. Expressing his feelings in a calm, thought-out manner.*

"Fuck that."

*His internal temperature bubbling to a boil.*

"Tristan, please get up and get dressed. I will meet you in the car."

"I'm not going to counselling."

"Why aren't you going to counselling?"

"Because it's bullshit."

"I'm going to ignore the fact that you're swearing in this house. Tristan, counselling is something the three of us do together. It's important."

I sit up. This conversation is not intensifying at the rate I want it to.

"Important? For what? What are we going to talk about?" I start waving my hands around theatrically. "Oh I don't know, our mom dying. Let's talk about that. Let's talk about our feelings about that for the fifteenth billion time. Hey, your mom died, tell me about it. Join the circle of healing. Tell me how sad you are."

He doesn't answer, so I do. I make a motion, my hand jerking off a penis.

"Circle of healing this."

He comes forward. I stand up, get off the couch. I'm almost eye level with him now, but he's still got a good fifty pounds on me.

We stand there. Two parallel towers itching to lean in. I'm intimidated as hell but trying to hide it.

Two feet between us and pure unadulterated chaos.

This isn't the first time we've had a standoff, and it probably won't be the last unless I get the fuck out of this house. Sooner or later one of us will carry this into violence. I need to leave. It's unavoidable now.

I hear the door open. My sister comes into the room in a huff, grabs my father's arm. He doesn't budge.

"Dad!" she says, tears starting to show.

She grabs him again, pulls hard. He relents, keeps his eyes on me.

Pulls him away and out the front door. I hear her speak from outside.

"Get in the car!"

Comes back in. I'm still standing there. I hear the car door open and close.

Liz comes up to me. She's holding back tears.

The pain in her eyes fucking hurts. It rips deep in through my aorta in a fraction of a split second, filling both ventricles.

She pokes her finger into my chest, accentuating each syllable.

"Ass. Hole."

</>

This national highway a horrible amusement park ride of monstrous things. Please keep your hands and feet inside the cart at all times.

Lynnwood.

Up the freeway north. We pull onto a rural street, secluded area guarded by a line of trees and a few farm homes. Towering thirty-foot evergreens and acre long front yards of fertilized grass.

We get out, pop the trunk, and munch on rubbery beef jerky, sloppy peanut butter, and warm bottled water. I devour a bag of chips and we split a few cans of fruit, my dad opening the tins with a hunting knife.

Eating in silence, as always. Sitting on the back hood, on a semi-rural road about an hour north of Seattle. Dew soaked green fields and trees, massive backyards with ride-on lawnmowers and freshly painted barns.

I think about Brianne. I wonder where she is, who she's with. Will I ever see her again? Did I throw away my one chance at love for selfish reasons, because I didn't want the same life she did?

Our fights play over in my head. Endlessly looping around the circumference of my brain, piano wire strangling me, strand by strand. Wipe my hand over my face, try to brush the thoughts away. It's useless.

Life before today a fabrication of endless streams of code. It's all gone. The Pfizer Twitter feed, my Facebook account with my 27 profile pictures. My witty retorts on Twitter, my neatly photo-shopped Instagram musings, my meticulously shiny LinkedIn profile. If this is our denouement, a subliminal *Matrix*-slash-*Terminator* in which the machines turned on us by turning off, it's straight out of some Shakespearian tragedy.

All that we created to bring us together has left us *so alone*.

Technospeak. Signals and noise. Rubber science blog posts. Stats, statisticians and Asymmetrical Digital Subscriber Lines. Bandwidth, baude and bits per second. Wide-area networks, multiplexing and digital compressions. Jpegs, mpeg, tiffs, raw, gifs, pngs and bmps. None of it matters one *fucking* bit anymore.

Rickrolling, Engrish, all your base are belong to us. Oh really, Leeroy Jenkins, epic fails, I accidentally a whole cake.

When the dust settles our species will be remembered by our memes.

Escape. Backspace. Re-do. Re-write. Edit. Open. Open Recent. Save. Save As.

Untranslatable hieroglyphs. reCAPTCHA text indistinguishable to the next generation of anthropologists.

Delete.

I shake off the violent severity of the situation like dust. Back to the present, to reality. Whatever's left is real. I'm sure of it. So sure I'd accept death to prove my point.

But I'm terrified of death, absolutely petrified, always have been. I do want to live. I enjoy happiness. I just couldn't find the right program to complete the task.

I can't wrap my feeble, shrinking brain around it. The actuality, the being, brass tacks, certainty and perceptibility. I will go back to being a PR hack, spin doctoring pro-pharmaceutical angles to ensure projected profit margins. Back to debating the merits of kids and marriage with whomever will listen. Of saddling my personal GDP with a backbreaking fixed term mortgage, buckets of credit cards and consumerist must-haves for what?

Or not.

The food in my stomach's allowed the anxiety and ache to subside. I dip some jerky in peanut butter. He passes me a can of pears; I slurp it down.

He's munching on crackers and drinking bottled Açaí Berry Vitamin Water. Staring forward the way he does, with that fucking look of pensive thought. Trying so desperately to ignore the wrestling match going on in his head.

I remember the last time I saw him. Christmas two years back. The three of us got together at Liz's place. But her duplex was too small, so my dad and I stayed in a hotel. She came over to the room on Christmas morning; we had a continental breakfast and he gave us money. No gifts, just cheques. A thousand each.

It was the closest we'd been to family in a long while.

I hear my father inhale and sigh.

Faded burn marks line his arms. Tragic topography.

"You okay?"

Continues looking forward.

"Yeah. Yeah, I'm okay."

Nods in acknowledgment. Stress in his eyes melts my disconnect.

I want to pat him on the back, do something to show I'm here with him. I get it. We need to find Liz. This is the only goal. I'm trying to find words, but I can't remember the last time I reached out to my father on an emotional level. I don't even know where to start.

"We'll get Liz. Brad's not too smart. He'll get smashed up in a fender bender or something. I mean, I never hated the guy, but intelligence is not one of his strengths."

"Yeah," replies my dad, nodding in acknowledgment that conversational small talk about our predicament within this apocalypse is warranted. "He's a cop, though. With a Middle East tour under his belt. He might be an idiot, but he's a well-trained idiot."

I open my mouth to respond but nothing comes out.

He's right. This well-trained idiot has real world experience from the dirty side streets of Kabul. Pumped full of PTSD, a uniformed officer with his unborn child on his mind. We're racing a nightmare packed with explosives who no longer speaks the language of reason. He answers to emotions, guided by impulsive instincts.

Thunder a few miles away. Not loud, but enough to stop us from munching. A small gust of wind rushes through. Electricity in the air, and the sickness—what feels like airborne mercury poisoning. I'm guessing a nuke went off somewhere in the region and we're in the blast radius. But then I realize I have no fucking idea how to substantiate any of that.

Another rumble, closer this time. I feel rain five hundred feet above me. He stands up, puts the food back in the trunk, closes it.

I stand, watching the sky.

We're heading towards a crash, I can feel it. The gut, the instincts telling me, us, as the unstoppable force, will surely run into the immovable object sooner or later.

A matter of time. A moment of instance.

Brad. Liz. Dave. Brianne.

Tristan.

In a matter of time we'll all encounter the script of fate.

</>

*Two-year anniversary. You made it past the first year, which was like a celebration. Now you're counting for the sake of counting.*

*For once I'd taken a vacation. We'd decided on Kauai. Brianne felt like we needed sun instead of culture. I was okay with that.*

*At the Aston Islander on the Beach, off the east coast of the island. We'd walked back from the Wahoo Seafood Bar & Grill. The ahi tuna was undercooked, but the wine was good enough. We strolled along the Kuhio Highway, traffic crawling in and out of Kapaa due to construction a few miles ahead. Hand in hand, chatting about the day's activities, staying on the surface.*

*Both suntanned from an afternoon at Tunnels Beach. I spent a few hours getting my ass kicked by waves while trying to hold onto a surfboard. She lounged on the beach reading Vanity Fair, listening to her iPod.*

*This trip was supposed to save us. Two years in and the honeymoon phase was officially over. She'd moved from Virginia to Seattle for me; well, for a marketing gig she'd found with an NGO. But it was for me.*

*She hated the rain. Missed her family. We tried our best, spent the better part of the first year watching TV on the futon together, enjoying the quiet company of each other. But it didn't last, cracks started to show. I was working too much, she wasn't working enough.*

*We were in love, there was no question. But circumstance had other plans. She wanted to settle down. She wanted me to ask her to marry me. She wanted kids.*

*I didn't. Why couldn't we just be together? Why wasn't that enough? She said this is what people do when they turn 30, they settle down. 'They' had been telling me what to do all my life and I was sick of it. I wanted a new course. A different path.*

*After a few months of continuous fighting and futon sleeping on my part, I booked us on this trip. Get away from all the shit. Re-tool. Re-adjust. Re-commit.*

*But the spark was gone. Our arguments going in circles, our opinions and stances hardening with each fight.*

*We walk back to the hotel bar by the pool, the ocean mere feet away in the dark. You can hear the waves but all you can see is the starry sky.*

*The whole trip was a bust. But every time we went back to the hotel and I checked my email, there were new Facebook notifications. Brianne kept posting Instagram shots of us smiling together, enjoying the sun and surf, like this was the best trip we'd ever taken.*

*A façade. Lying to the world through digital filters.*

*I order a screwdriver. She has a glass of Pinot Noir. We're tired of talking so we just sit and listen to the other Americans yell about their lives.*

*I look at her. She's still beautiful. Blonde hair down to her shoulders. Skin glowing with a healthy tan. I can't figure it out.*

*What happened?*

*Can you be in love with someone who isn't right for you?*

</>

Everett is freefalling.

Seattle's little underdeveloped brother in total blackout.

Windshield wipers on full, whisking back and forth. Metronomes of unease. The rain's started underneath the achromatic sky. Thick droplets; temperature has neglected to drop. Warm, wet, but not windy. Sheet lightning imprints the heavens in blazes of vibrant neon, amber and yellow. Crackling, booming noises descend in three hundred and sixty directions.

Techno rave of light deejay'd by Zeus himself.

This city decidedly catastrophic. Blackened fast food restaurants that'd normally shimmer with fluorescent lighting off the rain-soaked granular pavement sit dark, abandoned. No stop lights. Dank colours, drenched, desolate yet populated, in the middle of the day. Power cord—off.

Ghost town inhabited by the living.

A group of young men gang-beat a white male outside of a car in a parking lot. Bat cracks across his head; his body falls awkwardly to the ground. My father looks, but does not acknowledge. Boots descend upon his body in a trampling stampede.

"Fuck."

We continue like we just saw a deer on the side of the road. A passing glance, then back to normalcy. The instant I blink, the image of the baseball bat taking the guy's head into the pavement flashes through my mind. Imprints deep inside, tattooing my anima.

Numb from the cerebral cortex north. Whisking the entire memory into a zip drive in the back of my mind where a small ball of post-traumatic stress disorder is developing into a tumour ready to light up my brain like a firestorm.

We head into the first set of congested lights. Traffic a holy mess. People aren't acknowledging the four-way stop. Blue pick-up truck comes up off the curb, around another stopped car, clipping it, grinding its side. Speeds through the intersection, reckless, irresponsibility and negligence all wrapped in a single decision. It nearly T-bones a van, is forced to screech its wheels and hydroplane to a stop in the rain.

My dad waits, looks, then goes. Full commitment. Horns honk, we just about clip a Jeep, and tires squeal in the peripheral vision of my ears. All compounded by the pulse pounding rain splish-splashing everywhere.

A couple more blocks and we're back into the sprawl, watching the looters go nutso. Even the Jack in the Box isn't immune, people running out with full registers, baking equipment, cardboard boxes of what can only be uncooked frozen meat.

My dad, ever alert. Crow's feet off the sides of his eyes, debilitated and worn—cagey. Disorganized by the stress, held together by shoddy wiring. Frayed and slightly dismembered.

Hungover on fifty cups of coffee.

He's been fighting all his life. Fighting criminals, fighting me, fighting his mind. Now he's fighting Brad. Running, never sitting long enough to analyze with any real conviction. Metaphysically jogging on the spot. Constantly treading water to stay alive, never able to feel comfortable. Let his guard down, be vulnerable, or cry. He looks fucking stressed out.

When we get back on the highway, a thought crosses my mind. I blurt it out before thinking it through, trying to break the silence.

"What are we going to do with the guns and the cash when we try to cross the border?"

I realize instantaneously in the constant stress of the past six hours, my dad has overlooked a huge component of our plan. Human error alert. Crossing the border is difficult to begin with. Crossing the border with guns, ammo, and cash?

Plan A has encountered a problem and needs to close. We're sorry for the inconvenience. For more information about this error, click here.

"Dad, we don't even have our fucking passports."

He closes his eyes, slowly. Grinds the enamel on his teeth.

I let out a snicker. I mean, what can a guy do in a time like this? Such a silly error for someone who's built his life planning one step before the other. A simple mistake.

Looks at me with a face full of anger.

"Is this funny?"

"No." But I'm smiling. I have this image of the Customs officer asking him if he wants to declare anything upon entering Canada.

"It's not fucking funny. Your sister is over there, by herself. Scared, not knowing what to do. And that fucking idiot Brad is going after her, too. If we don't do everything we can, he might get there first and then . . . Do you realize the gravity of the fucking situation we're in?"

Looking away from the road at me in between syllables, his skin a slight percentage of souring red.

Retry—no. Wait until the application closes? No. Ignore. Ok.

He pulls the car over on the side of the highway, cuts off another vehicle in the process. Horn blares at us in disgust as it swooshes by in the rain.

Car stops, he cuts the engine, keys jingle in the ignition. He stares forward, like he's trying to blow the glass out of the front window with his glare alone.

I think about Customs asking us if we have any fruits or vegetables.

Firearms, weapons, ammunition. Alcoholic beverages. Thousands of dollars in stolen cash.

Maybe a cucumber or two.

Have we visited a farm, or do we plan on visiting one in the near future?

We have enough ammo to take down a herd of cattle.

Snicker again.

Something inside me is broken. I'm finding this funny for some terrible reason.

Then my dad is smacking the shit out of me. Hitting me. I'm trying to defend myself, throwing my arms back at him.

*Whatthefuck!*

He grabs my neck, pins me against the side of the window, air ceases to travel upwards from my windpipe.

Flailing my arms around. My vision starts to go as white as the sky.

My dad's grip loosens.

He backs off.

I rub my neck. Let out a few gasps to regain some type of normal breathing pattern.

Fuck this noise. We're back at Rodney's gym. We're in the ring.

I crack him upside the face with a right hook. Hand ricochets off his cheek and hits the roof. That distinct smacking sound of bone on bone, poorly cushioned by two small layers of flesh. Half smack, half crack.

Smrack!

I can tell the punch caught him off guard because he threw up a late hand to block it. But it's much too late.

We sit, staring at each other. Thick as punching, choking thieves.

I rub my knuckles, stinging with pain.

Laborious breathing.

"Look," I say, regaining my oxygen intake. "Whatever the fuck is going on, I'm with you. We need to get to Liz. We gotta stop Brad. I get it. But fuck. I mean, what the fuck."

Complete incoherence—sentence fragment, consider revising.

Somehow my dad understands my butchered grammar.

"Okay."

He coughs, hacking out some unknown feeling he suffocated long ago. Rubs his head where my fist imprinted like a typewriter key.

Opens his mouth to stretch his jaw. I caught him good.

"Let's have a look at the border. If we can slip by without losing all this stuff, we do it. If not, change of plans; we cross the Strait at Drayton Harbour, maybe Birch Bay."

I nod.

"Sorry for punching you," I say.

He nods. Doesn't apologize. Tries to start the car back up.

But it fails. Noise fizzles from the engine; a hiss, then a bloom of white smoke diluted and sizzled by the rain. He tries once more, but now the alternator isn't even turning over.

"Fuck!" he yells at the hood.

Bursts out and heads up to the front. I get out, instantly drenched in rain.

The hood won't even open. We've pretty much written this car off.

Stands there sopping, soaking to the bone. Vehicles zoom by on the highway, splashing water in our vicinity.

Plush white smoke out of the hood like an uncovered pot on the stove. Thick steam mimicking my father's emotional state. It surrounds him.

Crackle of thunder. Clouds light up; pillowcases with flashlights inside them.

"What do we do now?" I ask, water falling into my mouth as I open it.

Looks at me, then at the highway. Starts to wave with both arms, trying to flag someone down.

Cars pass.

Keeps waving his arms.

I decide the best thing to do is join in. I start waving my hands as well. More cars pass. None stop, and it's too rainy to see inside to gauge the drivers' reactions.

"Nobody is going to stop today," I say, still waving my hands in the rain.

Ignores the statement, continuously waving. Steps out into the highway to show his severity to the passing cars. Gets a few honks from the people in the right lanes, but still no one stops.

I stop waving and stand, staring at the cars as they whizz by.

I watch him as he keeps waving. Arms flail with a consistency only a father could muster, one of sheer commitment. He'd wave for months if it was the right thing to do in his twisted parental mind.

Thunder and lightning play out in our theatre of desperation.

Ground shakes. Crack lines of electricity imprint like veins.

I sigh. Close my eyes.

I could be praying.

I could be pleading.

I'm definitely doing something.

And then a signal light blinks, a car pulls over. Passes us, whisking rain water up, drenching my dress pants. Stops fifteen feet in front.

A scrawny, middle-aged man with glasses gets out. A young boy, maybe ten at best, in the front seat of the car. He's turned around and watching everything—obviously told to stay inside.

"You okay?" the man says, shoulders down so as to remain non-confrontational.

My dad walks slowly towards him.

His gun comes out. Guy instantly stops in his tracks.

"Whoa *whoa* I'm here to help," he pleads.

My dad speaks to me, still facing the father.

"Tristan, get the stuff out of the trunk and put it in this car."

Unwilling to comply.

Looting was cool with me. Stealing goods from mindless corporations, fine. But I am not cool with this.

This act would turn my moral compass south.

"Dad, there's a fucking kid in the car."

My dad checks, registers. But it doesn't faze him.

"Tristan, get the shit out of the trunk and put it in this car!"

This guy, hands up still, interjects.

"Look, we can give you a ride if you need. There's no need for this; I'm with my son, okay buddy?"

My dad fires a round off into the air on a slight slant. The guy ducks as if it might hit him.

"If I hear another word out of your mouth, I'm going to shoot you in the face."

Silent compliance—from both of us.

Not cool with this at all, but my dad's not budging, and I want this to end. I take the hockey bag and open the back door. Car's surprisingly similar to mine, silver four-door nondescript sedan.

The kid watches. Tears well up in his eyes.

"Sorry," is all I can muster.

I close the door and stand there like I'm waiting for further orders. My dad walks by the guy, gun pointed at his face as he passes.

I hear the doors lock. I look at the kid. He's scared, but obviously trying to take action against this serious misdeed.

My father stands there in frustrated disbelief.

Taps the barrel of the gun on the glass window.

My father now the villain in this scene.

"Open the door, kid."

Nothing. Kid stares him down, scared shitless. I want to tip my hat; little fucker has gonads.

He heads back to the father, grabs him around the neck and drags him to the door completely against his will. Points the gun at his temple and pushes his face against the window. Glasses fall to the ground. Facial features smear against the glass in an odd assortment of fleshy skin.

"Open the door, kid."

I hear the doors click open. I grab the kid—yank him out. He falls, sliding down a grassy embankment.

My dad gets in. I get in. Car still running.

We speed back into the traffic. Father runs towards his son, still on the ground, covered in mud now. He wipes the dirt from his son's face, holds him tight in the rain.

I'm shaking my head, my dad driving, gun in hand.

"What the fuck?! *What the fuck*?! WHAT THE FUCK?!"

Whatever the opposite of pay-it-forward is—we just did.

The vehicle's foreign, garbage on the floor, smell of other humans; my seat is warm. My father's emotions scattered around the interior, but in physical standstill, as if he just threw his morals and ethics out the window for a scrap of bread. As if he broke the laws he'd taken an oath to uphold. I'm uneasy around this wolf; he's obviously not stable, obviously hell-bent on his objective.

The precipitation drips off us both as we soak with rain and shame.

Liz is the goal, but at this cost? There had to be other ways. I didn't know we were already willing to go this far. To push things this deep into moral mud.

Thick water droplets litter the windshield like AK-47 rounds. Pulse-pounding, heart thumping, head racing. Mute inarticulateness, a lull and speechlessness when only words might dissipate this awful act.

We are now criminals.

At any cost. To get to his daughter. To my sister. To her unborn child.

At any cost.

</>

The rain's subsided. God cranked the faucet off. Splashed some cold water on us to try and chill everyone out.

Useless.

There's military at Aldergrove. Nondescript border crossing. Customs declaration signs, livestock permits, landed immigrants status. Shrubs, hedges, and nothing but a sterile looking line of red and grey colored buildings built for simple practicality. Duty Free shop with all the windows smashed. Along the front entrance a trail of cigarette cartons lead out into the parking lot.

One road leading up, State Route 539. Cars line the highway, some parked, some trying to inch forward along the meridian. People outside, trying to get their cell phones working. Some have set up shop inside their vehicles, screens blocking the windows, peering out through the cracks. Portable antennas perched on the roofs trying to find reception. Most of the cars have British Columbia license plates. Back a few clicks there's scattered stores, conglomerate gas stations and American fast food eateries—Rodney's Steakhouse and Jim's Old Time Burger Shack.

The direct lead-up is farmland, vast green fields, towering steel silos and rusted old grain towers.

A grey cloud of smoke billows up from the horizon off to the northwest.

Thieves in this stolen car. Lost my Blackberry in the switch, and I'm developing a bizarre sense of nakedness without my cell—apparently coined and termed now: nomophobia. Sounds like a fear of gnomes in tight places. Not the first time I've lost my phone, but this time I sense the permanency. Can't post on Facebook letting all my friends know I have no mobile device for the time being.

*Lost my phone, get at me on here if you have to!*

At least my sense of sarcasm survived the end times.

Took the cop's advice and went to the smaller, less used crossing. But they're already here—the army. Barbed wire barricades and all. Doesn't look like much—a few dozen men. We sit outside the car, watching the patrol. Cars up to the front, people out, talking to the military.

Nobody's crossing.

We have a mission, a goal, a common thread. A small solution in this free-flowing consternation.

My father is willing to forgo logic, morals, and ethics to beat Brad to my pregnant sister. The question isn't what we are willing to do, but what we aren't.

My sister, as foreign as my dad. The more I think about it on this headlong rush to the border, the more I realize the only tangible way I kept in touch with her was through Facebook.

Her status updates—everyone has a theme—understandably early 20s. Half prototypical school stress, *Biology 203 midterm paper, I hate you. fml.* The other half about her fragmented relationship with Brad. *My bf is the best in the world, flowers and chocolate. He knows the way to a girl's heart.* Or the other side, semi-cryptic ones that made you cringe in embarrassment. *Why is it that some people you just feel like you can't trust* or *Wondering when I will ever be truly happy.*

Don't get me wrong. Liz was no pushover. Growing up with two lost boys disguised as men she had to be a fighter—tough, relentless, like any Schultz. But my father defaulted his parenting skills and raised her as a boy after my mother's passing. She never got that feminine outlet, was forced to fend for herself emotionally. She had fucking moxie, just lacked the experience.

But a kid? She was going to be a doctor. I'd be quivering at her success in years to come.

Something must've gone wrong. I should've been there or felt available enough for her to reach out. But I wasn't. I was off dealing with my own relationship messes. Yelling at Brianne, arguing into the early hours. I was not a good brother, nor a decent boyfriend.

Watching Liz grow up, I wanted to message her sometimes, comment on the photos of her out drinking at the campus pub, climbing monuments in the street, Brad lifting her slender frame up. But I didn't. I didn't really know her and I felt no obligation to butt into her life because of some misguided sense of blood. Instead I watched like a voyeur as she went through the laundry list of growing pains any twenty-something goes through. At least when I was younger there was no online social medium to echo mistakes into the stratosphere.

Her last birthday. All I did was write a lame-ass note on her wall like all her other friends. Couldn't even be bothered to pick up the phone.

Now she's pregnant, almost finished pre-med, riding a wave of academic scholarships. She grew up without my involvement.

Social media gave us a reason not to be social.

And I'd failed another woman.

We stand, watching. Mess of people, cars, military.

"What about Sumas?" I ask.

"Probably no different."

The kid I tossed from his father's car. Without hesitation. I did it, not because it was the right thing to do, but because our circumstances required it.

I think about him sitting in the rain, covered in mud, staring at me, wondering why I'd be such a fucking asshole to someone I'd never met. I'm a bad person and I deserve no good karma from God—wherever that moronic deity is.

"You go up. Have a look around."

"What do you mean?"

"We need to know if they know anything that might help us."

The scene does not look helpful or welcoming, or any version of the two.

"Okay."

Drives closer, pulls over to the side of the road before the congestion starts to bottleneck at the crossing. Stops. We get out.

"You're gonna go up and ask some questions. Ask them whether or not people can pass, what the situation is."

"Why me?"

Does not further the discussion, pulls out a pair of binoculars and heads towards the side of the road, into the bushes. Disappears into the abyss of a grassy knoll.

I start walking towards the border.

Cars parked along the road, travellers gathering in groups of huddles masses. Military personnel addressing people at the first roadblock. About ten feet behind them there's military guards in full regalia with semi-automatic rifles. People talk to them, then leave in a huff. Doesn't look positive.

Make my way to a group talking to one guard—tall, lean, dressed in full attire.

"Sir, *please* calm down," is the first thing distinguishable from the white noise of conversation. "We cannot let anyone cross the border under any circumstances."

"I was shopping with my wife. I'm Canadian! You can't not let me back into my own country, on what grounds?"

"Sir, protocol strictly states that in times of engagement, the border is closed to civilians. I'm sorry for your family, but there is nothing I can do until we get further word on the situation."

"What is the situation?" I ask, butting in.

Soldier makes eye contact. Checking me out in my suit and tie, white shirt splattered with blood.

"Sir, there is limited communication as to the nature of the solar storms currently in the atmosphere and their extent, so under our rules of engagement we're obliged to hold this post as if this is an emergency management situation."

"What do you mean, solar storms?"

Shakes his head like he's not sure of his own answer.

"All we know is our telecommunications systems are down. The only communication we've had between the other border crossings is through hard line telephones, which went out about an hour ago. They're in the same boat as us. Please return to your car and await further instruction."

"From who?"

Puts his hands up like he doesn't know the answer, but gives one anyway.

"When we know, we will surely let the public know."

"Really. What, are you taking email addresses?"

unimpressed@military.com

We lock eyes. He takes a breath in, but I beat him to it.

"Solar flares? No nuclear war or something?"

I look to my right. Off to the side: a Washington State cruiser. A hand appears on my shoulder, I turn: Brad.

*Fuck.*

His face bruised. Eye blackened. This kid can take a beating. He's not fucking around, he's on his way to his child. To Liz. Regardless of our consent.

"Tristan! Okay, man, just listen to me."

I look over his shoulder, checking whether or not my dad can see the two of us. But he's nowhere in the vicinity.

I step back.

"Tristan, look man, I want to make things right. I mean, Liz only got a restraining order because she was scared. I didn't mean to say those things to her on the phone that one night."

"Restraining order?" Blood spit-firing into rage.

"Yeah, man, I said some things, you know? And I mean, that time I accidentally hit her in the eye. I mean it was totally not what I was trying to do there, man. She moved really quickly out of nowhere."

What? Restraining order? Hit her?

I shake my head. My father kept the worse of this mess from me.

"You did what?"

We look into each other's eyes. Simultaneously coming to conclusions about this situation. I am no longer conflicted about Brad's presence. He is a menace, his goal now competes with ours. Brad sees this, crossing the Rubicon. Knowing I might have been holding out hope for him, but now with the realization of how far he went—there is no second chance. He is no longer redeemable to my father, or me, and thus the person we are pro-tecting—Liz.

Now I'm right in his face, inches from his nose.

"Are you telling me you hit my sister?"

Brad's falling apart from the inside out.

He shakes his head, the realization now comes in the form of words.

"You two are never going to let me be apart of this, are you? Let me be with Liz and my child?"

"I think Dave was right, you don't deserve to be a father."

Something inside him snaps, I watch it manifest across his face.

Brad slaps me. Across the cheek.

The border guard jumps in to separate us. "Hey! Enough!"

Face stings with pain.

"Who the fuck are you?" he yells. "Liz said you just fucking abandoned her and her old man. Fucking absentee brother. You're a piece of shit if you ask me. After I told you all that shit outside the restaurant, man, fuck you!"

Fists clench. I bring my hands up, ready to throw punches through the guard.

He pushes the two of us away from each other. "Hey you two, enough!"

I hold my cheek.

"Did you just slap me? Who slaps someone, what are you some 18<sup>th</sup> century aristocrat?"

Brad looks confused.

I laugh. "You don't even know what an aristocrat is, do you? You're a fucking joke."

This royally pisses him off. He tries to get through the guard again, but gets distracted by something.

Four-door car speeds down the road beside us, weaving in and out of traffic. People scream, scatter like pigeons. Someone's clipped by the front hood, shoes above their head in a nanosecond. Car accelerates up to the roadblock; military start to shout, yelling at the driver to stop, guns raised and pointed.

Rules of engagement about to be engaged.

Vehicle continues, gloriously smashes through the barricades, sending kindling bits of wood and metal in all directions.

Open fire.

Litters the cab with bullets. Bullets rip-roaring through metal like wax paper. Windows combust in flurries of fragments. The noise is deafening. I cover my ears.

Car rams into a pillar, horn blares, airbags go off like some cheap defence mechanism.

They stop firing.

Middle-aged man staggers out of the car, spilling blood all over the concrete. Falls to his knees, tries to get up, resorts to crawling. Falls over like a drunkard's last gasp. They close in on him with their M4s. He's motionless.

"Fuck."

Blood pooling on the ground, crawls through the cracks in the pavement. Most people gone from the area, running as fast as they can. I turn.

Brad zooming away in his police cruiser.

Fingers me as he passes.

*Motherfucker.*

I run.

More gunfire, screaming. I don't turn around. I keep running, catch up to a young boy and his parents. The boy trips on his own feet trying to keep up. Takes his mother with him. I stop, turn, and grab the boy, pull him up to his feet in an instant.

"Thank you," says the mother.

I force a smile, turn, and start running again. The car and my father come into view. He's standing, alert, watching me and the scene, gun at his side.

Checking back over my shoulder, I jog up. Lean over on the hood, catch my breath. Treadmill-induced lungs only permit 5.0 speed on a 1.5 incline.

Look for Brad and his cruiser in the distance. Nothing.

I glance back, make out my dad looking around through his binoculars.

What is this death doing to my fucking sanity? The blood pouring out of the border runner like a leaky faucet, dripping ruby red gobs onto the cement. It doesn't look like it does in the movies. Not as dark, not as thick. Red—in all sensory explanations of the colour.

I regain my breath. Turn around. Military personnel huddled around the car. I can barely see.

"What did they say?"

Sigh. Let out a noise of frustration.

"Something about solar flares. Also the border is only open to military personnel. Something about no communication . . . even between the other border crossings."

Lowers his binoculars. My breath has slowed.

Splattering blood on the pavement. Clumps of red dropping out of his mouth, multiple teeth and parts of his tongue. Sound of bullets riddling the side doors, echoing off the buildings. Glass and shards of metal spastically exploding off the frame. Bullets ripping through metal at upwards of 3,000 miles per hour. Deadly spitballs puncturing instantaneously—in succession, one after the other.

Bam.Bam.Bam.Bam.Bam.

What it would feel like if it were your chest or stomach or the side of your head. Shrinks your composure—emotional dysfunction.

"Fuck me."

I start walking away from the car, away from the scene, away from my father. I don't look back. I just start walking south.

Soccer dad on the lawn, hanging from a tree. Religious nut on the bridge, his crazy mumblings. Kids beating the white guy to death with a baseball bat. The son I dragged from his father's car. The man at the border, dripping blood; red filtering into the asphalt. This race, this race with Brad, it's real, it's *on*.

He's gonna steal my sister and their baby. The next generation of Schultz.

A restraining order? Stuff I shouldn't have said? Accidentally hit her?

Fuck him.

"Tristan!"

I keep walking. Tributaries of blood, signs of death, lifeless eyes. Everywhere inside the mind, imbuing me with dread. A sense of finality. Formal acceptance of mortality.

Someone wipe my hard drive clean.

Run a magnet over my mind.

"Tristan."

He puts his hand on my shoulder and turns me around.

I whip it off as I pivot.

Desensitized to death and its terrifying shock—to suffering, terror, anarchy gone right. All those dead bodies over the years, wrapped in black body bags. Toe-tagged, marked for fingerprints, soaked in formaldehyde. Glazes over with a cloak of compliance. Remains calm.

I'm fucking losing my mind.

Modern life 101: kids and marriage, shitty job writing shitty press releases, updating social media statuses and compiling press clippings for a mindless multi-national capitalist monster of a corporation. Pumping brand-name pharmaceuticals into a diabetes riddled populous of Wal-Mart idiots who couldn't save their life to save a Diet Coke. The apathy, the fatigue, the news media, the cycle of violence, of fear, of commonplace attitudes. Culture of consumerist entitlement, of tech-savvy lemmings following the Pied Piper of Hamelin into cancerous tumours caused by too much cell phone use. Dying en masse of cardio-vascular disease while our planet cooks in its own stew while politicians wave puppeteers of Muslim terrorists to distract us from the real news.

This is what we've come to.

God threw us into the Recycle Bin. Deleted the contents. Ditched this galaxy to start over somewhere else. Realized he had no free will to begin with. Left us in the ether of an unfinished program, unable to update its own software, forever outdated to the current operating system.

Code:End

*Jet lag, hangover, time zone shifts I can't seem to track. Two years and two months but I still wake at three in the morning like it's five in the evening. Perspiration in my cargo pants and tank top. Stained with debauchery. Off the coast of the Phu Quoc beach in Vietnam there's a storm brewing. Ghostly looking clouds rumbling in like the horseman themselves. Muggy heat, standstill of oxygen recycling itself. The waves usually bring the wind in from the shore, but not today. Bombastic drumbeats of thunder crackle conversations as I sit on the beach, watching the firestorm roll in. Behind my red trimmed North Face backpack, worn to shit. Passport, toothbrush, codeine, the essentials. Everything I own within a 41-litre rounder carrying bag.*

*Honda-67 70cc motorbike. Jet black new. Now dusted and faded. Strip lines from mud puddles. Rust accumulating below the exhaust pipe. Vietnamese guy who sold it to me said it wasn't good for long hauls on the open highway. I didn't care, it fit my frame; we were in love. He laughed at the notion of loving a machine. Old man even got me in the ring one night, traditional Thai kickboxing match in Da Nang. Buck-forty Vietnamese kid never saw it coming. Found out I knew how to throw. Found out I knew how to breathe between punches, push the air from my stomach in that distinct hissing noise. He unwittingly consented to a one-on-on donnybrook. Two and a half minutes in I was dirty boxing him into early retirement at the ripe age of 18. Vietnamese guys offered to train me, said I could tour, maybe go pro. I'd fought enough in my life, just wanted to remind myself I could still awaken the physical beast within my soul. I could still be an animal.*

*Counted the days yesterday. Eight hundred and one, seventeen hours, sixteen minutes since I drove across the border and abandoned a 1989 Chrysler Dynasty in the Bellingham International Airport. Stripped the barcode and license plates. Donated it to the United States of America. Six countries, one skipped arrest, four time zones, three bouts of food poisoning, so many unforgettable nights. I missed my eight hundredth day off the grid. Slept the entire twenty-four hours in my cabin; some beautifully fit*

*German girl named Maya left when she realized I wasn't getting up for breakfast, or lunch. Took her Molly and headed back to Bangkok.*

*Visa card, email account. No camera. Haven't been on the internet in more than four months. Two nights ago I drank snake blood, slammed cheap whisky and motored down the National Highway 3 in the dark towards Phnom Penh in Cambodia with Maya. Weaving in and out of crowded buses. Horns honking, a clarification of intent, not distress. Malaria-filled air whisking through my jet blonde locks. Apparently I look like Brad Pitt. Apparently every white guy looks like Brad Pitt. I tell people I'm Canadian, they can't seem to grasp the dual citizenship thing over here. We partied at a rave until sun up, had a threesome, then sweated out the excess in a massage parlour on the outskirts of the city. Made it back to the resort in time for a shower and drinks at the swim-up bar.*

*Maya was running from a bad relationship. I didn't ask, I didn't care. I told her I lost my mother. That was enough for both of us. We just wanted to fuck instead of fight. Enjoy the blank stare of someone you don't know. Something fresh. Something foreign. She left her email, but I threw it in the trash. Didn't want to spoil the perfectness of our three weeks together. Things get weird. They always do.*

*One of the groundskeepers from the resort tells me it's going to rain soon, and that I should come back inside. I tell him I'm going to check out and bike the National Highway 2 all the way to Ho Chi Minh City. I'd heard of a massive house party at a mansion owned by a Hong Kong native who was dating an American girl I knew. She invited me three weeks ago. He nods like he somehow understands my incoherent Westernized babbling.*

*No DiscMan, no headphones. I only listen to music in the company of others. The highway frees me from thought, too concerned with the present, making sure I don't get sideswiped or pushed into a ditch by a commuter bus packed with Vietnamese families and lonely farmers. Peripheral lights off in the night, lining the way to the city. Palm tree outlines in the dark. Side-street shops with languages I could never fathom. So many sights, sounds and smells I can only focus on the present.*

*Maya asked me when I planned on going home.*

*I told her when I forget why I came here in the first place.*

</>

Deep breath of air from the pit of the stomach.

Fresh oxygen flash floods the lungs.

Hands on the head.

My father stands in remission, slight annoyance.

Offline for ages in real time. Headed back to the car to catch my thoughts, feet out the passenger side door. I needed time to reflect on this—whatever *this* is.

"What?" I say, dropping my hands in a fit.

Drag my tie knot until I can take it off and whip it to the ground. I have a serious urge to break something with some substance.

"Keep it together, okay?"

I glare at him.

"Fuck. You."

Raise my middle finger.

His expression barely changes. Puts his hands up, olive branch extends out his mouth.

"Stick to the plan. Steady pace."

I clear my throat.

Calm my thoughts.

He needs to know this.

"Dad, I saw Brad at the border. He's got a new cruiser. I spoke to him. Look, he's fucking batshit crazy. He told me about the restraining order. Did he hit Liz?"

He shakes his head as he realized this race is actually on, and for keeps. "I could never get Liz to admit it, but I think he clipped her pretty good in the face. It might have been accidental. I have to believe it's accidental, because if I don't, I will end up killing that boy."

My father puts his hands on his head, realizing Brad could be crossing the border as we speak. Looks to the left, to the right.

"Fuck."

Pupils scatter to the sides of the retinas.

"We need to cross the border. Now."

I agree.

We agree.

</>

My dad's just finished shaving our heads.

Run the fingers from back to front across the skull.

The thought of what we're about to do has me rampant with anxious fear. Looting, stealing, carjacking, eventually I can make peace with those. Now we're about to commit multiple federal felonies, all of which could get us shot or killed.

As he shaved my head, he told me to step outside myself. To pretend it's not real. To shit my pants and swim in it. I'm about to see if I'm man enough to enter this new world and grab it by the fucking throat.

The wind on my scalp, whisking across the short hairs, tickling each follicle.

I take a deep breath in.

*Violence*, he says. It's the one thing people respect.

Hidden around the corner from a military line haul tractor off the side streets right by the crossing. It sits, running. Rumble of the engine on concrete. Pump-action Remington shotgun pointed down towards my leg. The one he used to dummy the guy in the Wal-Mart parking lot.

There's blood on the stock. I don't wipe it off.

He goes. Taps me on the shoulder as we run straight for the front cab.

I jump onto the foot deck. The stock of my shotgun goes through the open window.

Barrel finds the cheekbone of a young American military soldier.

My dad's Glock's pushing into the temple of the driver, so much he slants sideways as he sits.

He speaks in a low, disgruntled tone.

"We're two very unstable men. All we want is your fatigues and your truck. You two have to decide if you want to be heroes. There's a cemetery not far from here."

No answer.

I open the cab door, swing to the side, and with one hand rip the soldier out.

He falls to the ground like the kid, but doesn't roll. My dad does the same.

I'm overtop in a split second, looking for any type of a firearm.

Veins pump blood. Autobahns of adrenaline. Wind tunnels for lungs. Autonomic nervous system on hyper drive.

Back to the downed soldier. Grab him by the scruff of his cargo jacket and pick him up.

"Jacket, now!" I say, shotgun barreling into his forehead so quickly he goes cross-eyed.

He's crying, the kid's no more than eighteen.

No time for feelings. Just pure heroin-grade human-produced epinephrine.

I'm hooked. There's no methadone for this shit.

Starts to take his jacket off. Once it's halfway I yank the rest.

The sound of duct tape wrapping.

I stand there, holding the jacket.

More duct tape.

I look at the kid from down the barrel of the shotgun. There's no way he's doing anything. Large pimple on his chin, a buck fifty soaking wet.

My dad comes around. His Glock cracks off the side of the kid's head. Kid bails to the ground, lifeless.

"Fuck," I say, lowering my weapon.

Starts duct taping his legs instantly.

"Check the other guy!"

Dart around to the other side of the truck.

Duct-taped soldier on the ground. Legs bound, arms behind his back. Tape over his mouth. No jacket. A poorly wrapped Christmas present lying there, staring up at me, helpless.

I point the shotgun at him, listening to the duct tape on the other side.

My dad drags the other guy around.

"Follow me," he says, lugging the soldier into the alley by his legs.

I grab mine by the feet. Uncomfortable noises as his clothes and body grind against pavement.

I stop and switch—start dragging him by the arms. This doesn't work either. I drop the shotgun and use both hands. I think I got the heavy one.

As soon as I get around the corner I lose my grip and the soldier slips back onto the ground. My dad looks back.

"What the fuck are you doing?"

"Mine is fucking heavy!"

He stops dragging his. Jogs back to me.

"Grab his fucking arm for Christ's sake."

We drag the guy towards the other one.

Once we make it into the alley, I see the pole. End of a concrete lined carport, behind a restaurant within a line of retail stores. Alley's secluded by garbage bins, high chain-link fences with wooden boards. Someone would have to drive down this road to see this. They'd have to be looking.

Drags the guy up to the pole, sits him against the slumped over kid. Eyes wide in compliance. The other down for the count, lights out. We just dummied two National Guard soldiers.

The violence my father's exhibited continues to escalate at an alarming rate. How far is he willing to go to get us to Liz? To beat Brad?

How far will a father go to save his daughter?

The answer might present itself.

Grabs the other guy and sits him up. Runs the duct tape around the two of them, pinning them to the pole.

Goes around about seven or eight times. Tight.

That sound. The sound of unraveling duct tape. Unforgettable.

One's mumbling something underneath his muzzle of tape.

This only irritates him.

"Get your shotgun."

Run back to the shotgun, pick it up off the ground, dart back. He's finishing his masterpiece. Putting more tape around their arms and legs, biting it off with his teeth. The one continues to mumble.

He grabs the shotgun. The stock comes down across the side of his face with quick intensity.

He has his jacket on. I left the other one back at the truck.
"Let's go."

I jog behind. He's got both guns. I reach down and grab the hockey bag full of our grub and weapons. Head around to the passenger's side, throw the jacket on, hop up into the truck. Cram the hockey bag down into the front of the cabin by our feet.

My dad does not hesitate.

Air brake pedal down, pulls the clutch knob back. Truck rumbles and grinds its teeth. Into first, gas down. Spins the large steering wheel.

Torque line on the steering column jerks us both forward before it rolls into gear.

I pull the coat hanger out, cloth tied to the end.

Around the bend onto the main drag. About 200 feet from the crossing. Barricades and the same group from earlier. Bullet-riddled car still on display. I check for Brad and his cruiser. Nothing.

We stop at a van parked on the side of the road. I jump out, engine running.

"Check to make sure nobody's in it!"

I look inside. Nobody. But—

"There's a baby seat in here," I say to my dad, looking back.

"Is there a baby in the baby seat?"

"No."

"Then do it!"

I nod. Pop the gas cap off the side. Coat hanger goes in, leading with the cloth. Push it as far as it will go.

Zippo. Cloth. Lit.

Diversion: about to be created.

Back up in the truck and my dad turns around. We head off the street; I watch in the rearview mirror as flames flicker through the van window.

Another corner and we're directly facing the back road. Military guards stand around. There's nothing stopping us now but them.

Nothing between us and Canada but spiked tire guards and M4s.

We sit and wait. Neither of us says anything, just sit with shaved heads. Stolen car, stolen uniforms. Clutch down, ready to shift into gear.

He doesn't take his eye off the prize, the route through to Canada. Maple syrup and beaver pelts.

Anticipation. Smells like diesel.

We watch the scene down the road; the side entrance across the border. Military men walk around like little figurines, back and forth. A Jeep comes across from the other side.

Eruption across the way on the main highway, a hundred feet back. I feel it pulsate the cabin of the truck, small vibration running through every particle in the air. That ding noise when the microwave is finished.

He's staring forward. Military men scramble, looking in the direction of the fire. Back to the explosion. Flames envelope the van, people scatter.

Still watching the scene at the back entrance to the border.

I look at him again. He does not look back, hands at ten and two on the large circular wheel.

Slowly drops his right hand down to the stick shift, vibrating inside the cab. Puts his hand on it but does not shift us into gear.

Still waiting. Patiently, intently.

Military guards scatter out of formation. Trucks start up.

Shifts us into gear. Rumble down the side street, passing cars. Some people on their roofs, trying to get a better view.

Another explosion.

File: downloaded.

The car closest to the explosion catches fire. Smoke shoves into the atmosphere. I'm rattling around in the seat, sweating, nervous. Climaxing on adrenaline.

Twenty feet away and we see a man in army fatigues with a semi-automatic rifle.

We get up to the checkpoint, one guy on each side. My dad's window already down.

"What happened?!" says the guard.

I can see the guard on the other side. He's distracted by the fire, smoke and commotion. I play into it, look back too.

"Cars are on fire, someone's lighting them up," my dad says. "Sergeant wants us to head across to get extinguishers over on Zero Ave."

"Where's your slip?"

Throat burns. I look back at the soldier on my side. He's looking at me.

My dad sticks his head out the window and points backwards.

"There's my slip. You wanna explain to Sarge why you sent me back to get a slip while half the block goes up in flames, you fucking idiot?"

I still can't see the solider he's speaking to.

This moment in time defined by anxiety.

Another explosion.

A hand starts to wave us through.

He shifts into gear.

I watch the M4 get smaller as we rumble over some speed bumps. I look to my left, at the actual border.

No passport.

No ID.

No baggage check.

Illegal immigrants to our own country.

Welcome to Canada.

Bienvenue au Canada.

As soon as we get far enough away I let out a noise of happiness, a quick "Wahoo!" and smack my hands off the dashboard. He keeps looking forward as we see the cars lined up on the other side of the border, all of them with Washington State license plates. People guarded and hesitant to make eye contact or draw attention to themselves. They're all watching the smoke signals across the 49th parallel.

We leave them in our rearview mirror. Exhale for what feels like the first time in more than twenty minutes.

Like something out of an action movie.

I'm looking for the credits to start rolling.

</>

*Soju. Clear elixir like soupy vodka. Green bottle like 7-UP. So cheap in Korea it was criminal not to drink it. You play this game where you guess the number underneath the cap—higher or lower up to 50, process of elimination, and the loser has to do a shot. More of a time-killer than anything else. Then you twist off the top, try to flick the protector from the bottle cap with your index finger. I was always good at it.*

*I'd been off the grid now for five years. People I once knew stopped emailing. I rarely called home anymore. I'd figured they figured I wasn't coming back, at all.*

*I wasn't sure if they were right or wrong yet.*

*The Incheon International Airport looks like something out of a bad 80s Tron remake. Dusted white tiling lining the way, clear lines, long conveyor belts and what feels like miles of glass exposing high rises off in the distance. From there, I'd landed a job in the Mapo-gu district of Seoul, serving beer at an American-styled bar. Tall and blonde, I drove in the Asian women like cattle. But the locals would never approach me, cultural thing, just liked to peer out of the corner of their eye, giggle and run off after a few flavoured drinks.*

*Atlanta guy named Mike I was rooming with in a long-term hostel said dating them was like dating a fucking, biting plush toy. Too much conversation and you'd wish the batteries would run out. He was about half of an LBH—loser back home—but still seemed like he knew what he'd gotten himself into. It was the guys who'd been there for close to a decade that scared me the most. Like they'd actually given up on the Western world. Karaoke bars their new Pittsburgh.*

*More than a thousand days. I hadn't set foot in North America in more than a thousand calendar days. Christmases, gone. Birthdays, gone. Weddings, missed. Babies, born. While everyone was growing up, I was growing away.*

*We head out after work into the nightlife and the Dongdaemun Market. South Korean kids dress like they're on runways. Pleated blazers with skinny ties and dark rimmed glasses. Fit for the frame of Asian indie-hipsters. We needed to keep up, keep our pants tight and our style current to blend into the scenery.*

*Two nights ago we'd caught a Doosan Bears baseball game. Team in the KBO that played out of Jamsil Stadium. Massive architectural beast lined by the high-rises of the city. Numbered high rises. Like what* complex do you live in? '80, oh yeah, I live in 54.' I still had no idea where everyone was parking their cars, except very poorly on the street. We watched a local butcher a parallel attempt to the ninth degree, laughed as we munched on Korean KFC.

We spent the better part of the pitching duel drinking cheap stadium beer, inhaling tiny American-styled hot dogs and laughing with a group of American-styled Americans. Teaching English oversees. Life experience, check. Stories to bring back home to the cabin at family reunions, check. Slowly forgotten cultural experiences, double-check.

The inflatable thunder sticks bang away in song structure. We sang along with the customary chants, inserting our own English versions. 'You pee too fast,' 'We watch bum holes cringe.' We laughed like we didn't care because, well, we didn't.

Mike and I heckle the import pitcher, one of three on every roster. Some poor Cincinnati guy not good enough for AAA in his home state was now getting culture shocked to the ends of the Pacific Rim. 'Hey Porter, we know you understand English. Go home, you fucking foreigner.' We laughed—he never acknowledged our barbs, guy was steely on the outside at least. Our group gambled on each pitch, a crisp green won for every at-bat. Hit, ground out, fly out, walk, strike, etc. The Koreans loved to watch us cheer and exchange bills each out. Gambling was illegal for locals. Weird cultural shit, it was everywhere.

After the game we went for galbi and then to a bar called 'Country Club' which had the words 'Well come' scrolling across the top of the door in fluorescent lighting. Mike had been taking pictures of all the spell fails, his favourite still 'vegeterian' at the underground COEX mall. Like being vegetarian was egalitarian, we laughed. We'd drink our way on and off of the Seoul Metro rapid transit; they had sliding glass doors to get on, as people tried to jump in front of the subway cars so much they couldn't trust them anymore. I understood their pain, such a controlled culture. We periodically got told to quiet down in broken English when we were too loud on the metro, like it was a fucking library or something.

The only thing I missed was my Honda-67 70cc. Traded in for a few hundred won. It bought us a decent TV at our place, which we barely watched as I couldn't understand the majority of the channels. The only comprehensible ones were out of date American movies like TimeCop and Abyss.

I'd taken to squid at the 7-Eleven, and wandering home after work through the back alleys and lights. So many plush toys and cellphone cases. Friendly Roy G. Biv colours illuminating my face like some Hello Kitty ad. I'd get drunk at work just to enjoy the scenery.

On our three days off, we'd take a bus down to the coastal city of Busan, enjoy the neatly crafted garbage-free beaches. I missed smoking pot but not as much as I enjoyed smoking Bohem Cigar mojitos. When in Rome, someone once said.

Mike and I would frequent the bars close to the shore, the love hotels where couples went to cheat on their significant others. Weird draped carpeting covering the entrances to the parking lots. We had a hell of a time trying to get a room with two beds and just gave up and got separate ones.

I couldn't remember what it felt like not to be surrounded by thousands of people at any given moment. Bright lights, big city was right. Seoul my mistress, she took care of me, nurtured me with her escapism and seventeen million souls. I was so anonymous, only recognizable as white, a foreigner, American, Canadian, European. It didn't matter; I was something out of place. Eye contact was minimal, but I knew they could sense me. I loved the blatant inconspicuousness.

Seoul, her buildings and architecture kept me marvelling at the endurance of mankind's will to continuously out-construct itself. I fell in love with each towering skyscraper, shielding me from the sun and memories.

The white guy named Anthony who owned the bar we worked at had taken to calling me by my middle name—David. Didn't like Tristan, said it reminded him of his hometown of Baltimore. He left some thirteen years ago, had been in Southeast Asia ever since. Came running from the IRS. I caught him wiping tears from his eyes one night as we watched Seinfeld on the overhead TVs during a slow night. He said there was onion in the kitchen, I didn't fact check his bullshit plea not to push the conversation. I just kept making pink-colored martinis for the little Asian girls in the corner, thinking about home.

Thinking about how foreign I'd really become.

</>

Pfizer's clinical trials are imperative in the ongoing search to make important medical discoveries to help people live healthier lives. Only through the careful study of how medical treatments affect humans are researchers able to determine whether medications that show promise are safe and effective.

As a world leader in clinical research, Pfizer is committed to upholding the highest ethical standards and we regularly review and update our protocols to keep pace with the increasing salaries of our executive leaders.

Before the fire. Our lives defined by it.

Pre-fire and post-fire.

Now a chance for a new definition.

Pre-disconnect, post-apocalypse.

I always imagine what life would've been like if my mother hadn't died. The four of us, together. My dad and I would be close. Liz would have her mom. I've thought about it so much I've created fake memories. The four of us travelling together, taking trips, my mother diligently researching each country we visited.

Watching my sister graduate from high school.

My mother helping me through university, helping me figure out what I really wanted to do with my life instead of using my charm and smarts to spin doctor for profit shares.

Dad and I meeting up for beers, checking out local fights, sparring and training together.

My sister and I having dinner, maybe catching a flick on a quiet Friday night, planning our parent's twenty-fifth wedding anniversary.

The fucking pain of it all.

Now north.

Magnetic north.

Pulled along the Number 13 like mice through a maze. Confidence boosted by multiple federal felonies. We made it across. Bought ourselves some time. Jumped the biggest hurdle and were now on a downward slant towards the goal.

I imagine Brad barreling through the border behind us, gunned down in his cruiser by National Guard troops. The whole thing some international relations nightmare; American cop killed by the military.

Or did he get through? Is he already ahead of us? If we show up at Liz's place and she's gone, how far down the rabbit hole will my father continue to venture? Does his sanity ride on the outcome of this race?

What do we do if we never find Liz or her baby?

Can we do anything?

Wild coniferous trees line the asphalt, evoking the rural sensibility of Canada. Farms and horses penned in, power lines and irrigation ditches. Dark homes. This chaos, not national.

Pull a hairpin left turn on 264<sup>th</sup> Street and start heading back south.

"Where's that map?"

"We left it in the car, remember? The one we traded that guy for."

He keeps driving like he's not going to acknowledge me for a bit.

Head onto 4<sup>th</sup> but I notice the yellow No Exit sign and point it out.

"Fuck."

Back out onto the Number 13.

Flat-lined semi-rural farmhouses with detached garages. Multiple trails of smoke in the distance lift up in the peripheral vision. White sky, forever drowning the sight with a blank stare of clear opaque nothingness. A car in a ditch, no occupants, all the doors open. Glass and metal everywhere, all over the asphalt.

Up to 13<sup>th</sup> Avenue. Young boy stands on the side of the road in a ratty T-shirt, holding a long wooden stick. Kid stands, locking eyes with me, shirt with scuff marks of dried and crusted dirt.

No shoes on. Ruffian of the Armageddon.

I stare him down until he's out of view.

Up to North Bluff Road and a left, heading west. Eerie chill on this highway. All cars speeding. No pedestrians. Trees line the way. Tanker truck down an embankment off a small creek that runs parallel to the road. Driver's side door smashed. Corse blue liquid pours into the soil, staining it, killing it with its acidic base of corrosive chemicals.

We pass one intersection, a large sign on a telephone poll. It's for a lost cat—Kizzy. Unspecified reward for his or her return.

"Where are we going exactly? Your boat's at the White Rock terminal, right?"

Seventeen-foot bow rider cutter he takes out saltwater fishing when in town. Last time I went was years back for his retirement party. Caught a boatload of Chinooks and off-season bluebacks. Smoked them up on the backyard grill, marinated in lager beer and barbecue sauce. Hung out with his police buddies and my sister. Brad even made a brief appearance during his shift. I'd come up to Vancouver for the weekend, back to our place. I mean, I couldn't miss his swan song. Used his retirement party as an excuse to reach out.

But we never got time to talk, and before I knew it I was back in my car on my way home, waiting at the border, thinking about another missed opportunity for reconnection. My sister posted a neatly crafted photo of the three of us on Instagram, tagged us all.

It was as close as we'd get to looking like a real family.

"That thing's going to get us across the Strait?"

"Hopefully."

I look at the wild white yonder, crystallizing into a creamy black within the bleach. Our planet's atmosphere is sick with some communicable disease.

"We gonna go tonight?"

"No," he glances up. "We'll find a place to stay in White Rock, head out at first light. Tomorrow, we get to Liz. I doubt Brad made it across the border, but we keep the same pace, steady, cautious. Traveling at night is not a good idea unless we absolutely have to."

Travel at the pace of this thing.

"You think she's okay?" I ask.

I watch the stress of the question crawl across his face.

His daughter, pregnant.

Ready to burst as the whole world tumbles down around her like a revolutionizing country.

He doesn't answer.

The road rumbles on. Exhausted, we settle into a suffocating silence.

Streetlights sit unlit in the distance.

No moon quietly perched in the celestial sphere. No massive star signalling sunset.

One sheet of colour, black. Bleak.

Full-blooded earth set adrift in the dark, abandoned in the corner of the universe. Society stripped away like a decaying layer of paint. Crusted to the edges, our initial fabric exposed. Exposed for who we are.

Uncontrollable.

Unreachable.

</>

She is in pain. Walking hurts, sitting hurts, standing hurts. The only thing that doesn't hurt like hell is lying on the bed, head propped against a pillow.

The baby hasn't kicked in a few hours, allowing momentary rest.

This kid wants out. Boy or girl, she doesn't care anymore.

Internet doesn't work. No power, no TV, no running water. Battery life on her Macbook Pro slowly drops. Thirty-two percent remaining. Decreased the brightness, fiddled with the Activity Monitor, anything to give it more time.

Looks through pictures on her hard drive. She deleted all the ones with Brad after he called her one night at 2AM. The ramblings of a drunken mess crossing the line: after she told him she was pregnant with his kid but too far along to have an abortion, he wanted to marry her. She had saved his life. She had ruined it. He loved her. He wanted to kill her.

Earlier she listened to the voicemail her father told her to keep. The one she played for the cops when she got the restraining order.

*"Liz! You fucking take this kid away from me, from my one chance to be a father! I'll take us both! I'll end us both! I love you so much, baby!"*

Put her phone on the bed and cried.

Where did they go so wrong? Where did she go so wrong?

He once brought her flowers after she aced a midterm exam. Played her a silly song on a ukulele.

Now it's this. This is what it's come to?

Family photos console her in the echo of fear.

*Her dad. Tristan.*

The family she so desperately needs right now.

Old pics scanned from albums scavenged after the fire. Her mother, beautiful with long white-blonde hair, standing beside a bunch of men in suits, receiving an award for her work with the City of Vancouver. She looks powerful, head held high.

Twenty-two percent battery life.

Puts her iPhone in sleep mode, hoping to save it for an emergency call if the phones ever work again. Security told her to conserve power on her electronics but they also told her they might not ever start working. It was all incredibly confusing.

Her father, and a young Tristan stand sideways in a boxing showdown pose. Tristan with his shirt off, gloves on, blonde hair sweaty across his forehead. The next is Tristan in the ring, helmet and gloves on, referee lifting his hand in victory.

Fifteen percent battery life.

Her mother stands behind her and Tristan at the Vancouver Aquarium. She chuckles, looks silly in her rain boots, hugging her mother's leg. A huge ice cream stain down her shirt. Tristan sticks his tongue out at the camera.

Eight percent battery life.

The four of them on the Oregon coast. Her dad holding his wife. Tristan in a tracksuit, dragging a long walking stick across the ground. She looks into her young eyes. Has no memory of this day, this trip. But she knows. She knows that trip was the last time the four of them were ever together.

You are now running on reserve battery power. Please plug the power adapter into your computer and into a power outlet. If you do not, your computer will go to sleep in a few minutes to preserve its memory contents.

Scrolls forward to the newer photos, ones taken after her mom passed away. Pictures with dad, out fishing together in his boat. Her high school graduation, honours, valedictorian. Her father holds her around the shoulders, a massive grin on his face.

Tristan's gone. Like he's been plucked from memory.

Her laptop screen goes black. Blinking light fades into dark.

She closes the computer, holds back tears.

</>

Rain's given everything that wet stank. Grass and manure ferment in the nostrils. Damp concrete, bark-soaked trees. Sinking feeling in the stomach, downward magnetic pulse dragging the spine towards the centre of the earth. Headache in the back of the neck, cresting forward to the temples. Hard alcohol, cigarettes, too much sugar, not enough carbohydrates, lack of electrolytes. Too much stress and running around.

I'm a soccer mom.

Started this morning in a full suit. Now I'm down to pants and a bloodstained dress shirt, Army fatigue jacket with JOHNSON in bold black lettering on the breast. Head shaved. Peeling the skin off the former world and emerging into a brave new one. One I'm still not able to fully comprehend.

West along North Bluff Road. We navigate each four-way stop—or lack thereof—with cautious, bitterly sober enthusiasm. Cars try to wave us down. People on the side of the road trying to get our attention or jump into the cab. Slithering down the slimy path from rural to urban sprawl. Smoke and unrest choke the consciousness. Unnerving feeling climbs—a fresh patch of blood stains the asphalt, surrounded by crushed particles of glass. Remnants of something terrible.

Up ahead at Campbell Valley Park, a wooded area cut down the middle by the provincial highway.

I can see the fires.

Trees burn a smoky, crimson red on the south side of the road. I've never seen a forest fire this close up. Flames leap from treetop to treetop, leaving patches in between unscathed. Grass runs wild with a deep dark blaze. Dense black smoke that looks like it weighs more than water, devouring elements at a rapid pace.

He slows the engine, gears down.

Line of flames across the pavement.

A literal firewall.

"Fuck."

Another long drawn-out U-turn grinding the gears of the stick shift. Clench my teeth, wondering how long before he completely dislodges it and I'm forced to toss another tweener into a muddy grave so we can carry on toward Liz.

"Where are we going now?"

"Back to 216<sup>th</sup>. We'll drive around this."

Pacific Northwest a bonfire of cherry red. Not extinguished by the rain, its own heat generating a protective shield. Ready to incinerate the countryside to the end of the wick.

We turn left, head north on 216<sup>th</sup>, countryside backdrop. The same scene, dusty grain silos and long wooden-poled electric fences.

Northwest to Bradshaw Road, then another left to the small township of Brookswood.

Tiny community buried within the forest of the district. Power lines dip across the side of the road, sending out small sparks every few seconds, like it's trying to jumpstart itself.

Massive pileup of cars at the first stoplight. Vehicles overturned like exposed turtles, crushed like kid's juice boxes. Puddles of blood, connected by streams across the pavement. A man dizzy-steps around with a white, bloodstained towel pressed against his head. Another sits on the side of the road bawling, holding an unconscious woman in his arms, head slumped awkwardly to the side. Two overweight middle-aged men yell at each other. Start pushing and shoving. The small group of people around try to separate them; it pisses them off even more.

They start to wave us down like we're the police. Like the Army will sort everything out. These people craving civility and lawfulness—fiendlike addicts assaulting reason.

First you hate the cops for pulling you over while speeding. Now you'd suck the balls right off Johnny Policeman for a few drops of law-and-order.

We're the culture that wants what it doesn't have.

"Keep fucking driving," I say to my dad, knowing full well he will.

A young man dressed in a ripped blazer runs up beside the cab and jumps onto the plank. Bangs on the window, leaving a handprint of blood. I hear his muffled voice.

"Let me in!" he yells, holding onto the side mirror as my dad navigates the intersection.

I push my body up against the door and pop it open with one mighty move.

He flings off the cab onto the pavement. Both his shoes fly off in a full-on yard sale. Blazer stays on.

The outside air too foreign, the noise too much. I grab the door, slam it shut in an instant, once again regaining the fishbowl of sensibility within our vehicle.

I'm breathing heavily.

"Fuck."

Rows of smashed windows, freshly abandoned cars. No lights. No power. People run across the middle of the street. Cop car darts across a side street, lights flashing but no siren.

How quickly things fall apart. Seventy-two hours of no connectivity. All reason—lost. Take away something as simple as the ability to call 911, and we're unable to adapt to a new environment collectively. Reverting to primal motives, as if we never really left the cave in the first place.

Society a fragile bird dropped from the nest, broken wings. We're the kids who've overthrown the daycare. The lions born in captivity suddenly freed into the Sahara. Give us a chance and we will thoroughly disappoint you. Give us a chance and we will throw it away for one last hit.

Nothing more than a calamitous disaster waiting to happen. William Golding was right. Fuck the idyllic high functioning societies of the future where we bathe in soapy symbiosis and tolerance.

We'd rather roll around in the shit.

Until we wake up back in the Dark Ages.

</>

Exhaustion. Whisked together with stress. High anxiety, low energy. The body fights the mind for control.

I will remember this day for the rest of my life.

This day will define the rest of my life.

All I want to do is crawl into bed with Brianne and forget everything. Not some things. *Every*thing.

If I could go back, I'd do it differently. I'm sure of it now. Work less, play more. All those hours, all that time working towards goals, trying to increase my stock, my pay grade, shine up my LinkedIn profile. None of it matters anymore. None of it ever mattered. It's gone like passed flatulence.

I wanted happiness. I figured I'd be happy if I kept working at it. I had it all wrong.

I had everything wrong.

If nothing else, the end of the world is a chance to begin anew.

If nothing else, I am not sentenced to my previous life for eternity.

The workforce, the minions, the regulars sent up a prayer to the heavens. 'Save us from this hamster wheel.' God answered.

*Oh*, did He ever.

A T in the road, 200$^{th}$ Street.

South, cresting smoke from the forest fire burns through residential areas like one match igniting the whole book. Lifts up drywall residue, metal rebar and fried concrete excrement into the air. We sit at the junction, foot on the brake, watching the blush cherry and copper haze as elements heat to burning degrees.

"You think it's gone that far west?"

My dad keeps looking, answers slowly.

"Yeah."

And with that he shifts back into gear. We turn right, head north again.

Signs for Langley.

"Not a good idea," I say. "I don't like going where people are congregating."

Doesn't answer, continues driving, one hand on the stick shift.

Langley pushes into the vision, dense uninspiring cul-de-sac housing complexes. Abandoned stores, boarded up restaurants, the usual. McDonald's, Shell stations and sit-down corporate chain eateries being violated by the common folk.

Semi-truck carrying something flammable sits on its side by an intersection. Not a soul around.

My dad's hair short to begin with, but now he looks like a veteran criminal with a shaved head. Burn marks scorched into his arms. He's in the zone, driving, periodically checking his blind spots.

$200^{th}$ Street seems to miss the epicentre of Langley. Off to the right a water-warped beige high-rise apartment complex flares with flames, brimming out windows, crawling up the exterior, floor by floor.

Left on $56^{th}$ Avenue, a main feeder street into Vancouver and more tightly-packed urban density.

"Isn't the Fraser Highway up a bit?" I say, pointing to an applicable sign.

He waves it off.

West on $56^{th}$. To the south elongated produce fields of blueberries and strawberries, new two-storey condominium complexes to the north. We crawl up to a light, proceed slowly, look both ways like respectable citizens.

A flash of colour rapidly invades my view.

All I can do is throw my hands up to block whatever this is.

Tires screech like ravenous tribesmen.

Car smashes into the passenger side, noise shatters the eardrums.

Truck lifts up, hockey bag unapologetically jams into my leg.

Growl out a curse.

*Fuck!*

Throw my hands out straight, hoping to find solid ground to brace against.

No luck.

Head whips back, hits the window behind us.

White dots imprint my vision as I squint.

Windshield wiper flies by like a bird darting off into the sky.

The truck up on one side for a moment. Stomach makes a mad dash for my neck.

Grabs the wheel and rights us, but we're still moving, heading towards the side of the road.

Pumps the brakes; snake hiss of air. I'm bracing the cabin frame as we head off road.

Slow to a stop, inches from a ditch. Glance back; a blue four-door BMW, front hood crumpled. Dislodged airbags.

"You okay?"

When I twist my neck, my left shoulder moans in pain. There will be a bruise there tomorrow. Rub it with my hand and turn my upper body around. We look out the back window. A figure in the passenger's side, obstructed by an airbag. Unconscious. I'm blinking over and over to right my blotched vision.

My father lets out some kind of noise.

Twists his shoulder, pulls his arm down, lets out a massive bear growl. A pop.

The sound of cartilage reasserting itself.

Rubs his face in displeasure, tired and cranky of all this fucking shit. I'm about to join him.

"Did we seriously just get in another motherfucking car accident?" I say. "Should I go buy us lottery tickets?"

Looks at me. Almost smiling. I see a smirk. I smile too. The absolute absurdity calls for nothing less.

"Yeah," he says. "Yeah, we got T-boned. *Again.*"

"Apparently four-way stops are too tough to follow," I say, rubbing my neck.

"Yeah, thank God we're in this beast."

Looking for witnesses.

"Check the side," says my dad.

I start to open the door.

"No, don't open the door. Roll the window down."

I turn the crank, lower the window; surface damage, door dented, concave imprint in the metal. Other than that it looks fine.

"I think we're good."

"Okay," he says, and we're off.

Scene disappears behind. A car stops. Guy gets out, looks like he's trying to open one of the BMW's doors, but by that time we're too far away to tell.

Leaving the scene of the accident. No cops, no first responders. No swapping of insurance info, no playing up potential whiplash symptoms, trying to place blame on the other party. No spectators passing by shooting apathetic glances, more worried about the time they lost in the subsequent traffic jam than actual human lives.

We just leave.

Contours of criminal activity becoming much more subjective.

West on 56th. A telling silence fills the cabin of the truck. We both dart our eyes everywhere, like another BMW could leap from the bushes and surprise T-bone us.

Cloverdale, on the north side. Rumble along. Cars zoom by. Up to Number 15, highway that weaves north to the Trans-Canada and straight south to the border. At the four-way stop, my dad slows, takes a deep breath. A car's coming from the north; he waves it through with his right hand. Vehicle creeps out and darts through the intersection like a mouse moving between furniture. He checks once again and hits the gas while shifting into gear.

I blink. Everything saturated with a slight dim. I lean forward, white scale across the top of the world infused with a musty tint.

"Is it starting to get dark?"

He leans forward, looks up, like he's searching for a plane or helicopter in the sky.

"Yeah, maybe."

"What time is it?"

Scans the dashboard. No clock.

"Where's your phone?"

"I left it in the other car."

"Why would you leave it in the other car?"

"I didn't leave it, I forgot it."

"Why would you forget it in the other car?"

"Fuck, because I had no idea we were going to trade cars with someone. You didn't really include me in the planning on that one, carjacker."

His answer? Silence—as usual.

Infinite penumbra over the alabaster horizon. Dark rising tide. Dimming, downgrading the lucent glow. Unnatural, a shadow cast upon, hovering and filling the cracks and corners with dusk.

Southwest of Cloverdale. There's no way we're going to make White Rock before dark. Surrey is close by.

Town was bad to begin with, riddled with East Indian gangs, violent turf wars, daylight muggings and balaclava armed robberies. I'm guessing it's fine and dandy now—all-out Middle Eastern warfare with no oil to bring in the hammer of foreign powers. They're *really* on their own.

"I don't think we should be travelling at night, especially through Surrey."

He nods, turns south on a side street as fences start to separate the homes instead of fields. Heads down a half-industrial road on the edge of town, warehouses spaced far apart. Two lane roads with large shoulders, granite rock and dust kicked up covering the traffic lines. Worn chain link fences with padlocks. Stain oil patches and long commercial buildings with no signage.

In the distance the mountains remain poetically picturesque, uncorrupted. As if untouched by this unfettered madness. Too monumental and grandiose to end up in the middle of squalor. Mute reminders of the physical geology that will stand through this era regardless of our eventual outcome.

A hotel. Accent Inn. Tight and compact, four stories. No cars in the parking lot, covered drive-through right by reception. Out back a clump of oak trees, and off to the left and right vacant warehouses. It's quaint, given the circumstances.

We drive into the parking lot, continue around back.

"Why are we going around back?"

"This truck draws attention."

Tucks us into the alley beside the hotel, partially covered by a few large dumpsters and a high brown fence. The rest of the peripheral vision blocked by the oaks.

Engine cuts off. Our friend silence slides between us. Thickset air inside the cab. He leans forward, rummages through the hockey bag. Finds the money, wrapped in a plastic bag. Twenties in messy stacks. Andrew Jackson and his windswept Hamptons hair, the original pompous ass. The irony of his disaffection for paper money and the National Bank. I remember the story on Reddit. I only made it through the first paragraph. Couldn't bring my brain to read anything substantial lately, preconditioned like a frenetic monkey chained to an iPad; taurine jacked on crushed pharmaceuticals and too much internet porn.

Everyman idiot of our generation. Educated in headlines.

Brain chock full of tiny tidbits of useless information.

Gum stays in your stomach no more than two days. Jonathan Taylor Thomas went to Harvard after *Home Improvement*. Salt Lake Stadium in India holds over 120,000 people. Bill Gates' house has a stream running through it in which salmon spawn. Marilyn Monroe had six toes on one foot. The youngest Pope was eleven years old.

My Brain©: Powered by Wikipedia.

A hand smacks the window beside me.

*Yelp!*

My dad, up on the step, opens the door.

"Tristan, get the fuck out of the truck."

I jump down, shut the door behind me.

He's stuffed some of the money in his army jacket.

Makes sure to lock the doors, a wise move considering the heavy artillery we're packing.

We walk around the side of the hotel. Feels weird to be out of a moving vehicle. My back and ass deep-tissue sore; headache still choking the arterial veins around my hairline. Dried blood-stain on my perma-pressed white shirt and the muggy post-precipitation air caressing my shaved head with particles of fresh oxygen.

We come around the front of the hotel. Sliding doors closed, my dad leads, but they don't open. He walks right into them— bird smacking into a window.

I can't help but laugh.

"You sell your soul to Milhouse or something?"

He turns back, face squinting, holding his nose.

"So help me God, Tristan, I will fucking kill you."

I know he doesn't get the reference, but it's funny to me.

Someone comes out from the side counter, slowly. Holding a gun. East Indian.

"We're not open," he says in busted English. Turban and dress shirt colour-coordinated.

My dad takes the cash out of his jacket pocket and slams it against the window. Medieval PayPal. We flash currency like a credit-riddled middle grade rapper.

The guy steps a few paces closer, gun still down by his side. I can read his name-tag. Mandeep.

"How much?" says Mandeep.

"One thousand dollars. We need a place to sleep for the night."

I turn around, evaluate the firmament. It's sundown, minus our dwarf star's glowing rays slashing beneath the viewable sphere. Overcast celestial orb blankets the entire sub-stratosphere. Imminence bearing down on us like hard truths, grinding away at the surface, millimetre by millimetre.

I turn back. Mandeep walks up close. I can see him checking me out, noticing the blood on my shirt.

"I don't want no funny business, okay?" he says.

"Scout's honor," I respond, holding my hand to my heart.

Walks back to the front desk and pushes the button. Door opens.

We walk inside.

"You have power?" asks my dad.

"Generator downstairs in the laundry room. Industrial area. These warehouses throw power all the time."

His English is heavily accented but you can tell he's been speaking it for decades. Hard and crusted into his poor tense selection and singular/plural confusion.

Lights come on.

"What time is it?"

Mandeep looks at his watch.

"About five o'clock."

Back out the door, dimmer switch emitting with increasing intensity.

Achromatic light, no splotched sunspots to gauge the time of day. Just a clarion, shrill sweep of ebonized azure cascading over the vision above our heads.

Like something out of a Radiohead song.

Never have I seen skies like this in my entire life.

My dad puts the thousand down on the counter; promptly snapped up.

"I'll take you to your room," he says, eyeing us like frat-boys ready to rock star his establishment. Quite possible given the amount of firearms, liquor, and stress we're packing.

As we walk I make small talk, but the other two aren't buying.

"So, you know anything about what's going on?"

"No, I got a call from night manager who said the power went out around Friday night. I come down, whole block is down. Everyone kind of checked out except for few guests."

Societal annihilation applied in more realistic circumstances for Mandeep. Business as unusual. Whatever's directly irrelevant is not worth a thought. Dunno where the guy is from originally, but chances are he's seen shit go sideways. He knows the game, has a clear strategy. Stay put, centralize your priorities. Wait it out, trust no one. Much better call than running four-way stops in a BMW or blitzing the border like a defensive end on third and long.

Holding pattern. Decrease movements. Limit interaction. Lockdown. Lockup. Alert.

Hand forever on the trigger.

Stand still and maybe the apocalypse will walk right by you like a massive Tyrannosaurus Rex that preys on movement.

Four flights of stairs to 431.

"Why are you putting us on the fourth floor?"

Mandeep looks at me like this is not a question I should be asking.

"First three floors having hot water issues. Okay? Elevator shut down because it uses too much power." Hands my dad the key.

"Sounds good enough for me."

"You wanna stay another night it will be one thousand again."

Our faces crinkle in disgust.

"Can we get a wake-up call? When does the continental breakfast start?" I ask.

"Is he serious?"

My dad looks at me. I don't give a fuck.

"How late is the pool open?"

"Pool is closed," snaps Mandeep.

"Mini-bar?"

"Tristan, shut up."

I walk past Mandeep, eyeing him up theatrically.

Fuck. This. Shit. We got robbed. For a thousand bucks the bed sheets should be jerking me off while Elton John plays "Tiny Dancer" on a pink piano in the corner.

I guess the idea is *not* to negotiate. The cash bought us no questions, something that's obviously imperative to my father.

Two beds crammed into a room. Not much else but horribly outdated wallpaper patterns.

Head for the TV.

Nothing.

No signal detected.

I drop the remote on the bed in a sign of concession.

My dad walks out to the balcony. Peanut shaped pool in the courtyard. Folds of newspaper float on the surface. I look across, someone peering out of their hotel room, staring us down. As soon as they see we see them, the door closes.

I sit on the bed. He comes back in.

"I'm gonna go get the bag from the truck. Stay here."

Empyrean heavens gone. Gloomy obscurity has set in, tint pigmentation over the geographical compass. Illiterate colour scheme. Drab, bleak. Inky charcoal.

Tiny clover blots dangle across the left side of my vision. I dart my eyes over, but it's gone. Look around, confused by the optical illusion trickery. Lean against the railing, assessing the other rooms. Dead quiet, no rustling, no room service, no week-end getaways, no normal ambience to sooth the psyche. The pool sits there, lawn chairs on their sides. Off to the corner there's a pile of clothes littered across the courtyard lawn, like someone threw them from the deck in a huff.

Barren noise. Reticent static. Soundtrack for the deaf.

Alone with my thoughts for the first time in ages. No cell, no internet, no TV. I'm not used to spending this much time with my thoughts. We'd drifted apart over the years, started seeing other people, didn't keep in touch. Can't check my newsfeed on Facebook, can't randomly surf the net for funny ad-lib Vines. Can't download music to my extensive iTunes library. Can't browse the comments on Gawker. Or the postings on Failbook.

Alone with this stranger—my conscience.

He comes back with the hockey bag, opens it up, pulls out food. Inside the guns and ammunition and a couple bottles of vodka. Looks like we lost our medical supplies somewhere in the day. I shuffle over to the bed and start to snack. My dad heads to the bathroom, closes the door.

"Are you shitting?"

No answer. After a while I hear the shower running. I sit back on the bed, turn on the TV again, hoping to catch something. Nothing.

Turn the nightstand radio on. Squirrelly, whistling feedback.

Open the desk drawer. Phone book and Bible.

I figure why not. Crack it open to a random page.

Revelation 7:1-17.

'After this I saw four angels standing at the four corners of the earth, holding back the four winds of the earth, that no wind might blow on earth or sea or against any tree. Then I saw another angel ascending from the rising of the sun, with the seal of the living God, and he called with a loud voice to the four angels who . . .'

Boring.

This has got to have something to do with the sun. Our one and only leader. Giver of light. Now taker of life? It was always going to be science. Something right in front of us; the elephant in the corner of the room.

The uncertainty of this idea allows it to drift into the warm summer evening—a firefly lifting into the muggy sky until it's swallowed by the night's black hole.

Silence on the bed beside me. The noise of a shower. I'd kill for some music, a TV show. I'd even watch fucking commercials.

Child of nominal distraction, give me something to keep me 33.33333 percent occupied.

Pace the room, inspecting the cheap wallpaper. Plastic coffee maker, cone shaped faded beige light, corner chair, small table. An Ethernet plug.

I pull the vodka out and rummage through my dad's jacket for his smokes.

*Success.*

If I can't engage my mind, I'll numb it.

Nicotine, ethanol, intoxicating the personality. Trying to think like a reasonable person did before 1998. My ex-girlfriend. My fucked-up family. My Microsoft Outlook-calendar complacent non-unionized position. Transient lifestyle, drug-fuelled trips in humid Third World countries that rely on Waspy tourism to stay afloat. Over thirty now and my whole life has been one compartmentalized experience after another. I am an application, produced by my surroundings, a product of simulated, counterfeit culture and fortified environments. I can be downloaded and deleted within a matter of minutes.

Forgotten before conception.

My dad comes out clothed.

"You should shower. Not sure when we might get another one."

Into the steamy bathroom. Mirror fogged over. I wipe my hand down the middle and my face appears. Bloodstained dress shirt, the cut on my face producing a dark red mark accenting my bottom lip. I look tired, worn.

I am tired, worn.

I shower efficiently—water runs down my shaved head, a new sensation momentarily distracting me from reality.

I'd masturbate but I'm helplessly lost without YouPorn.

I need a release. Something to help me reconfigure. I'm dragging old world mentalities into a new one. My millennial tendencies, my predictable habits of procrastination as I run the clock out on my life, they're not going to cut it anymore. I can't resort to mind numbing.

I try to breathe in. I try to breathe in air.

Get out and put my clothes back on, head into the room, see my dad checking the magazines in the guns. All the food packed onto the table. He's turned some of the lights on as it's now completely dark outside.

"Dark before five, eh?"

"Yeah."

"What do you think that means?"

"I dunno."

Half-ass nod. I'm too tired to administer CPR on our conversations. I sit on the bed, then lie down. I can hear my dad eating crackers, munching away.

Awareness starts to slip. Wavers, wanders, fades like a falling boxer, ready for the canvas. Memories become unstuck, feelings gist like exhaust in a windowless room.

Carbon dioxide singing me to sleep, dancing me in and out of consciousness in a slow waltz. Hard alcohol lullaby outweighing the nicotine, tiredness usurping the stress.

Do you want to . . .

Restart. Log Off. Shut Down. Cancel. Sleep.

Sleep it is.

*Singapore. Changi International Airport. Sits on the edge of Southeast Asia like a diving board. You either jump, or turn around and never look back. There is no middle ground. It's my favourite airport. Better than the sterile, stinky carbon monoxide infused white tiles of Beijing or the ugly brown carpeting and culture shock of Delhi. Singapore is the pristine pinnacle of overseas travel. Private stalls where you can shit, shower, and shave in solitude for eight Euros. Watch a free movie—* Wedding Crashers. *The breast scenes cut and swear words dubbed. You get lost in Changi—everyone transferring, on their way somewhere else. Somewhere between here and there. Purgatory of the aviation industry. Every passenger a stranger, even yourself.*

*Connecting flight. Yes. Checking luggage, no. Carry on, yes. Please just let me carry on.*

*Between the Gucci handbag store and the Lacoste shoppe lies a line of chairs, rows of laid back seating, not long enough to lie down, but long enough to lounge. Somewhere between Gate 45 and the end of the road. Purple seats, just plush enough to let your back rest from the cramped seating of SEAir. There I was—me and a half-eaten, half-toasted six-inch Subway BMT with bacon that tasted like dried pork.*

*It had been close to six years. Straight from high school into the pit of the Third World. India, Taiwan, Vietnam, Cambodia, Japan, South Korea, Fiji, now Malaysia. The question wasn't where I'd been, but where I hadn't. So many cultural milieus I'd forgotten how to say hello. Forgotten I had roots to begin with. Washed clean of identity, I existed as a flight number, a seat—38A. A hostel door, room key, an empty seat in a crowded café. I was as fluent as a universal sign of greeting. Everyman of the globe. Incandescent traveler.*

*Scathing blonde hair, tanned skin, skeletal frame. About fifteen pounds underweight, I'd been surviving on suntan lotion and saltwater. Faded t-shirt and dark cargo shorts where I could hide my wallet and passports in too many pockets for street thieves to count. Worn, imprinted sandals. No jewelry. I was never a sentimental guy, not one for keepsakes and trinkets. I had the memories; they faded, but the impression, the essence, never died. The smell of the wind coming off the Indian Coast. Sounds of countless bodies scuttling by a crosswalk in Tokyo. The taste of Kava in Fiji around the fire at night. The lights of Shanghai, glimmering and shimmering like topless dancers underneath black light.*

*What had I gained? Knowledge. Americans will talk about themselves and only themselves. Bangkok will fuck any man who dare take her on. Japanese women will cry after sex.*

*Somewhere I'd lost my soul, wiped clean for a new start, destitute of reality.*

*It was the most beautiful thing.*

*I'd lost my way, turned around, and everything was foreign. Nothing made sense, and I'd never been happier in my life. The beaches laid out for me, the drinks came when I wanted, and the birds chirped quietly when I needed to sleep. The world had taken me in and churned me around until I knew nothing and accepted everything. Lost in the fray and couldn't be more content.*

*No longer earmarked by tragedy, I'd accomplished what I'd set out to do when I came running here in the first place.*

*Six-hour layover. Enough time to get accustomed to the clean floors and sterile settings. Before Singapore would shit me out like all the others, back across the Pacific in a cattle call of itineraries. I didn't fear home, I just didn't feel it. But the money had run out and my time was done. I'd begged, borrowed and stolen my way to the ends of the earth, hoping to get lost in a bus terminal somewhere between the swim-up bars of Jakarta and the snorkelling routes off Suva, where the clown fish looked at you like they'd never seen a human before.*

*Six hours until twelve hours until San Francisco. Two hours to Seattle. Too many time zones to prepare for—only Xanax and Heineken. Then where?*

*A chance to take my degree at the University of Washington. A full-ride in the Bachelor of Arts program. The Jessica Schultz Memorial Scholarship. The university set it up in her name, as her alma mater. I knew if I applied for it, I would get it. They could not say no to the son; I could tug enough heartstrings to get into the academic world and start the next chapter of my life.*

*A father, drifting through the last years of his career. A sister deep in the throes of undergrad. Who were these people?*

*I hadn't seen my best friend from high school in over half a decade. He was married now. I missed his wedding. Missed the birth of his son. Missed it all.*

*It wasn't time to go home, but it wasn't time to stay anymore, either. The globe would swallow me whole like* Moby Dick. *Chew me up and spit me out along the Trans-Siberian railway where some Russian dissenter knifed me for my passport and wallet. I had to go home before I forgot how to get there. My time had come and I knew when to cash in my chips. Tap out.*

*So: home.*

*Okay.*

*Now . . . where do I begin?*

</>

Drifting solo in a flat-bottom boat. Splinters fray like electrically charged particles; rickety frame, oars off to the sides. Tide breeze a cavernously deep purple. Sprung through with milky reds, hard orange smears of luminous colouring. Rainbow tipped to one end. Firestorm ember dye, clouds singed ash hue of blue. Dexterous ability gone. Vision a mirror; left-handed when I'm right. When I go up, it's down. East is west, inside is out. Trying to pick up the oars but I can't control my hands. Everything is upside down and backwards at the same time. At intermittent times in the thought pattern the sea is the sky and the sky is the sea.

As one of the world's leading pharmaceutical companies, Pfizer's mission is to develop and discover innovative medicines and other products to improve the quality of life for people around the world. Our diversified health care portfolio includes biologic and small molecule vaccines and medicines for humans and many of the world's best-known consumer products.

Every day, Pfizer employees work to advance wellness, prevention, treatments and cures that challenge the most feared diseases of our time. We apply science and our global resources to improve the health and well-being of Americans at every stage of life. Our commitment is reflected in everything Pfizer does, from our disease awareness initiatives to our community partnerships, to our belief that it takes more than medication to be truly healthy. To learn more about Pfizer's goals, please log off and commit multiple sins against your body and mind.

Installed backwards.

Free mind born in captivity.

Life rafts on deserted oceans.

Water when all I need is oxygen.

The horizon, once again my foe. Seas a stygian gel of blue. Floating on acrylic paint.

Boat starts to tip, to creak and sway as the waves come up. Whitecaps of fermenting paste. Noxious smells as they rise. Bracing the sides, but I'm so disoriented I spill into the water in a slow-motion mess.

Lungs flood with a calcifying liquid. I fill up entirely, unable to breath. Gasp. Nothing.

Try to open my lungs.

Panic.

Nothing.

Eyes dart open.

Ingest a huge gulp of air.

Heart almost tipped its own scale, but it returns, righting its rhythm through an unhealthy murmur. Look over at my dad, his mouth stuffed full of jerky as he sits on the side of the hotel bed.

He looks as confused as I do. Speaks with food in his mouth. "You okay?"

"Yeah," I say, rubbing my face with my palms. "Bad dream."

I sit up in bed, vodka and cigarettes on the table. I take a pull, light up a cigarette. Drown the memories.

Throws over a can of beans and peaches. Catch them with my lap, one hand on the bottle and another smoking a cigarette. Throws over a spoon. Then he gets up, leans over and starts to cut both cans open with a hunting knife. Doesn't make eye contact. I sit there—little boy being served dinner.

Leaves them on the nightstand. I trade the addictions for the beans. Shovel it into my mouth.

His stance has changed. Looking out the sliding door to our balcony.

"What the . . ."

Walks over. I dump the beans and follow.

Skylight dances as performing arts, floating in unrehearsed rhythms.

Aurora borealis. Emerald swoosh so apparent it's reflecting off the sides of the hotel. We stare at the sight. Neon green flotsam and jetsam on top of black. I'd seen the northern lights before, but this was surreal. Smooth, semitransparent snake wiggling across the night's theatre in no particular direction. Grand symphony of illuminating colour, forever bouncing between red and violet.

Across the courtyard someone's looking up, hands on the railings. I nudge my dad, motion with my chin. He looks. Stares a while. Guy puts his hand up in a non-threatening manner.

"Hey!" he yells across the courtyard.

I raise my hand, white flag of acknowledgement.

Chlorinated pool water a mirror image for the scintillant show above our heads. Grass-tint of light; fluorescent shadows. Most of the hotel dark, nothing to distract from this sensory experience. Quiet orgasm of phosphorescent radiance.

My dad turns and heads into the room. Comes back with a bag of chips, the vodka and the smokes. Sits down on one of the cheap plastic chairs on the deck and settles in.

I pull up another chair somewhat close to him. He passes a smoke, the vodka. Takes his wallet out, puts it on the table. It falls open, revealing two pictures.

My university graduation photo.

One of my sister, receiving her pre-med scholarship in Victoria. Brad with his arm tight around her shoulder.

He notices me noticing the photos. Reaches over, closes the wallet. Doesn't make eye contact.

Fuck.

We need to find Liz.

*If it's the last thing either of us does.*

</>

Darkness has set in.

*Keep the blinds drawn.*

She's scared to light candles, doesn't want to draw attention to her presence in the midst of this unexpected anarchy. The nightmarish noises outside have paralyzed her with fear.

Aurora borealis brought out something in the student body tonight. A signal, a sign from the heavens that this disconnect and subsequent chaos was real, that it is in fact what we all thought it was: the end.

Out the back bathroom window, she can see the fires. Thick black smoke puffs into the air. From the campus parking lot behind the stadium she hears explosions. Smells gasoline, imagines cars scorched and burning in the night.

Tribal screams, the cutting sounds of chaos. They close in. She can make out voices. People laugh and yell. Windows smash.

Chanting. Can't pick out the words.

Pokes her fingers through the shades. Squints to see.

They walk in groups, holding torches.

A few turn onto her block.

Pulls her hands away. Clutches her iPhone, turns it on. Holds her stomach as she adjusts herself in the bed, feet on the floor. She's worried for her baby's safety and it hasn't even left the womb yet.

Dials 9-1-1.

Nothing.

Starts to cry.

The voices close in. Hears them knocking on doors. Smashing anything they can.

"The end is near! The end is here!" they yell.

"It's about fucking time!"

A bottle smashes off the side of her condo.

She gasps, covers her mouth.

It's too much.

Closes the eyes, drifts away.

A child again, with her mother. Holds her hand as they walk through a field in the summer heat. Her mother's blonde hair drifts and dips in a gentle breeze. She looks down at her daughter, smiles at her.

Sunbeams everywhere. Birds chirp. Soft wind whisks through the blades of grass.

"It's okay, Elizabeth. Everything is going to be okay. Your father and Tristan are coming. Trust me."

She smiles. They walk. Pillowy clouds form incoherent shapes as they glide overhead.

"You need to be brave for me, okay?"

Nods.

Holds her mother tight.

Opens her eyes.

The voices are quieter.

Fading away into the black.

Exhales.

She finally exhales.

</>

Cheap vodka, hotel ice and warm Vitamin Water.

Went back in and made us some legitimate drinks.

Sloshing in style.

Still on the deck watching the show in the sky. Directed by the heavens.

"So what do you think this all is?" I ask, conversational tone so as not to incite stress while we de-stress.

Mulls the question. Looks up as if the dancing colours will explain it all like some final monologue.

"Tough to say. Obviously the sun has something to do with it."

I sip from my drink, ice cubes clink around the glass.

"Yeah, the military guy at the border said something about a solar flare."

"That would explain the lack of communications," he says. "No radio, no cell. If something took everything out of the sky, this is probably what it would look like."

"You think it's all over the world?"

"I dunno. We can't think about that right now. To survive this—it's about absolutes. Your sister and her baby are the only absolutes. After that, yeah, maybe we sit back and assess, draw up a game plan, see if it looks like this'll be a long-term thing. Look, Tristan, what we've done . . . we'll atone for it later."

"Atone?"

He takes a deep breath. He's going to get something off his chest. I can feel it.

"The things you've seen me do today. The things we've done. Tristan, they're not without purpose. I'm not without remorse."

He's opening his emotional shell, hard outer surface revealing exposed guts. When was the last time this happened?

Takes a sip from his drink, looks ready to continue his train of thought.

I wait patiently.

"What we did to that father and his son. Stealing their car. Leaving them there. And those soldiers at the border . . ."

He trails off, stares into the night sky.

"We'll answer for those sins later. If that is our fate, so be it. But I can't leave your sister alone in this, in whatever this is. We will get to her at all costs. I won't lose another . . ."

Hard as fuck feelings stop the world's rotation. Time itself ceases as his sentence trails off, slowly starts back up again.

"I won't let fate decide this time."

The ghost of my mother. His wife, his lover, his partner. She sits beside us.

This man, with the end of the world staring him down like a massive monster, doesn't blink.

"Yeah," I say.

I decide to leave it at that, divert the conversation.

"You talk to Liz a lot lately? When did you hear about this mess with the kid and Brad?"

Takes a drag off his cigarette before answering.

"She emailed me last week. Told me the whole story. Said Brad wouldn't stop calling her. I had to help her get a restraining order. Wanted me to go down to Washington and talk to him. Come see you, too, tell you about the baby."

"So what happened with Brad on Saturday?"

"That kid isn't right in the head. He wants to marry Liz. Thinks a baby will sort everything out. He needs psychiatric help. He eluded that he might have actually hit Liz. I lost it, I knocked him out cold at the coffee shop we were at."

"Why did you even get him a job as a cop in Canada then?"

"That was before I knew him really. Liz pleaded with me. It was before I found out he watched half his battalion get smoked in Afghanistan."

"What the fuck happened?"

"I had a buddy who's high up in the CF pull the AAR. Apparently he got pinned into an apartment complex with a few members of his squad in Kabul. They got separated from the patrol by an IED in a parked car. From what it read, the firefight went on for over ten hours, and Brad was the only one who walked away. Two slugs in his vest, fractured ribs, exit wound from a bullet in his leg. Army doc declared him mentally unfit for battle on the spot. Honourably discharged."

"Jesus fuck . . . so how did he get on with the Washington State police?"

"His dad was American. I guess they're hurting for applicants in the force or something. His military background makes him an ideal candidate."

"Wouldn't they know about his PTSD and all that shit?"

"Not if he kept it from them. Don't get me wrong, he's not entirely stupid. I mean, I think I can see what Liz saw in him."

"Was she not on the pill?"

"I don't know?"

"I don't know? You mean you didn't ask her?"

"Yeah, I assume she wasn't."

"Fuck."

I lean back, put my feet up on the balcony railing. Puff my cigarette.

He's trying, we're trying, to bring this back to life. Bring us back to life. If anything, through all this shit, it's impossible not to feel a renewed bond with him.

We were father and son. We *are* father and son. It's never too late to forgive or forget. To repair.

Family. I'd been avoiding it most of my life. Now it's the only thing left worth fighting for.

He kickstarts the conversation again.

"Were you enjoying Seattle?"

"Yeah," I shrug. "I mean, does it really matter anymore?"

"No . . . I guess not."

Philosophical meanderings about the past tense are obsolete, my current thoughts more exciting. A brave new world. I was timesheet coding, a department number, a budgetary concern.

Now I'm an uncle. A son. A brother.

He drags from his cigarette and fills his tummy with hard liquor. Speaks again.

"Were you happy?"

I'm taken aback by the question. He's getting sauced. Alcohol loosening his vocal chords along with his tough exterior. Peeling back layers of apprehension.

"Happy? What do you mean?"

"Were you happy? With your job, your life? This girlfriend you had?"

I mull, trying to signify that I'm taking the question seriously.

"About as happy as anyone in my position."

He nods.

A telling nod.

"What about you? Were you happy traveling?"

Serve returned, a disarming question met by an equally per-plexed look. Probably never been asked that in his life. Turns it over in his oven of thought, rotating it slowly—plotting a response.

"Yeah," he says. "As the next guy I suppose."

Understanding shoves silence off the chair between us.

"How come you don't box as much anymore? That Rodney guy says you only go once in a while."

Sports a good segue, our only common denominator through the long hard years.

"Yeah, I mean I still spar a bit. It's too much with the job. I can't come to work all busted to shit from three rounds with a MMA shithead wannabe."

He smiles.

Moving body across the courtyard, walking slowly. Out in the open to appear neutral, I'm suspecting. My dad has his Glock underneath the chair. Leans over, arm outstretched in case he needs to engage it.

The body stops below us, by the pool. A guy, mid-thirties, nominal at best. One of a million. Everyman left stranded by the unthinkable.

"Hi," he says, lifting his hand with an open palm.

I lift my hand in response.

"Hey, are you guys drinking?"

I look at my dad like I'm asking him if it's okay to verbally engage this guy.

"Yeah," says my dad.

"Huh. Well, my name is Ira."

Holds his hand up again.

Neither of us responds.

My dad looks at me, then back down into the courtyard.

"Ira, what is your business with us?"

"Yeah, hey sorry, I understand. I'm by myself, I'm from Seattle, got stuck up here in Canada. Flight was grounded Friday. I was just wondering if you guys had a drink. I could really use a drink and a smoke. I mean, I mean you guys no harm."

Appears as dangerous as a kitten on morphine.

"Are you carrying a weapon?" asks my dad.

Throws his hands up. "No, shoot no. I mean, I don't even know how to fire a gun."

My dad looks at me. "What do you think?"

I look down at the guy.

"You're from Seattle? Where?"

"Clyde Hill."

I nod.

"What do you do there?"

"Well, I was a writer."

"Oh yeah, I know tons of writers in Seattle, part of my job. What's your last name?"

"Robbins."

"Robbins," I say in my dad's direction. "Why does that name ring a bell?"

I hear Ira chuckle.

"I uh, that might be a good story over a few drinks."

I look at my dad. He shrugs.

"Okay," I tell him. "431."

"What do you think?" I ask as Ira moves out of sight.

More shrugs than you can shake a stick at.

"Probably not a good idea to trust anyone, but that doesn't mean we can't have a drink or two with him."

He turns, stands up, has to right himself. Alcohol tipping his weight scale.

Walks back into the room and shoves the hockey bag to the side of the bed against the bathroom wall. Walks over, opens the door, swings the latch around; comes back and sits down. I lift a plastic chair over myself and hand it to him.

We sit in silent anticipation. He picks up the gun and puts it on the table beside us. In a mad dash one of us would get it before this Ira guy, the way the chairs are placed.

Door opens.

"Hey," Ira says.

We look back. He's walking slowly, cautiously, looking over our room. Comes out to the balcony.

Late thirties Seattle Gen-Xer. Trimmed spotty beard, loafers, short sleeve t-shirt, dark rimmed glasses. I can tell instantly if shit went down, this guy would just shit his pants.

"Hi, I'm Ira," he says, reaching over to shake our hands. I notice he notices the gun, and he notices I noticed him noticing the gun.

Flashes a stunted glance only a pacifist who's never encountered an ounce of violence in his life could flash. Looks up at the sky as the green snakes dance.

"Pretty crazy, hey?"

Ira sits down in his chair.

My dad hands him the vodka.

"Oh man, thanks so much."

He takes a swig. My dad hands him the pack of smokes and his Zippo.

"Oh man, I'm in heaven. Been a tough day."

Lights up a smoke, takes another pull from the vodka.

"Have you been here since last night?" asks my dad.

"No. I was in Vancouver this morning. Until the riots started. Got the heck out of there pretty quickly."

"The riots?"

"Yeah mid-afternoon is kind of when they came to fruition. Mostly downtown on Granville. East Hastings. Freakin' madness. Cops all over the place. Fires."

"What were you doing in Van?" I ask.

"Well," he says, chuckling, "I write for the *Seattle Times*, and they sent me up there to cover a story."

"On what?"

"Funny story," he says, chuckling again. Guy is a chuckler. "I was sent up there to cover this lady; she'd been diagnosed with this condition. She was addicted to standing in line-ups."

We glance at each other with curled brows.

"I know. Weird, hey?"

"Like a line-up at the post office or something?"

"Yeah. She would go to the bank just so she could stand in the line-up."

I'm laughing. It's too funny. Of all the shit to get addicted to. Crack, sex, huffing gas, Facebook, this lady's hooked on the mundane. I try to draw some type of analytical, sociological conclusion that expresses how this mirrors modern culture.

Instead I let out a monstrous burp.

Like someone stepped on a constipated frog full of Pepsi.

BEEEEEEEEELCH!

Both of them smile. My dad even laughs.

"Anyways, line-ups," I say, wiping spit from my lips.

"Yeah, apparently she enjoyed the comfort of being close to people, being able to make small talk and mingle in a socially appropriate setting. Stemmed from her childhood, her parents weren't big talkers, so she gravitated towards social settings where she could make small talk without the fear of abandonment."

"So what's wrong with that? Seems fine," I say.

My dad half-disinterested, but alert. Dog watching another dog on a leash.

"Well apparently it was starting to dominate her life; she would miss work to go stand in line-ups. Spend hours looking for line-up hot spots."

I try to think of line-up hot spots.

"Man, I bet she loved the airport."

Ira chuckles.

"Yeah, and the DMV," he says, still chuckling.

I smile. We sit in stillness. I know my dad isn't going to kick this dead horse, so I start up again.

"So, you hear anything about what's going on?"

Ira wipes his hand across his face like he's cleaning the mental filth from the day.

"I probably don't know more than you guys. Friday all the flights got grounded, then the power went out at the airport. I got into a hotel downtown. Saturday and Sunday I kind of waited, hoping the flights would start back up again, but they never did. Monday rolls around and nobody knows anything at the hotel, and the hot water wasn't working. So I rented a car with cash this morning when people starting looting stores and this is as far as I got."

"The power thing, with it being on some places, and not in others, we've seen that too," I add.

"Yeah must be something to do with telecommunications. I mean it's pretty obvious there're no satellites in the sky anymore. No radio, shortwave. I mean, the cops, the ambulances, they were just driving around looking for crime or patients. They have no dispatch, they told me."

I nod.

"Yeah, the GPS didn't work in my car."

"The white sky, though. I haven't a clue about that."

My dad chimes in, finally.

"The sky's normally blue because molecules in the air scatter blue light from the sun more than they scatter red light. So maybe now all light is being scattered. Or none at all."

Ira and I nod at the scientific explanation. It's the best intel I've heard yet.

"Why do I feel sick half the time?" I ask.

"Well, if this is solar, it would be the electromagnetic pulses making us sick."

"So you guys feel it too, the sickness, like a bad stomach flu combined with a hangover?"

Ira and my dad look at each other, and kind of nod in unison.

"Okay then."

All three of us pull from our drinks.

"Ira Robbins," I cut in after a few seconds of silence. "Why's that name familiar?"

Looks nervous, scratches his short beard.

"Well . . ." he says, then trails off. Takes another swig of vodka.

"You ever hear of a band called Nirvana?"

"Yeah, maybe," I say, playing into his lukewarm sarcastic bomb. I bet my dad has no clue who Nirvana is.

"Yes, so I wrote the *Rolling Stone* review for *Nevermind*. Back in 1991."

Light goes on in my head.

"You're the guy that only gave it three stars!"

He smiles, no chuckle.

"Fuck, man, shitty. Sorry. Who knew it was going to be so big?"

"They've changed it online to four stars. But it's still there in the print edition."

"Yeah, I read that article they did on you—talking about all the backlash in the past while, as the album grew and shit. After Cobain's suicide."

Ira just nods. I throw him a bone.

"Whatever, man, nobody fucking cares now. The internet doesn't even exist anymore."

He seems to lighten up a bit. I continue.

"Man, if anything we've all been given a clean slate. Chance to right some wrongs, chose a different path."

My dad's paying close attention to that sentence for some reason. Ira nods in agreement.

"So what have you guys heard? Where in Vancouver were you today?"

He has no idea we crossed the border.

"Yeah, we were in Seattle this morning."

"Seattle? How the hell did you get across the border?"

I look at my dad like maybe he should take the mic for this one.

"Yeah, we crossed at Aldergrove," he says. And that's all he gives.

Ira looks puzzled, like there should've been an addendum.

Looks back towards the courtyard, then back at us.

"I see. I take it that's your military truck in the back parking lot, the alley. You guys military?"

I look at my dad, but then I interject, "We're just borrowing it. You know."

Ira smiles. "Borrowing it, I see. So I take it crossing the border isn't that easy right now?"

"Yeah, when we were there they weren't letting anyone cross."

Ira nods in recognition, filing this important information away on his desktop for future reference.

Rumble off in the distance.

Foundation of the hotel vibrates.

We all look around, not sure of the noise's orientation.

Sounded like a blast, muffled by a few miles of distance.

"What was that?" I say, standing, looking out over the courtyard to the horizon.

Nobody else stands up. I look over at Ira. He looks shaken.

I sit back down, light up another smoke.

"What a day," says Ira.

Looks like he's about to cry.

Big ol' man tears.

Nothing more embarrassing.

"You okay, man?" I say.

Scratches his head, adjusts in his seat, fiddling with the uncomfortable notion of offering personal information to people he just met.

"Yeah . . ."

Ira shakes his head like he's ready to jump off some fiscal cliff or throw his savings into some African country's GPD.

"I found out my wife is filing for divorce, like on Friday morning, but that's the last I heard from her."

My dad's staring into his drink, a half cut, half somber, dozy-looking bear in his seat.

"We've had a tough go the past few years. We're newspaper reporters. She was at the *Post-Intelligencer* when it went online in 2009. So was I. We lost our jobs. I mean, neither of us were super tech-savvy so we kind of got lost in the shuffle. I do freelance jobs for the *Times*; she's running a daycare out of our place, but it's been tough."

My dad and I flash each other looks of puzzlement. Should we be serving wine and Haagen-Dazs?

Ira continues his sob story.

"And our mortgage shot up like a year after that. We had to sell and move into her parent's basement, with two kids. Then thank God her parents moved into a home and gave us the house."

Incredibly typical of the last decade. Economic downturn, housing crisis, aging parents, blah blah blah. US of A sob story. He should be a bullet point on Wikipedia under Americana.

I consider telling him about Brianne, trying to identify with him. But part of me feels like I might be Ira in another life. The life in which I did get married, have kids, buy a house. Would this be me in a decade? Sucked into decisions I didn't want to make, tied to a wife who resented me because I married her and got her pregnant because that was the thing we were supposed to do at that time in our lives?

"Anyway," he says, standing. "Thanks for the drinks and the smokes. Can I take some for the road?"

I'm surprised he's calling it a night so quickly. We expected him to wear out his welcome, not smoke, drink, and run.

Neither of us stand to see him out. We just supply him with sufficient vodka and cigarettes to lull him into a stupor.

"Nice to meet you guys," he says in the most pathetically mundane voice I'll ever hear.

I look at my dad; he looks at me and then resumes staring at the sky. I face the courtyard. My dad gets up.

"I'm going to sleep," he says. "You should, too. We have a long day ahead of us."

I watch him weave his way towards the bed, struggling a bit with his footing.

"You know, it's not even seven," I say.

Doesn't answer. Grabs some ice from the bucket and puts it in a plastic bag. Ties it up. He lies down, pushing one shoe off with the other foot. Face up, as if in a coffin. Places the bag on his shoulder. Separated in the car crash just past the border.

I sit, pondering my next move. Decide to make my way to my bed, the two of us lying there, parallel to each other in our puke green and beige flower pattern tombs. Staring at a white hotel room roof that cloaks a blank white sky, well into day three of disconnect.

Mentally tired. Unfocused. Exhausted. Sore. Bloodied. Cramped. Headache. Drunk. Nicotine shakes. Uncertain future.

The stress of it all strangles me.

Asphyxiating under the weight and gravity of the situation.

Choking on this realization.

Gasping for answers.

Clogged with questions.

Crashing.

Power: Off.

</>

Sense the light on the inside of my eyelids.

Open my eyes.

Teenage East Indian kid with gelled hair pointing a gun at my nose, looking like the biggest gangster his scrawny frame will allow.

I look over.

Hotel owner sticking a gun in my dad's face. He's standing, hands up, beside the bed.

*Fuck.*

"Stand up!" shouts Mandeep.

I'm not having any of this. I think the thought over again.

I. Am. Not. Having. Any. Of. This. Shit.

I stand. The gun pointed at my nose follows.

"This is fucking gay," I say.

Mandeep looks at me.

"Shut the fuck up. Where is rest of your money?"

Looks at my dad.

"I fucking knew it," I say, pointing my finger straight out. "I fucking knew you were going to rob us or some shit like that. Fucking thousand dollars for a night and you're fucking robbing us on top of that!"

"Shut the fuck up!" he barks, pointing the gun at me.

As soon as he does, my dad lunges without a molecule of hesitation.

Violence. Commenced.

In one well-trained motion the barrel of the shotgun pulls Mandeep's face into striking range. My father's open left palm, fingers curled back, smashes into the nasal bone. Shotgun changes hands; fist reloads, strikes the windpipe as hard as humanly possible.

Mandeep falls. Nose broken. Throat, obliterated. My dad has the gun.

Kid turns to my dad.

Right hook—starting from my external oblique, sending the right hand into his cheek at close to the speed of sound.

Hair gel never saw it coming.

Shot fires off. A hole magically appears in the wall beside my dad. He flinches.

My index finger's cut open.

Kid plummets to the ground, backwards, knees buckle like a folding lawn chair.

Another shot fires into the bed. Cotton explosion.

Gun falls between all four of us.

My dad fires a round into the leg of Mandeep. Kid looks like he's going for the gun.

I football punt his head with faultless ferocity, leaving nothing back. The top of my foot hits him square in the nose. Bone breaks instantly under the pressure.

A sound I've never heard before. Sharp bone puncturing squishy cartilage. Pushing into it, penetrating it.

Mandeep yells out in pain, blood splatters the walls of his hotel. Pollock-like upwards spray rainbow from the ground, pea-cock array of dark red.

My dad keeps the shotgun on him. I reach over and pick up the gun. Kid is face down, on the ground. Motionless.

He's still pointing the gun at Mandeep who's screaming in pain. Holding his leg. Blood pools all over the carpet, onto the sheets. He wipes his bloodied hand on the bed as he tries to roll over.

I do not quip about calling housekeeping.

Black SIG Pro semi-automatic pistol in my possession.

I look at my dad, he's still on Mandeep.

"Hey!" I yell to get his attention.

My dad walks past Mandeep muffling his voice into the carpet in a half prone position. Walks over to the kid, lifts his body with his foot.

His nose an ugly malformed mess drenched in blood. Flat, pushed up into his forehead. Eyes bloodshot. Red streams from his face like each hole's a faucet.

"Fuck."

My dad looks at me. Bends over and checks his pulse.

"He's dead."

I stare at his face. At first I want to look away, but now I can't. He's *dead*.

Did his nasal bone puncture his brain? Did the force of my foot snap his spine?

It doesn't matter. A life has ended.

Thoughts dawn over me like a massive spaceship ready to encompass every existing atom of my soul.

I fucking *killed* someone.

My dad lowers his gun, stares at the kid.

We both stand, staring, amidst the ambient noise of a screaming man slightly muted by carpet.

Breathing heavily, I start thinking about all those people in movies who killed people.

This kid. Who was he? What was his name?

I start thinking about jail. About going to jail. For murder.

Hyperventilating.

He looks at me. Mandeep rolls over, wails in pain.

My dad turns, fires the gun at his chest.

I yelp, cover my ears. It's too late.

Sound echoes throughout the square footage. Colossal splurge of noise.

Blood splatters various parts of the wall around us, litters my father's face as red specs.

My father's joined me in murder symmetry.

Does not want his son to suffer alone.

I've never seen so much blood. I step back from the kid between the beds. Back up so much I bump into the nightstand, sending the lamp onto the mattress.

Dry, destitute waves of sheer complexity hunt me down and take me for all I'm worth in a matter of seconds.

No bearings, unapologetic thoughts, unplanned course. They run a rampant ramshackle of destruction—uninhibited. Dancing around the fire in the night, speaking in tongues. Pure, unadulterated crazy. A sacrifice, offering of sanity. No looking back.

This is what it feels like to take a life.

My dad turns to the door, runs out into the hallways, leaving me along with the carcasses. Comes back with a bottle of bleach from the cleaning cart, and starts dousing the whole room with it.

Erasing the forensic evidence of our sins. So they remain within the mind, but are unprovable beyond a reasonable doubt in a court of law.

He turns to me.

"We need to get the fuck out of here," he says as he splatters the room with that distinct smell of chlorine.

I just stand there.

Thunderstorms of destruction. Typhoons of delirium. Acid rain of hallucinations. Melting from the inside out. I fry like a plasticine figure in a microwave.

Was it self-defence? Was I justified?

He grabs my arm. Drags me past both bodies to the door. I stand there in comatose compliance.

Shutting down.

He packs up the food, the guns.

Two East Indian males lie in pools of blood on the hotel room floor.

We're leaving.

Mandeep twitches underneath the blanket. Flinches. I back up.

Blood stains the white sheet covering him, seeps out in all directions. His body continues to spastically move.

My dad turns around. Leg twitching on the dead body.

He continues to pack.

Throws my shoes at me.

One hits me in the chest; the other hits the wall behind me.

I do not need instruction. I put them on.

There is blood on the laces. When I tie them, I get blood on my hands.

There is blood on my hands.

"Tristan! For fuck's sake!"

I look up. Stand up.

"Open the door!"

I open the door. Turn and head outside.

Blink as a towering curtain of blood flash floods my consciousness. I can feel my foot penetrating his nose. It replays over and over on some horrid loop, still stinging from impact.

My dad comes, physically pushes me out of the room.

Smacks me in the face.

Hard.

Shoves me into the wall. Points his finger straight at me, eye level.

"Get your shit together! We get caught at a crime scene, it's lights out for both of us."

In the process of getting away with murder.

Our fingerprints and DNA all over the room. We flee, praying the apocalypse and chlorine will wash away our sins.

Down the stairs, rumbling around in counterclockwise circles as we descend to ground level. Burst out of the door into the courtyard, heading into the back parking lot.

I notice the pool in the dark. The green light above has turned different shades of blue and purple.

A body in the pool.

Floating in the middle like a starfish, arms and legs spread open. A man in a short-sleeve shirt. I stop.

Ira.

Blood swims from him in all directions. Beautiful liquid red bouquets shimmering in the night.

My dad stops, looks at the pool, looks at me, comes back, grabs me by the scruff of my neck, and starts dragging me along.

I keep watching the pool. Body floats on the surface. Newspaper pages strewn across the water.

A singular crime scene with one suspect.

*Suicide*?

Case closed.

We head to the truck in the dark. He lets me go; I stub my toe on the curb, stumble forward, tumble to the ground. Hit my cheek off the pavement; palms of my hands rip themselves up on the rough concrete. Tiny bits of gravel ground into the epidermis.

I'm whipped up before I can even spit chucks of dirt out of my mouth. He pulls me to my feet. Opens the door and throws me in.

"Where are we going?"

"The ocean. Now."

</>

Drive into the dusk. Drive in the dark silence.

Vancouver-Blane Highway. West. Then north.

Unlit industrial yards. Mechanical monsters sit in the dark. Chain-link fences shimmer off the headlights.

Reflective street signs guide us to the ocean. Away from it all. The lights haunt. All at once. Dirt grave of indignation uncovered and open like a fresh wound. Solitude for all the universe to squeeze into. Solace of one, hearts of many, torn, blistered, impaired. Ground hard to the enamel. A quick breath. Destitute plea for grace. Life no more. Blood no more. Air no more.

As our nation's leading pharmaceutical company, Pfizer strives every day to help Americans live healthy, balanced lives.

We do that by discovering and developing innovative medicines. As a company, we're dedicated to building healthier communities and empowering Americans to make healthier choices every day. At Pfizer, we believe that to be truly healthy, it takes not just medication, but consumerist indoctrination.

Dances across the uncovered spine, dips its scaly fingers into the corners of the rib cage. Seeps through concrete, pushes through thick metal steel. Its residue unstoppable. Obstructed, saturated hue, hijacked—all within a singular cell. Pirate operating the controls. Passenger in my own body. Eternally tied to the insides of everything that is, was, and will be.

On a cellular level, the molecules, the genetic makeup. The fibre of what I was in the womb, of the place conceived. As far back as my scientific lineage goes, this goes too.

*Murderers.*

Dashing towards an end.

A sister.

I swallow blood down my throat in an exasperated gulp.

Not all of it my own.

There is no sun this morning.

</>

She needs medical attention. She needs help.

Though she's barely able to navigate the stairs, she heads out into the sunless morning. The blank white canvas stares at her. Summer heat sticks to her skin in a sweaty filament. Waddles into the parking lot. Looks left, then right.

Squished bladder and racing mind left her unable to sleep last night. That and the fires, the voices, the screams. Tears in her eyes caked themselves dry.

She was supposed to check into the hospital today. She is supposed to give birth.

She knows these things for sure: that her father was on his way. That he was going to stop in to see her brother for a few nights. He was going to tell Tristan she was pregnant. She wished she'd told him herself, but she never felt comfortable reaching out to the brother she barely knew.

She hadn't told her dad what happened. That Brad showed up one night, and in a moment of weakness and alcohol-induced decision making, she slept with him again, without a condom.

So careless, so childlike. She always prided herself on being the grownup in the family, on following in her mother's footsteps. But he kept saying he loved her, that he was going to counselling for his PTSD. That he'd moved to Washington State and was on the force again. He was picking his life back up, putting the pieces together.

She'd loved Brad so much at one point. He gave her the emotion, the passion she'd lacked for so long. But he couldn't keep his mind in check. Just like her father. Bottling up unhealthy feelings until they backfired, discharged all over anyone within striking range. Always at inopportune moments. She couldn't remember how many times she'd dumped him and taken him back. She felt like a failure, repeating the sins of her family.

She knew her brother had broken up with his girlfriend, or so his Facebook statuses and photos implied. But she never called. She didn't know what to say. 'Hey, heard you broke up with Brianne. Well, guess what, my ex got me pregnant. Let's talk.'

He was alien to her. She knew what happened, how after the fire he started to resent their father. She watched him pull away, he stopped wanting to connect. When the insurance money came, he vanished overseas for the better part of half a decade, left her alone with their broken dad.

He rarely called.

When he came back he was a different person. He'd wiped his memory clean. He went to the States, wanted to start anew in another country. Go to school, get a job, live a normal life.

She has a few memories from before the fire. Of father and son. Of boxing, their bond. They trained together, went to fights. But after the fire he went and trained on his own, went and grew up on his own.

It was like he blamed their father, but she could never tell for sure. Like he knew something about that night no one else did.

She walks carefully to the end of the parking lot, watching the circular road that loops through campus. No one in sight.

Tried to drive herself to the hospital earlier that day. The contractions stopped her in the parking lot.

Smoke crawls into the air. She hears a man yell at the top of his lungs a few hundred feet away. It startles her.

She can't do this. She might harm the baby.

Heads back to the apartment and locks the door. Heads slowly up the stairs. Into the living room, down the hallway. To the right, the bedroom, to the left, the bathroom with an empty white linoleum tub.

She nods ever so slightly, like she knows what she has to do.

Salty sea up to the calves. Pants up to the knees. Dress shirt—gone. Washed away in the gentle tide of the Pacific. Saline fills the eyes and nose. Brisk cut of air, lightly tainted by sodium chloride, cleansing the nasal passages.

The horizon a parallel line of amber blue. White sky slowly returning. The chameleon—from grey, the slumber of dawn awakens from hibernation.

Forgiving the dusk for its lack of inhibitions.

I can't remember the last time I was up this early.

Shoreline north and south. Muddy sand squishes between the toes; water numbs the calcium in the bones, chilling the marrow. Sandbars and White Rock off to the north, a railway line embedded within the grass along the shore. Cordilleran greenery extends to the water's edge. Driftwood lines the beach like scattered bones of Mother Nature. Dry, cracked, swollen.

A bald eagle sits atop a log. Perfectly perched, elegantly still. He's resorted to scavenging for tiny crabs that have washed up at high tide. Crunches the crustaceans in his beak. Seashells and soft rounded rocks. Dark green seaweed, Dead Man's Fingers, kelp like wet, matted hair. I turn back the other way, slowly walking where the shoreline would be in high tide.

On the edge of the sea.

Staring at this quiet giant, trying to theorize how the ocean fits into all of this. Two-thirds of the planet. Something like 70 percent of the world covered by it. We were destroying it at an alarming rate, an infectious disease eating its host's organs one, by one, by one.

It sits there. No expression change. No response.

It exists.

My father spoke to me.

Told me we did what we had to do.

What *needed* to be done.

For his daughter. For my sister.

His grandchild. My niece or nephew.

He stands in my peripheral vision, gun down to the side. Looks out towards the void. Staring deep into the ravenous fires of the unknown.

*Murderers.*

In the names of self-defence, self-preservation.

Manslaughter, maybe.

Murderers nonetheless.

Too many thoughts to count.

Fragments of condensation litter the walls of the lungs. The dampest air you will ever breathe. Amidst this horror, the ocean breathes at the exact same pace.

A plastic shopping bag floats by my feet. Cancerous jellyfish.

We are getting what we *fucking deserve.*

I turn around, step back up to the shore, shoes and socks across the dark sand. Military truck parked by the dock. He stands alert; wolf on the outskirts of the pack. The lookout, chin up.

This air haunts. The silence is blinding. Not even waves to calm an equatorial fever. Just thick, dense oxygen with nowhere to go.

Ocean stares us down.

A mundane sound licks the back of my ears. In the distance, bellowing out quietly, the drone of muted, smooth static.

Then a whistle. I turn to the noise. Pointing up in the sky. Off to the north, a few hundred feet off the shoreline. A hundred feet up.

A helicopter. Too far to distinguish its make. We watch. Completely tuned in to its quiet drift across the sky, a straight line, circular hum of chopper blades pulsing into the eardrums.

"Where's it going?" I yell.

He doesn't answer right away.

"The island, I think."

The string breaks. It starts to flutter, veers on an awkward angle. Tries to right itself, tips further towards the ground, a falling mechanical leaf, spinning in uneven circles.

My insides elevate. Hot coal furnace of fear and anxiety ramps up. Helplessly watching it plummet in awkward zigzags towards an aquatic grave.

Bombs into the ocean. Propeller blades splash up water, whipping white sea froth into the air.

You have exceeded the size limit of your mailbox.

Would you like to AutoArchive old memories and replace them with these new horrible ones?

The helicopter drifts on the surface, floating carcass half submerged, a bloated whale about to wash up along the shore. Bodies trying to escape the cockpit. I do not move, I do not look away.

Enough.

He moves down onto the dock. One boat tied to the end. Outboard fishing vessel. Walks as the wood speaks under the pressure of his steel-toed boots. The pillars of the pier stick up like teeth, coated in barnacles, plaque from the ocean. Seagulls dance around, pecking at scraps on the harbour walkway.

I head to the shore, put on my shoes and socks. Throw on the black t-shirt my father scavenged for me. Stolen jeans and running shoes, shaved head.

We made it to the ocean. Grabbed some clothes from the marina. Articles without blood on them, lacking direct evidence supporting the truth of an assertion directly. Sat in silence on the dock, waiting for the white sky to return. Waiting for the dawn to fall asleep. Ready to make a mad dash across the waters for my sister.

To our goal. The one thing that will surely save us from a life destined for Hell.

The rebirth continues; we fit ourselves to this new uniform of the present. From top to bottom I'm being broken down, emerging from a chrysalis.

A new being no longer roped or strangled by the technological rat race.

Just a son with his father, looking for his sister.

Make my way back to the walkway that divides the beach from the parking lot. Still dew on the grass. The truck, its passenger's side bashed in. The feeling of lifting in the cab washes over me momentarily. I shoo it away.

Boat starts up. Propeller blades rumble and gargle, gas being shot into the injector. Huff of black smoke as the engine clears its dirty lungs. Down to the dock. I glance to see if the helicopter's still in view down the coastline.

Gone. Sunken below.

He's rearranging things to make room. As I get close enough, he throws a lifejacket onto the deck.

Slips his over his shoulder, wincing in pain as he stretches his arm.

Hops down into the boat. Weight pushes the port side; my dad braces himself with the seat.

THUD!

I'm on the ground. Split-second black out.

Violent assault in one swift motion.

Back of my head numb with pain. Ears ring.

Roll over.

*Brad*.

His gun on my dad.

My dad has the shotgun on him.

I rub the back of my head.

Shotgun loads into the chamber.

"Last chance motherfuckers!" he screams. He looks worn, eyes dart around like there might be another Schultz ready to tune him up.

I sit up. Fog blotches the vision.

Brad points the gun at me.

"Stay the fuck down, Tristan!"

I'm staring right at him.

"If I get the chance I'm gonna absolutely skull fuck you until you wish you were back in Kabul."

Brad chuckles, but now it's a completely menacing chuckle.

"Like you know what it was like over there you fucking pussy."

"Tristan get in the boat," says my dad.

"Don't either of you fucking move!"

"Fuck you, jarhead."

"I swear on my father's grave, if I have to, I will fucking kill you all and raise that goddamn motherfucking kid myself!"

This guy. This guy is crazy.

Crazy with a capital C.

"Brad," says my father in his police uniform tone. "You kill someone, you won't be able to erase that mistake. Think rationally here, think about your kid, about Liz's safety and wellbeing, she's days from birth right now. Remember what they taught you in field training. De-escalate this situation."

Brad keeps alternating between pointing the gun at me, and then my dad.

I stand, slowly. Brad watches.

"Stay calm," says my dad. "Let's talk this out, okay?"

Somehow, in this melee, Brad's backed up right to the edge of the dock. I look at my dad, he looks at me.

*BLAM*!

Fires a round to the left of Brad.

I fall forward, right into the boat.

Brad falls backward, right into the water.

Boat rumbles away before I can even find my footing.

I watch out the back as Brad splashes around, trying to get back up onto the dock.

Touch the back of my head.

Blood on my fingers.

More blood.

This time all of it my own.

</>

"We've got a good hour on him. I don't think he knows how to navigate a boat across the water like this. He won't pay attention to the weather conditions. He's still his own worst enemy."

*Steady pace.*

Fuck that. I want five minutes in the ring with him.

Except no bell to save his fucking ass.

Holding a towel against the back of my head to stop the bleeding.

Plan is to head southwest back across the border in Semiahmoo Bay, curling around Point Roberts. Quick stop there, then if the weather is good and the water is calm, a mad dash for Lighthouse Point. From there we follow the ferry route to SaltSpring Island, weaving our way through a myriad of semi-populated isles. After that another push for Swartz Bay to find a car. Then south on the highway to the circular shaped University of Victoria campus.

The major worry is taking a pleasure craft on open seawater. When you get out past the tide and into greasy waves rolling all the way into the Strait, the ocean can be an unforgiving beast. A quick weather pattern change and we're fucked.

Still, we're stocked with enough gasoline to cruise the coast to California if we wanted. We have paddles, a cover, and lifejackets. We're prepared, but at the mercy of Mother Nature.

Concentrated blue seawater surrounds. No whitecaps today in the summer heat, but the cold air comes up fast.

Outboard engine hums across the waves, skimming elongated ripples as we leave the protection of shallows for the gaping hole between the mainland and Vancouver Island.

Mountain ranges a quiet pulse line across the purview. Lurid green barreling hills right up to the ocean. Cut across like a knife slice, pale white fixation of nothingness, one giant cloud imbuing the vision.

Steers us towards the void. I try not to think about the past three days. I try not to think about what's transpired. He sits with one knee on the seat, peering over the windshield. Aviators to break the wind.

Off to the north, smoke lifts into the air. Plots of grey airborne and liquid particles seep up, releasing gases in uneven lines. Combustion, together with the quantity of oxygen entrained or otherwise mixed into the mass. Smoke signals of collective distress.

First sign of land north is the Boundary Bay Airport, a diamond-shaped runway in the grassy fields of a peninsula. Pointing directly south, nothing but dead airspace. No planes, no takeoffs, no landings.

Naked sky. No contrails. Just riotous smoke stacks from the city. Magnetic pulse pushed everything to the ground, the inhabiting air carrying robust amounts of harmful particles. I feel the weight in my stomach like an undigested peach pit of atmospheric poisoning.

Trapped with my thoughts again. No technology to distract from reality. The wind's hum forgoes any conversation.

No more cheesy internet gossip. No more endless swirls of newswire stories, cycling around in uneven, unending circles. No breaking updates interrupting regularly scheduled programming. No constant feeds filling us up like pigs at a trough. Shitting out information into a tub that circles around endlessly.

No connection to things that don't really exist. No quick answers to deep questions. No search engines to power and guide our thoughts.

No battery life.

You are running on reserve power.

Please switch to another source.

The ill informed, the underprepared, the over-educated, under-trained. The silver spoons of my generation with their supple, soft mouths sucking on the tit of the information revolution.

Weaned from the mother of invention.

Ripped from the warm bosom of connectivity.

Thrown from the nest.

We fall.

Gloriously.

Prophecy: fulfilled.

</>

Point Roberts. Pene-exclave; the tip of a peninsula that's technically the United States of America but originates geographically from Canada. Some homes, a marina, a sprinkling of bed & breakfast three-storey townhomes.

We follow the shoreline along scenic Edwards Drive. No power here either, homes abandoned or blinds drawn on every window. Coast past the marina, an odd manmade inlet that resembles a teardrop. A few people out tending to boats, stocking supplies into the cabins in a concerned rush.

Nobody is waving these days.

He conducts a fast pace up until the southwestern corner of the peninsula, where a small airport landing strip stretches out to the end. Unfinished line into the sea. Looks around to see if anyone is in the vicinity, anyone who might cause harm. Turns the boat into the shore, docking slowly on the rocks; we slide up in the gravel. Tucks the anchor under a rock and sets out on foot with a pair of binoculars. The waves make focusing onboard impossible. Lies down along the sand with a compass and looks out towards the ocean, searching for Lighthouse Point, our next destination.

I stay on the boat. I've spent enough time on American soil.

To the north a line of shadowy cargo ships—each one still lit with diesel-generated power. Tsawwassen ferry terminal outstretched into the sea; a thin arm across the horizon, tongue rolling out into the straight line of the Pacific Ocean.

He stands up, dusts off some sand, heads back to the boat.

"How's it look?"

A motion with his hand signalling so-so.

I nod.

Hops back in, pushes off with a paddle after I free the line. Engine starts and we plunge into a superhighway of water. From my perspective it doesn't look that far, maybe ten, fifteen minutes. But depth perception is shot by the white sky slicing across the field of vision. Sky and sea, oil and water. No saturation from white to blue.

2D view in a 3D world.

Southwest at full throttle. He brings the binoculars up at intervals and systematically nudges the steering wheel according to the compass. Magnetic south, to the latitude and longitude of a sister. A daughter. An end point.

Deep open water entices my mind's attention. I stand up and look overboard to see. Blue. No consciousness.

Gulf Islands. Smattering of mushy green, rocky pieces of land separating Vancouver Island from the open sea. We're going to deke our way through them, through the guards of the break-water, and into the coastal island comfort. Buoys float and bob with the waves, exposing rustic sea lines. Seagulls perched on them like landing docks; they scour for dead fish and bugs. Oceanic vultures.

Worn from sleep deprivation. Eyes weary from an early morning start and the nightmares. I sit back down; wrap my upper body in a blanket, lifejacket tight around the chest. Drop my eyelids; try to let my other senses drown me. Red and white blood cells raging a nasty civil war within the veins.

My father commands the boat with compass in hand. Clothes ripple in the wind.

Whatever's running up the walls of his mind trying to besiege his internal kingdom is sufficiently contained by the current task.

*Father.*

The word repeats itself.

Brad has faded off into the forest, giving into a troubled mind scarred by the horrors of battle. I left mine to drown in the smoggy haze of foreign countries. I think of what my son might be like.

Would I make a good father? Did Brianne see this in me, an ability to raise a human life? She obviously did—something I'd never thought about.

What mistakes would I try to erase with my son?

What errors would I commit, or force upon my son?

He steers us towards the end, and I head back to the past again.

The freak tragedy of the fire. Brought a full-blooded male to his knees. Bad luck, shitty karma, poor fate. Call it or don't call it, it doesn't matter. That night set him back decades. Now he has a chance to reclaim his family. Raise a grandson or granddaughter up close and personal. Isn't necessarily being given a second chance, but this crisis has allowed prioritization and the ability to find a discernible goal. One that doesn't require family coun-selling or overtly introspective self-help books about dealing with remorse and loss.

Just a big fucking hammer.

That—he could bring.

He needs this, his rewrite. I see it in the scarred muscles on his forearms, tightly gripping the steering wheel, guided by compass, governed by tasks. Scampered back from the other side of the International Date Line, the third generation of Schultzes his chance to start fresh. Go over some mistakes, right some wrongs. Go over this kin with a fine tooth comb. Raise something without a serious elbow in the road.

The sway of the boat starts to rock me to sleep.

I close my eyes, try to think about nothing.

Sweet, beautiful nothing.

</>

*A clownfish dwells in an anemone. Sleek, black-tip reef sharks slither across an invisible line. Fishes from the coasts of Africa, Madagascar, Central America. Roy G. Biv of biodiversity hotspots.*

*I push my face up to the glass, smushing my nose into the cold pane separating me from the gallery of gill-bearing aquatic craniates. My mother gently puts her hand on my shoulder—I'm just now into double-digits, but still young enough to marvel at the spectacular beauty and playfulness of Gaia.*

*"Tristan, step back a bit, respect the fishes' habitat."*

*I step back. My mother's knowledge was intrinsic, robust. I'm sure if she said it, it was true.*

*She points to the left as a green sea turtle dives to the rock bed. My sister comes up beside me, rain boots and ice cream-stained shirt.*

*"Did you know green sea turtles can live up to eighty years old?" my mother says to both of us.*

*"Older than Grandpa," my sister blurts.*

*She smiles. "Yes, older than Grandpa."*

*A giant Indo-Pacific reef. Fishes carry children in their mouths. Corals, endangered sea horses, mouth-breeding cichlids.*

*We walk by a school of serene pajama fish. An Asian turtle crosses their vision, and they scatter into hiding.*

*My mother tells us about the devastation from shark finning, cichlids from Lake Victoria and Banggai cardinal fish vulnerable to over-harvesting.*

*I'm so enthralled by the information that later that night at dinner at the Teahouse in Stanley Park, I quiz our waiter as to the origin of every fish on the menu. Poor guy heads back to the kitchen three times to fact check himself. My mother smiles, gently nudging me towards an educational mindset.*

*We head outside to Penguin Point. Made to look like Boulders Beach in Cape Town, the birds waddle on the rockwork and swim in the surrounding water. She holds our shoulders as the two of us try to lean as far as humanly possible over the railing.*

*"These penguins are from Africa," she says.*

*"Africa?!" I say, still-developing brain so confused I go cross-eyed.*

*"I thought penguins lived at the North Pole?"*

*"Actually, that's the Antarctic. There are no penguins at the North Pole."*

*My youthful mind being blown. Cartoons lied to me.*

*My mom bends over and points to one as it lifts up its feathers to trap a layer of air.*

*"That's how they keep warm."*

*Another dive bombs into the water, splashing everywhere. My sister laughs at the absurdity of penguins. Aquatic birds wearing tuxedos, waddling around like little overweight football coaches.*

*My father couldn't make it out for the day; he's working night shift. I didn't know what night shift meant. All I knew is I'd come downstairs sometimes to find him on the couch at all hours of the morning, smoking, drinking alcohol. He said he had trouble sleeping. I was too young to prod.*

*Earlier that day we fed squirrels in the park, facing south towards Coal Harbour. My mother made us peanut butter and jam sandwiches. I chased a peacock down a grassy hill until he turned and stood his ground, which sent my butt back to the picnic blanket and my mother's comfort in a hurry.*

*He came back across our field of view; I pointed him out, like my mother should go have a stern talking-to with him. He made that noise that peacocks make, one of high octane barrel-chested squealing.*

*While we ate, my mother played counting games with us. If I had seven grapes, gave two to my sister and ate one, how many would I have left? She laid them out on the blanket. I refused to give two to my sister; she could only get one, sibling rivalry starting to take shape.*

*"Four grapes," I say proudly, counting them out as I plop the remainder in my mouth. My sister eyes her small pittance.*

*"I ate four grapes."*

*Later I relent, let her read Calvin & Hobbes with me on the blanket as my mother turns the pages of a book. I tell her Hobbes is only real to Calvin, but it doesn't matter, his parents are slimy and gross. And Susie is gross too because she's a girl and has cooties.*

*My sister runs to my mother.*

*"Mom, mom, Tristan said I have cooties."*

*I hold my hands up theatrically. "I said Susie had cooties. Not her. She doesn't have cooties, I don't think, not yet."*

*My mom smiles; my sister buries her face in her chest as my mother lays her book gently down, face up.*

*"It's okay, Elizabeth, you don't have cooties. Tristan is just teasing you."*

</>

Thud!

Vision—blurry.

Rub my eyeballs with my fingers.

Look up to my dad, still steering.

"You might want to have a look at this," he says.

Lighthouse Point on Mayne Island comes into view, only a few minutes away. Must've dozed off.

Something else enters into frame. What looks like a white block against the rocky shore. It's a ferry, on its side. An imposing vessel, blue trim, multiple decks with railings, blue smoke stack.

We pass a lifejacket. And an oar.

A body, face down.

I rub my eyes again like I might be stuck in another horrible nightmare.

The Spirit of Vancouver. Some 18,000 tons. 550 feet. Belly exposed like a carcass.

We weave in and out of the debris, turning the boat left and right in a slow, deliberate manner. I head up to the front, looking forward. A little bit of everything floats on the surface—food trays, clothes, full Pepsi cans. I look at the ferry, hull exposed, scars along the bottom, water marks like geological time scales.

Massive architectural grave on the edge of the island like a beached whale. Still pristine metal in some points, rusty and faded in others. I watch as we pass. Lying there, half-submerged, taunting me with its quiet terror. Birds circle and dive at the garbage feast, dropping down to pick up scraps.

The hair on my arms stands up.

Another body floats by. I turn forward.

File—deleted. Recycle bin—emptied.

Click, ignore.

Try to ignore.

Fail.

Application—fail.

"Should we slow down, see if there are any survivors?"

He doesn't look back, keeps weaving through the debris.

"No. This must've happened Friday night. Radio interference probably sent it to land, hard. Anyone who survived is already gone."

He points to the shore, a line of life rafts.

"This is just wreckage now."

Galiano Island, due north of Mayne, acting as a bottleneck. The ferry sits locked into the island like an errant jigsaw piece. We pass on our left. Giant white ghost bellows a silent cry. Along the shoreline scattered remnants of passengers moving onto the beach, but no bodies, no souls to be seen.

Untouched green forests creeping all the way to the breakwater. Jagged, rocky cliff formations, small scattered shoals, the odd house entombed in the trees. Tattered and weatherworn, some with postmodern angles.

Veer right at Village Bay, following an inverted S route between the two main islands. Sea breeze pliable in the cover.

Prevost Island, largely untouched, no dirt roads or power lines. An island of archaic arbutus trees and sandstone beaches. Line of Garry oaks, their origins covered by a small field of wild lilies. Offshore a kelp bed.

Still the sense of pulsating radiation bubbling in the bottom of my stomach like an endless CT scan. Lessened on the open water. As if the ultraviolet poison dripping from the roof of the planet is being washed away by the Pacific.

We curve around the southern side of Prevost Island.

Off to the left, Port Washington, a slew of single-level ash brown cabins on North Pender. Someone out back of a house chopping wood. He looks up at us. I wave. He stares for a few seconds, then waves back.

Returns to his chopping block.

We continue south, heading through the final straightaway. North is SaltSpring Island. Cast-off community of champagne socialists and hardcore eco-friendly hippies who drive new model hybrid cars. I can see the roads, some homes, not a lot of activity.

Fulford Harbour comes into view. A small group of boats and ships stationed around the bay.

Our destination. The terminal, docked ferries. Boats. Small ships. Debris litters the water. A plank of wood. Unopened bag of Lays Potato Chips. Fishing net. Styrofoam bits. A soccer ball.

We're going to slip around the west side of Swartz Bay to Shoal Harbour. Docking out of sight. We weave in and out of tiny islands. Homes off on the right, burrowed into the trees. Roads, power lines. One house comes clearly into view; a man stands on his front porch, watching us intently as we motor by. I wave.

He does not wave back.

Into the harbour at Cedar Grove Marina. My father reaches down to the side, pulls up the shotgun. Places it barrel up against the bracket that holds the steering wheel. Looks over at me. I reach into the glove box and grab the Colt pistol. Safety off.

Half the harbour empty of vessels. Two sailboats drift on their sides aimlessly, leftover toys in a child's bath. Off in the distance yet another trail of soot lifts into the sky. Now that we've slowed, ambient noise has returned, seemingly normal—birds chirp, summer wind rustles.

Slow up at the dock. I step off with one foot. We tie up; I toss the hockey bag onto the planks. He hops up with the shotgun, Glock stuffed into the back of his belt.

We walk down the pier. Footsteps echo off the water below the wooden frame of the marina. My dad carries the hockey bag over his shoulder, I follow behind, head on a swivel. Doesn't appear to be any power in the boathouse. Not a soul in sight.

Up a path to a row of cars. Another sedan, silver. He tries the door, locked.

I walk around to the other side. To my amazement, it opens.

Inside there's a few maps, empty coffee cups, a small fire extinguisher. I reach across, open the door. He looks at the dashboard. No keys in the ignition.

His post-apocalyptic skills about to be showcased again.

Pops the hood and bends down to the hockey bag. Pulls out a black wire. Heads to the engine to locate the plug and coil wires. Wraps the exposed metal coiling of the wire around the positive side of the battery. The starter solenoid is on the passenger side fender wheel, near the battery. He attaches the wiring to the solenoid—a battery cable. Then the wiring with a set of pliers.

Finally he hops in the cab and jams a flathead screwdriver into the top centre of the steering column. Pushes the screwdriver between the wheel and the column, pushing the locking pin away from the wheel. Reaches in with a finger and grabs the wiring from the solenoid, crossing the terminals together. A spark, and the engine fires up, a growl of mechanical haste.

I pop open the glove box and a set of keys falls out.

"Are you fucking kidding me?"

Can't help but laugh.

</>

South on the Patricia Bay Highway. Line of cars snakes back from the ferry terminal. Families camping out, setting up networks of cars and tents, obviously waiting for mainland service to resume. Waiting for the Titanic. One group has a barbecue up and running. Pockets of civilization remain within the turmoil.

Garbage everywhere along the road, parts of fenders and bumpers, cardboard boxes, newspaper, glass shards. Off to the southeast, smoke about a mile down the road.

I try the radio. Static. Coins fill the ashtray, outdated Seattle Mariners Ichiro bobblehead on the dashboard. I grab it, toss it out the window. The CD player works but all I can find are audiobooks on scuttlebutt sailing. Neither of us in a nautical mood.

We pass the sleepy harbour town of Sidney. Lights out at the main junction. Smoke starting to come into focus.

A sign for the airport turnoff.

Over a rolling hill to the right of the highway, a small float plane burns to a crisp in a field.

Scorch marks across the hull. Debris on the ground. Nobody in sight.

Part of me wonders if Brianne might be dead. Did she try to get on a plane to head home to South Carolina sometime after Friday? The dwindling chance of me ever seeing her again tries to digest downwards. The thought too tough to swallow.

I spit it out.

Turn, face forward. Rub the residue from my eyes.

Every car I see, I'm looking for a Washington State police cruiser. As if Brad is following us like a shadow. One we can never outrun. Hearing footsteps at every turn. The nightmares we all have where we can never shake our pursuer.

We continue along the highway, under a pedestrian overpass. A large cloth banner hanging from the railing; words spray-painted in black:

In the deep glens where they lived all things were older than man and they hummed of mystery.

Some of the land remains untouched. Orchard fields with fresh green grass. Cows munch away, oblivious to it all. Relics of the previous day—what seems like light years prior, mankind pushed unapologetically through a wormhole. I crack the window, let the air in, check that it's breathable as if this thick fog of Hell might choke us all where we stand. A shady-looking guy passes by on the highway with his thumb out—no sign showing a requested destination. Watches us as we pass. I finger him for good measure.

Not a chance in Hell.

Highway signs signal a turnoff for the University of Victoria. I have no idea where my sister lives, but apparently it's on campus. I sit in stillness, Colt pistol on the seat between the two of us like a divider.

McKenzie Avenue turnoff and we head into Saanich. I'm counting busted windows and abandoned cars. Everyone who's driving is avoiding eye contact. Four way stops once again a serious point of stress.

We pass a church. Dozens of believers outside the white building below the cross, holding signs for the cars passing by. They read as per usual: repent, rapture, apocalypse, sins, repent some more. Some of them yell at me as we pass. I finger them, too. Then I stick my upper body out the window and yell at the top of my lungs.

"If this was the fucking rapture and you were real Christians you'd be gone by now, you fucking idiots!"

My dad grabs my belt and yanks my ass back into the car.

"Tristan, don't be a cunt."

"What?! It's true."

I sit back down, content with my comment.

He glances at me, then back at the road.

I sit, staring forward.

I hear a chuckle.

I look over.

My father lets out a sheepish smile.

"You're still a little shit," he says, shaking his head.

</>

Patches of black soot on the concrete signal where fires were lit. Ash tar smoke residue journeys into the air. Off one street a row of power lines creeps unnaturally down to the road. Fire truck overturned on someone's lawn, hose sprawled across the grass like a strand of spaghetti.

Campus signage. Centennial Stadium. An entire parking lot of cars torched. Sides of the stadium charred. Ash still polluting the air. Ground covered with black grunge and grimy sediment.

We weave around a fender. Someone went into the lot and set the cars on fire.

*All of them.*

The stank residue of burnt metal—carbon monoxide. A litter of crushed Pabst Blue Ribbon empties and a pair of used underwear. Bonfire of the apocalypse.

We keep driving.

Campus is a mess. A large oak tree toilet papered; windows smashed. A naked kid on a banana bike wearing nothing but a toque pedals leisurely by us like he's out for a reading break stroll. People visible inside the buildings. They've set up communal camps.

A student wearing a Superman costume comes into the middle of the road with a pitching wedge and puts his hand out like we're supposed to stop.

"Really?" says my dad with a chuckle.

He steps on the gas without hesitation.

Superman leaps out of the way in a single bound, takes a drunken swing at us with his golf club, falling to the ground in what must be a gloriously substance-induced mess.

I watch out the rearview mirror as he lies on the pavement, body covered in a bright red cape.

Something crosses my peripheral vision. To the left.

A figure running across the grass, bare feet.

Female. Completely naked.

Early twenties. Runs with wide strides that will surely bring her down soon.

My dad slows as she crosses the street—not looking either way, just running.

A male figure appears.

The female notices us, screams something, but we can't make it out inside the cab.

The guy is most definitely chasing her.

This . . . This does not look good.

My dad stops, parks in the middle of the street.

Adrenaline joins the conversation. Shoots bullets of ephedrine into my lung pockets. Wires up my heart with anxious CPR electricity.

My dad's out the side of the car, pulls his Glock, chambers a round.

I'm out the right. I grab the Colt pistol. Heavy steel iron cold in the hand.

The two figures run across our path. I make out a 'Help!' from the girl.

Shot fired into the air.

Both bodies drop to the ground.

I follow my dad as he walks forward onto a grassy hill across the road. I can see they came from dorm rooms on the other side.

The girl turns, on her knees, crying. Her nose bloody and arms scraped with cuts.

The guy stands, faces us, palms directed outward as a sign of concession.

"Hey man, it's all good," he slurs as we near.

He's wearing a faded t-shirt and a bandana. Bloodstains on his shorts. Looks about three Red Bull vodkas from a frat-boy rapist. Glassy eyes seeking anything with a pulse.

"Hey—"

*BLAM*!

Round echoes by his ear. The girl drops to the ground like she's trying to hide in the grass.

"If you speak again, I will kill you," says my dad.

A telling nod.

"Tristan, check on the girl."

I walk over, lower the Colt.

She looks up when she's close enough to see my eyes.

Tears and mascara destroying her face like errant charcoal on a white canvas. A cut on her cheek, still bleeding.

I crouch down on my knees, come in close to her.

"Are you okay?"

She nods, sobbing, covering her private parts. I take off my shirt and hand it to her, she pulls it over her shoulders and wounds.

"What's going on?"

"He was raping me."

I look back at my dad and the guy. All three of us heard her.

My dad raises the Glock.

The guy drops to his knees and starts weeping too, hands still up.

I turn back to the girl.

"Are you sure?"

"Yes!" she screams. "He came into my dorm room, broke down the door."

I walk over to my dad.

His chest heaves with anger.

Court is now in session.

We're mere feet from Liz. But we can't ignore this. If we're going to atone for our sins, now might be the time. We have the chance to right a wrong, to instil justice in this new world.

This new world will not survive without justice.

"She's bruised up pretty bad," I say. "I can't see how this plays out any other way."

My father nods.

Years ago, he broke in on a guy who'd been beating his wife. She wouldn't press charges. My dad put the guy in a wheelchair. Official police report said the perp came at him with a crowbar. Chances are that wasn't true.

It didn't matter.

There was no room for this type of stuff in his life, or ours— ever.

Unmistakable.

Unforgivable.

You never laid a hand on a woman.

Never took advantage.

Never.

I breathe in. She keeps sobbing, back down on her hands and knees.

My dad and I walk over to the guy. He's crying as he speaks.

"Oh God, please don't kill me, I wasn't going to rape her. I swear to God."

"Yes you were!" screams the girl, spit flying from her mouth.

I've never watched someone beg for his life. Never watched a soul face death so directly, with so little power.

I watch the urine trail down his pants.

"Please oh my God please don't kill me, please."

I look at my dad. Sense the fight in his mind. We've seen enough death, but . . .

"This is like a hundred feet from Liz," I say, the severity of the words heightening the anger within me as they leave my mouth. "What if this guy went after Liz? You know if we let him go he'll try something like this again, especially given what's going on now."

I look at my father.

He raises his gun. I raise mine, almost instinctively.

"Oh God no, please don't kill me!"

"Shut the fuck up!" I yell. "If I hear one more word from your shitbag mouth, *I* will fucking shoot you!"

Wait a second.

"Wait a second," I say. Both guns pointed square. My hand is still, unshaking. "We're gonna execute this guy?"

My dad looks over. I'm looking at him, too, searching for something to go on. A moral code to follow. But the more I look, the more I realize he's looking at me, and we're searching for the same thing.

"What's the alternative? Let a rapist go?" says my father, his mind apparently already made up.

I drop my gun.

Try to rub an apocalypse of stress from my face.

"Fuck, I mean, I get it," I say.

Silence. The guy sobs quietly.

"Fuck, dad, we're not Judge fucking Dredd here. What happened yesterday, we did what we had to do. But this, this is different."

"Judge Dredd?"

"He's this guy in the future, like a cop, but he's a judge and an executioner too."

My dad looks confused.

"Is he like Serpico?"

I let out a hiss of breath, the noise of stress wrapped in frustration.

"No, Dad, he's not like Serpico."

"Oh."

"You're a cop, and you don't know who Judge Dredd is?"

He shrugs.

Neither of us knows what to do here. We stare at one another. Standstill of conundrum. There is no police, there is no orchestrated law and order, we are sure of that now. The formality of justice has become objectionable. If we let this man go, who we witnessed trying to rape a woman, he could very well re-commit his crime. We would be forced to live with the decision, knowing we did not uphold justice when the time asked us to.

"Fuck me."

My father nods. His gun drops.

"All I know is I'm not leaving him here like this."

"Fuck."

We're fixed. Staring at each other.

The girl walks over. Wipes tears and mascara from her face. I can see a trail of blood running down from her vagina. Holds out her hand.

"Can I have your gun?"

I look at my dad. He looks at me, gives me nothing.

I meet her eyes.

Hand her the Colt.

*BLAM*!

The guy's head whips back, blood and brains spray all over the grass in a soupy mess. Body flails awkwardly.

Falls.

Shot echoes straight to the Gods.

She hands the gun back to me. Cold eyes.

Walks away.

We look at each other.

Searching for words.

</>

Whatever this is, we are in it. Whoever we were, we are no longer.

The severity of the present steals the past and future from thought.

Left with the here, the now.

Left with whatever we can scavenge for sanity.

My dad pulls a piece of paper from his jacket pocket.

We make a turn into student housing.

"She lives here?"

"Yeah."

Pulls the car into the lot. Homes like mini duplexes, small condos joined at the hip. Nothing but backwoods beyond.

We get out, my dad with the shotgun, me with the Colt.

He does a full 360 degree look with the shotgun. Walks around the lot.

The menace of Brad has us on permanent high alert.

He's been tracking our locations like any cop would. My house in Seattle, the best border to cross, my father's boat at White Rock. Now we stand at Liz's place, and I have no doubt he knows where this is. Following us like a treasure map.

But nothing.

Lowers his gun.

Heaves the hockey bag over his shoulder.

We're heading to 12A. Layered house, three floors. Short set of stairs to a front door. Off to the side a bike and barbecue with a plastic cover. I knock on the door.

"Liz!"

Try to open it. Locked.

My father comes up, drops the hockey bag. Pulls out a small tension wrench and a pick that looks like a dentist's tool. Pushes the tension wrench into the bottom half of the lock and turns it clockwise. Inserts the pick above it, feeling for the pins. I can hear him trying to lay the end of the pick on the bottom of the last pin to try and push it above the sheer line. The spring pushes up, a click; he takes one hand off and turns the doorknob.

It opens.

Pushes the door open gently. Slowly.

"Liz!"

We wait.

No reply.

Make our way inside, lock the door behind us. Drop the hockey bag and proceed up a set of carpeted stairs to what must be the living room.

Dank apartment, musty stench. Like the smell that accumulates when a shut-in does not open a window for days.

"Liz?!"

Up the stairs, modest living room breaks into a kitchen via a beige sofa. Feminine decorations. Wilted flowers. Landscape pictures. Carefully arranged colour coordinated trinkets. A thin layer of dust covers every surface, as if the apartment is shedding.

Smell of what I can only describe as warm meat left to rot in an enclosed area.

Bay window, shades drawn. Laptop on the floor. Dirty dishes on the counter, clothes all over the futon and glass coffee table. It's a mess, as if someone thought about leaving, starting packing, then abandoned their plans.

My dad lowers his gun as he looks down the hallway. To the left, a bathroom. To the right, a bedroom. Trail of blood across the carpet between the two.

I follow.

"Liz, are you in there?"

Streams of caked blood come into focus, dried and crusted into the carpeting. Blackened bile around the edges.

To my left.

In the bathroom.

Bloodstained tub, umbilical cord.

I dart my eyes away.

Cover my mouth and nose with one hand.

As soon as I blink the image floods the backs of my eyelids.

Handprints of blood.

Trail across the shower curtain. Human discharge. Yellow green alkaline secreted liquid.

"Ah fuck."

I turn to the room. Liz in the bed, against the headboard. Blonde hair strewn across the pillows in a clumped mess of sweat, tears, and plasma.

In her arms, wrapped in a towel.

A baby.

Blood splotches stain the sheets. My father drops the shotgun.

"Liz?"

Her eyelids flutter. Slender features mimic mine. I see the similarities in her face, always present, no matter how long we've been apart.

"Dad?" she tries to say, but it comes across as more of a hollowed-out moan.

Her hand lifts. He takes it, pulls it to his face.

The baby, my niece or nephew, wakes too.

"Dad?" she coughs.

"Tristan, get some water."

Into the kitchen. Turn on the faucet. Nothing. Not even a drip.

I open the fridge. Smell of rotten food smacks me across the face. I cover my nose and mouth. Gulp down the start of vomit in the throat. A bottle of warm water. I grab it, bring it back.

My dad takes the water, pours it into her mouth. She's on death's doorstep.

"We need to get her to a hospital."

My sister.

Here she is, right in front of us.

I'm trying to encapsulate this moment, but the present too vibrant to allow proper reflection.

He takes the baby out of Liz's hands. She tries to stop him but looks as if she might pass out in the process.

"Is it a guy or girl?"

"Girl," he says.

My sister gave birth to a baby girl by herself in a bathroom tub.

Officially the toughest Schultz of them all.

He holds the baby. A look on his face I cannot begin to describe.

A grandfather.

I sit down beside Liz. She's floating in and out of consciousness. I try to give her more water; it spills down onto her shirt.

My dad turns to me. I stand up and stare into the eyes of my niece.

I am an *uncle*. The word sounds odd bouncing through my brain.

"Tristan, I need you to do something."

I stare at my niece.

"Tristan?"

"Yeah."

"We need to get Liz and her baby to the Navy base. She needs medical attention, but we can't move now. It will be dark soon, and we need fresh water, baby formula, medical supplies to get her through the night."

"The Navy base?"

"Esquimalt has a huge Navy base. They might be up. Running on diesel."

"What about the hospital?"

Shakes his head.

"The Navy base, over the bridge."

My sister moans. My dad sits beside her.

"At first light we go. It's our only chance. They won't make it more than a few days without proper care. They're both going to need an IV, medical attention."

I look at my niece again, her tiny blood-streaked forehead.

"Okay," I say.

I stand there like I should know what to do—but I don't.

"Tristan, go down to the bag. Get a gun, the knife. Head to the closet supermarket; find the pharmacy. I want you to get baby formula, antiseptic wipes, and go behind the counter to see if you can get some morphine or oxycodone, topical antibacterial cream for post-pregnancy. Also some gauze and some instant ice packs. You'll have to walk, I might need the car if they take a turn for the worse."

I look over at Liz. She's unconscious now.

"Tristan?!"

"Yeah," I say, "I have no idea where the closest supermarket is."

"Your best bet is to head west back to the highway and go from there."

"I have no idea which way west is."

My dad points left against the wall.

"That way. Back the way we came, north to MacKenzie then west."

I nod.

"Don't we have stuff in the hockey bag?"

He shakes his head.

"We lost a lot of stuff when we left the hotel."

He looks at me. Eyebrows raise in confusion.

"What are you waiting for?! Go! Be careful, don't talk to anyone. Keep your gun visible at all times."

Deep breath of air in.

"Go now, before it gets dark."

I take one last look at my sister and niece, then turn for the door.

Colt pistol. Hunting knife.

I'm out the door holding the heavy weapon, almost pulling my shoulder down.

He's right; sky already turning shades of grey. Once again dropping the curtain across a blank backdrop.

Out onto the main road, circular two-lane street running around the entire campus. I keep to a slow jog so as not to exhaust myself entirely.

Most of the buildings newly barren. The odd person catches my glance. Lush green trees encase everything in an unnatural standstill, like the oxygen in the air has ceased to move. Sirens wail off in the distance. Smoke creeps into the air.

Start to pass some larger sports buildings, a gym. Signs for field hockey turfs. A car rolled over in one of the parking lots, windows smashed. A line of trees toilet papered. Newspapers strewn across the street, boxes smashed, litter everywhere.

Even the pragmatism of academia couldn't survive this chaos.

The past four days replay in my head. As if nothing ever happened before Friday. As if nothing prior to Friday even matters. The day everything turned off. I wonder what they'll end up calling it. They always have a name for it in the movies. Day

Zero. Day One. The Day of Disconnect. The Reboot. The Start
of the End.

Either way, none of it matters.

*I am an uncle.*

That's all that matters now.

Campus breaks into a residential road. I pass the parking lot
by the same stadium, on the other side this time. Burnt cars
smoke away like fried food sizzling on a stove.

A car speeds by on the road, so fast I can't discern the
colour.

Make my way onto MacKenzie Avenue. Four lanes.
Deserted. Black lines of concrete patching clutter the highway.
Faded yellow dividers. Stoplight hangs off, dangles down towards
the ground like a dislodged tooth.

As I walk west, another car speeds by. I don't make eye contact. I keep the Colt visible, an announcement of antagonism.

I am willing to be violent.

Head on a swivel.

Another car.

My mind's trying to figure out where to start. To begin sort-
ing this all out. My sister gave birth to a daughter. I no longer
work for a major pharmaceutical company. I may never return to
Seattle. Will I ever see Brianne again?

I have committed multiple felonies—*murder*. Will I stand trial
for my crimes?

It all leads to one question.

But I don't know what it is yet.

The only thing I know for sure is that if Brad gets in the way
of my father again, he will kill him.

There is no doubt he will take his life to protect his daughter
and granddaughter now.

Up ahead, I make out a strip mall. Look both ways, cross the
street at a brisk jog.

Tuscany Village. Three-storey condos, light pink and white
buildings. Ali Baba Pizza. Thrifty Foods. Shelbourne Pet Clinic.
Monk Office. Liquor Store. Pharmasave.

Bingo.

Errant bruised fruit scattered around the parking lot. Boxes of oranges rotting, breakfast cereal and crushed bags of chips. The liquor store's windows smashed, cases of beer all over the ground, spilling foamy alcohol into the gutters. The pet clinic, untouched.

Into the Pharmasave, sliding doors busted wide open. I stop, look around, hold the Colt up and survey the space from the front entrance. The surreal feeling of holding a gun with every intention of shooting it if need be.

Half the store is fine. The other half's a mess. Like a bouncing ball of unruliness ripped through the aisles randomly, leaving some racks untouched, others destroyed. Slew of pills litter the floor, myriad whites and reds. What looks like thousands of Tylenols and Advils.

I grab a couple shopping bags from the front counter. Registers smashed, a few crumpled colour bills scattered across the floor.

Back to the pharmacy. I search through. No oxycodone, figures, but a few vials of morphine. I find syringes, thinking my dad probably knows how to inject properly. Cotton swabs, antibacterial cream, antiseptic wipes, anything that looks like it could help, I grab.

Baby formula, soother, a baby bottle, diapers. Pretty soon my hands are full.

I hear a sob. Childlike.

Drop the bags instinctively and pull out the Colt.

Turn around, 360 degrees. Gun leads the way.

Another sob. It's from the corner, the vitamin aisle.

"Hello?"

I walk over.

Huddled in a display is a small boy, the whites of his eyes staring towards me as he sits with knees up to the chest.

I lower my weapon.

"Hey," I say.

No answer.

Put the Colt down on the ground. Both his knees scraped. He's been crying for what looks like days.

"Hey buddy, I'm not going to hurt you. What's your name?"

I come up close, his eyes widen. I slow and get down on one knee. Place my hands up in a non-threatening manner.

"Hey buddy, it's okay, I'm not going to hurt you, I promise."

He looks at me. Blonde locks fall across his forehead. Blonde, like me. Crystal blue eyes and freckles. Handsome young man in the making.

"What's your name? My name is Tristan," I say as slowly as possible.

My experience with young kids is minimal at best, and speaking to him like he might be a foreigner is possibly not the best idea.

"Sean."

I smile.

"Sean, I'm Tristan."

"Hi Tristan," he says, hesitantly. Packages of opened crackers and chips spread around him on the floor.

"Sean, where are your parents?"

He shakes his head.

"You don't know? When did you last see them?"

"I dunno, like yesterday? We came in, he told me to stay here. Then there was an explosion outside."

Fuck.

"So you've been here overnight?"

"Yeah, in the store."

"Are you hungry?"

He shakes his head.

"I ate some chips."

I smile.

Come closer. He backs up, scared again.

"Hey Sean, don't worry. I'm not gonna hurt you, okay? I'm gonna try to help you find your mom and dad."

"It's just my dad," he says.

"Oh," I say. Not sure if I should prod, might bring up an uncomfortable situation.

This conversation needs lightening.

"Sean, do you play any sports?"

"Soccer."

"Soccer, who's your favourite player?"

"Lionel Messi."

My soccer knowledge is not deep. I know Messi plays for Barcelona and that's about it.

"So who do you play soccer for?"

"I play for Bays United."

"Oh yeah, what position?"

"Striker. Sometimes I play midfield."

"Striker, nice. A goal scorer, I like that."

I stand up.

"Sean, do you want to come with me? I can try to help you find your dad."

He nods, stands up slowly, walks over to me and the bags. I realize I've made this decision without thinking it through.

"Okay, can you help me carry these bags? We can go back to my sister's place; my dad is there, and my sister just had a baby."

For whatever reason these words calm him, elevating his trust in me. He picks up one of the bags. I pick up the Colt and the other bag; we walk out of the Pharmasave.

Skies still nebulous, grey tinting everything with a shallow pigmentation. I wonder if I'll ever get used to this new background.

"Okay, Sean, let's cross the street, okay?"

He nods.

What the fuck am I doing? I basically just adopted a son. I'm in way over my head. We jog across. He drops the bag halfway. I hear its contents empty onto the pavement.

"Shit."

"I'm sorry," he says, bending over to pick them up.

"It's okay, buddy, no big deal."

I bend over, help him put the things back in.

I hear a horn, sounding over and over.

A car speeds down the road.

Swerves into the other lane. For some reason I instinctively stand in front of Sean, point the Colt at the car as it zooms by, honking profusely. Sean ducks behind me.

The car speeds out of sight.

I don't hesitate; I continue packing the bag up again. Then I start jogging to the sidewalk. Sean follows.

"I'm sorry."

"It's okay, buddy," I say, handing the bag back to him.

Is this what parenting feels like?

Sean points at the gun in my hand.

"Is that yours?"

I nod.

"Have you killed anyone?"

Fuck. Me.

Levees of emotion about to burst.

I plug the hole.

"Just bad guys," I say, smiling.

We continue walking. I keep Sean close. Try to keep the conversation light, but also glean information from him. He starts to loosen, talks more freely.

He went to the Pharmasave with his dad. His mom hasn't been around for a while; she left and moved to Calgary. I'm filling in the blanks the best I can. Sean went into the store; his dad went out to check something and never came back. I'm not sure if he was abandoned, or if his dad met some unfortunate fate.

Either one is not good.

Sean just turned eight. He plays soccer and is an only child. Lives in some area called Oaklands. His dad works. He had a girl-friend for a while but she doesn't come around anymore.

We make it onto campus, follow the same route back. Sean stares at the burning cars in the stadium parking lot.

"What happened?"

"Someone lit them on fire."

"Why?"

"I dunno. I think they were mad at someone."

"Who?"

"I dunno. Maybe God."

He nods like he somehow understood my response.

My parenting skills need work.

"You have a sister?"

"Yeah, she just gave birth to her daughter. I have a niece. Do you have any cousins?"

"Yeah, they live in Vancouver, but my dad and I don't see them very often."

Once again sounds like this kid comes from a pretty broken home. He seems well adjusted, all things considering. Still lacking the corruption of a young teenager. The fact that he looks strikingly similar to me at that age is fucking with my head. I'm thinking how 10-year-old Tristan would take the end of the world.

We get up to the complex. Knock on the door.

Footsteps down the stairs. Azure umbra falls in, polarized lens hue almost at maximum power. It's moments from a sunless dusk.

"Tristan?" says my dad through the door.

"Yeah."

It opens. My dad stands there with the shotgun.

"You okay?" he says, and notices Sean. "Who the fuck is this?"

I scrunch my face in displeasure.

"This is Sean; he lost his dad a day ago. I found him in the Pharmasave."

"You found a kid in the Pharmasave and decided it would be a good idea to bring him back here?"

Sean watches us converse in elevating levels of anxiety.

"He lost his fucking dad."

Abandoned. Like Brad. Left his blood to fend for himself.

Confused and filled with questions that will never be answered.

The one person in every boy's life that's needed for the proper creation of a man.

"So?"

I look at Sean like I should've covered his ears for that response.

"He's coming in," I declare.

My dad glares at us both.

We stand in silence. Sean still holding his bag.

My dad backs off. We walk in, up the stairs. He's cleaned the place up, let some light and air in through the windows. Scrubbed down the hallway and the bathroom. Cleaned the area where his granddaughter was born. I can't imagine the thoughts running through his mind at that time.

Liz is sitting up, holding her daughter in her hands.

"Tristan?"

"Hey Liz."

"Dad said you were here."

"Yeah, I went to get supplies."

My dad empties the bags out on the floor, starts looking through them.

"Good job, Tristan."

I nod.

"And who is this?" says Liz, looking at Sean.

"This is Sean," I say, putting my hand on his shoulder. "I found him at the Pharmasave."

It comes out like a joke but nobody laughs. Liz smiles.

I sit down on the bed beside her. My niece squirms in my sister's arms. Liz still looks about a gallon short of $H_2O$ and a quart short of oxygen. Eye sockets sucked back into her face. Skin cloth washed a pale amber. Sweat-stained hair.

"This is Jessica," she says, turning the baby towards me.

My mother's name.

Tears leave my eyes without consent.

"Do you want to hold her?" she asks, holding Jessica out.

The baby comes into my arms, wrapped in a towel. My dad must've cleaned her off. Her eyes look into mine, an expression-less face. I don't know what to do or say. Should I rock her gently, or hold her up close?

"I'm glad you guys came," says Liz.

I nod.

"Me too."

Liz is crying.

"I didn't know what to do," she says between tears.

My dad sits on the bed beside her, caresses her hair, brushes it out of her face. He turns, motioning for me to give the baby back to Liz. I do, as carefully as I have ever done anything in my life.

"Tristan, can I talk to you in the living room?"

I look at Sean. He's sitting on the edge of the bed. He seems happy to be in the company of others.

"It's okay," says Liz. She turns to Sean. "Hi Sean, do you want to hold the baby?"

We all look at each other. My dad leaves the room. I follow. He walks to the edge of the space, as physically far away from Liz and Sean as the floor plan of the house will allow. Turns to me, looks like he's going to speak but stops himself.

Bites his lip.

"Please tell me why you felt the need to bring that child back here?"

I glare at him.

"Because he was lost, and his father was gone. His dad's not coming back. The kid had been there for more than a day."

"This child is not our problem. Liz and Jessica are."

"He needed help, Dad. What would you expect me to do?"

"We can't afford to look after someone given our situation right now."

"It's not about that. This kid needed my help. I wasn't prepared to abandon him."

He nods, but not an understanding kind of nod.

"He could jeopardize our family."

I mull a response. I'm defending a young boy I've known for less than two hours.

"He needs someone to take care of him. After all the shit I've done in the past few days, the lives we've destroyed, the people we've *murdered* . . ."

I trail off as my emotions get the better of me.

We stand there, together, father and son.

"After all I've done, I don't want to forget that I'm human. We're not fucking animals."

"We did what we *had* to do."

"Yes, but that doesn't mean I can't do this, too."

Sean will not survive on his own in this new world.

He needs someone to look after him.

He needs someone *not* to abandon him.

My father nods.

I don't know what he's thinking. I never really do. But I'm sure he's trying to find the good in what I did, however misplaced or misguided it was.

Puts his hand on my shoulder.

"Okay."

And it's all he says before he turns around. I stop him with my words.

"What about Brad? Should we tell Liz about Brad?"

He shakes his head.

"Not now. She doesn't need that stress, not in her state. We need to sleep, get to the Navy base."

Turns and heads back into the room, rubbing his separated shoulder in displeasure.

I follow. Sean's holding the baby, rocking it slightly back and forth. Go figure.

"I'm going to sleep in here with Liz and work on getting her some of this medication and food. Tristan, you and Sean can sleep in the living room on the futon."

Another futon. Excellent.

My dad takes the baby from Sean, closes the door behind us.

"Daybreak, we go," he says through the wood.

Sean and I walk into the living room. There's a bunch of blankets and pillows on the floor by the futon. My dad thought this through.

Might be good to focus on something else before I share a bed with a boy I just adopted from a drug store.

"Sean, do you want some food?"

He nods.

I rummage through the hockey bag. Some chips and jerky, Vitamin Water. He munches down like a ravenous little animal. Too tired and scared to eat alone—but now he's filling his tummy.

While he eats on the living room floor I set up the bed.

Am I atoning for my sins with this kid? After all this, why on earth do I feel the need to look out for someone? Do we do good to try and erase the bad? Can we be good and bad all in the same sentence?

I shoo the thoughts away like a pesky fly.

Fate, karma. None of that applies anymore. This kid needs help; I will give it to him, because inside the core of me, it feels like the right thing to do.

"Where are we going tomorrow?" he asks, jerky dangling off the side of his mouth as he chews.

"The Navy base. We think it might be a good place to go."

"Why would we go to the Navy base?"

"I think because it might have power, run on diesel instead of electricity, like a car on gas."

Sean continues to eat, content with the information he's received. I come over and munch on some chips with him, pour some fluid down my throat. Take a deep breath of air in.

If there was a TV, we would've turned it on by now. But there's no power. Once again, I'm left with my thoughts, and a young boy who may never see his parents or family again.

Five days ago I was worried about the elevation in rent at my apartment, about setting up a dinner with Brianne, about preparing a communications strategy PowerPoint to outline third quarter media results. I was supposed to give that presentation today.

"I went on a submarine," says Sean.

"That's cool. What was that like?"

"It was fun; I got to look through the periscope. And they have bunk beds where everyone sleeps. They're really small. I used to sleep in a bunk bed."

I nod. Bunk beds, okay. His conversation like improvisational jazz.

Sean munches. I open some cans of fruit for him with the hunting knife, thinking about my dad opening food for me yesterday at the hotel.

We sit, eat in silence. Sean's appetite increases in intensity. He's obviously been running on stress the past few days and has realized his body is starving.

The more I eat, the more tired I get. Sean's belly starts to bloat as he shovels peanut butter into his mouth. Worried he might have a sugar high and be up all night. I stand and get into the bed, propping the pillow against the end of the futon. I don't get under the sheets; I just lie there.

Sean doesn't hesitate; he gets into the bed, leaving the food on the ground, and crawls under the sheets. The light has retreated, leaving us in a room full of unfilled shadows and dark corners.

"I'm excited to go to the Navy base tomorrow," he says. "I hope my dad is there."

I nod. Reassurance is needed now, however untruthful it might be.

"I'm sure your dad is there, and if he's not, he's probably on his way."

This Navy base. My father has us on a route. A pipe dream maybe. But something to aim for. For now, it will have to do.

</>

The dark. Devoid of the white.

No light to wake. No sun to shine through the window.

Just black. Just nothing.

Someone touches me.

Eyes open to my father. His hand on my shoulder.

"Tristan, the light came up early. We need to go."

Blink a few times. Look over. Sean isn't in the bed beside me.

"Where's Sean?"

"They're in the car. Let's go."

"Why didn't you wake me up?"

"I tried; you were out cold. Figured I'd give you a few extra minutes while I packed everything up."

Rub the sleep from the eyes. Hangover without the fun. High sugar-glucose levels crashed me to sleep. I've woken to a combination of sweats and pains. Headache. Groggy. Tired. I want bed so badly. Sleep pulling me back to the sheets.

"Tristan, let's go, now."

Roll out of bed, into my shoes. I'm down out the door following my dad in a matter of seconds.

Opaque scrim. This is my new morning, this white beast. Gone are shots of caffeine, long showers and microwavable muffins. Replaced with the sour taste of displeasure.

Liz sitting in the back of the car, door open, legs out, holding Jessica. Sean stands there like Sean apparently does, not sure what to do, waiting for instruction. Maybe he thinks his obedience will let him slide into this family, become a Schultz somehow.

"Okay," says my father. "Tristan, you're in the front seat. Sean in the back with Liz."

Nobody seems ready to argue.

We drive out of the parking lot.

A black pickup truck littered with scratch marks stops us.

Front door opens.

Brad staggers out, dressed in civilian clothes. Baseball bat in hand.

He drops it down like a tomahawk on the hood of the car.

Wood puncturing metal.

We all flinch.

"Motherfuckers! That's my kid in there!"

Looks like he hasn't slept in weeks. Like he's been through Hell and back to get here, then realized he'd left his keys and had to go back for them. Like he mugged some guy for that pickup truck too.

My dad's taking off his seatbelt. Holding his shoulder as I can hear cartilage grinding bone. He's in no condition to fight this morning.

This is now *my* war.

I grab his shirt. He turns to me.

"Dad. Stay in the car."

Before he can respond, I'm out the side. Brad faces me, baseball bat in hand.

I need to even this up.

"What's up, jarhead? Baseball bat, huh? Thought you were tough. Can't fight me one-on-one? What are you, cruiserweight, light heavyweight?"

Stares at me. Eyes fill with petroleum ready to be lit.

The bat rattles off the pavement.

I hold my hands up, take a breath of oxygen deep into my lungs; exhale slowly. Clench my fists.

Hot wash of terror rushes over me like a tsunami at a million miles an hour; it's cleansing my thoughts, turning me into a blank slate.

I'm gone.

No longer present. Third person in my body.

I *am* violence.

Back to simpler times. In bed with Brianne. Staring into her eyes as we hid from the world, ignoring the universe for a while.

The times when things actually made sense.

My oasis. I'll forever be under the sheets with her.

Cutting my heart open.

Letting it bleed.

Exhale.

Brad's skull smashes off the hood of the pickup.

His body falls to the ground, limbs first, core perplexed at its destination.

He tries to speak, but coughs out bloody chips of teeth instead.

My knuckles sting.

Veins pulse with savage, predatory blood.

Chest heaves as I pick up the bat.

Across his back. Wood breaking bone. Crushing muscle against it.

He howls in pain.

Again, for good measure. His body taps out; the feeling of breaking a hundred mile an hour swing of a bat against a human body shockwaves through me like a victorious concussion.

I stand, regain my breath.

My dad steps out of the car.

Looks at me. Looks at Brad.

Raises his gun to Brad.

I watch him stare down the father of his daughter's baby through the sight of a loaded weapon ready to fire.

The baby he wiped bile from last night. The baby whose eyes he finally looked into after all this fucking chaos. Her father on his hands and knees, bloody eyes looking up.

"Not like this," Brad says to me. "Not in front of Liz."

</>

Drive off campus onto McKenzie Avenue, past the Pharmasave. I don't say anything. Sean sits in silent compliance, like speaking might incriminate him in this assault.

Past the church, people still waving signs outside.

I'm panting like a dog. Adrenaline taints the bloodstream. Heart trying to slow down the valves, close the pipes, squeeze some calmness into the tendons.

"Breathe," says my dad. "Just breathe."

My father's hands tight around the steering wheel. He's about to find out if his luck will pay off.

I look back at Liz.

"How you doing?"

"I'm okay. My stomach really hurts. I don't feel good, at all. Who was that?"

"Nobody," I say. "It was nobody."

"Was that Brad? I thought I heard Brad's voice."

"No, honey, it wasn't. Don't worry," says my dad.

Liz needs to keep her heart rate down or she will never make it.

Hold my hand back, bloody knuckles and all. She reaches forward and takes it.

So cold, so weak.

"It's good to see you," I say.

"It's good to see you too, Tristan."

We pass over the Patricia Bay Highway. An apartment complex to the north burns to the ground.

Shopping malls, McDonald's, Quiznos, Tim Hortons. Windows smashed. Cars left in random, odd places.

Translucent wan sky. As pale as my sister.

Blank screen of sins and counterparts.

Everlasting reminder of what suddenly transpired and left us all without an explanation. We encountered the Rapture and not a single soul taken to Heaven.

Southwest to the Trans-Canada Highway on Admirals Road. A bad intersection to begin with. Stop lights on the highway are never a good idea. Centred in grassy fields off to one side; trees spill down a large embankment. A cut of greenery within the sprawl of the city. One field appears to have held a small fire, grass singed to a crisp.

The road's a mess. Cars everywhere. Turned over, doors open. A truck curved inwards, frame bent to shit. Crumpled four-door Nissan with no hood. Shards of glass, diamond sparkles litter the rubble.

Ambulance on its side nearby. Medical supplies strewn out the back.

We weave around the placed cars, abandoned in God's sand-pit, never to be played with again.

There's no traffic.

Craigflower Bridge. A lineup of vehicles about halfway through. Up ahead is what looks like a military checkpoint.

I let out a massive sigh of relief.

Order within chaos—located.

Your search revealed one file.

We stop on the bridge. I see the enormous army vehicles massed behind the fortified concrete roadblocks. Barbed wire over the fences like vines. I look down to the water, streaming into the ocean. The amount of precipitation in the last few days has made it animated, robust with colour and movement as it flows.

My father turns.

"Sean, you take the baby. Come with me up front. I don't want Liz going anywhere, and I want to make sure they know that we need to get in right away with a newborn. Tristan, stay in the front."

Liz carefully hands the baby to Sean, who holds her up tight to his chest.

The door closes. I look back to Liz. I smile. Not sure what to say. Liz jumps in.

"Dad told me you guys came all the way from Seattle."

"Yeah."

"Wow."

Liz nods, starts to cry softly.

"I mean, thanks," she says.

My sister. Mother to a new generation of Schultzes. Something for us to gather around. A flame to light our way.

Family.

This is my purpose.

Not some techno-junkie tied to a status update.

A brother.

A son. An uncle.

Part of something tangible.

My blood.

Emotions pour out of my mouth without any filter. The words come before I can comprehend what I'm saying. Open like a fresh wound.

"I'm sorry I've been such a bad brother," I say. "I never should have left you guys like that, run away after high school."

Liz looks at me. Tears cloud her eyes. This time, she reaches for my hand.

"It's okay, I understand why you did it. Why you had to go and be on your own, make your own life."

I nod. The best apology acceptance I will ever receive.

Something catches my eardrums.

Rumbling.

The pavement shakes.

I look back.

Black pickup truck covered in scratch marks barrels into the back of our car.

The car moves, universe shakes my body.

Life does not slow down, does not flash before my eyes.

Liz screams.

Thrown violently against the window.

Flash of white sky. Car turns, then falls without my consent.

Metal punctures my leg. Skin tears under the pressure. Calf rips open. I'm winded and can't yell.

The taste of my own blood. Again.

The water.

My stomach tries to jump into my lungs as we plummet. Gravity and I fall out of favour.

The water is coming.

*Du Maurier Signatures in an ashtray. Rye whisky. Tired looking, worn beige carpeting. A man sleeps alone on a couch in a home. Throw blanket, pillow without cover sheet.*

*TV flashes melodramatic, chromatic colours into the black pitch of the room.*

*He snores. Nasal decompression to the left nostril after a junkie swung a rock at his face. Perks of the job.*

*Cigarette dangles between his fingers. He's draped over a couch too small for his long frame.*

*Sleeping off something.*

*The dying ash of the smoke breaks off, dropping the filter onto the carpet.*

*It sits, smoking. Grey chemicals lift off, cancerous snowflakes.*

*Fire, hush of blue and red. Grows exponentially, hovers across the floor, consuming the dusty dry fabric in an instant.*

*Now the whole room is red hot with carpet glue-fuelled flames. Orange kamikaze dances of heat.*

*The man wakes up, first slowly, then quickly. Panics.*

*"Fuck."*

*Drapes light up, ground engulfed.*

*Darts to the kitchen and rips the fire extinguisher off the wall, metal holdings bust off, fling into the air like throwing stars.*

*A dragon spraying white powdered mist everywhere.*

*It's too late; the white clumpy smoke simply blocks his vision. Heat pulsating into his skin.*

*Walls start to bleed fire. Framed pictures fall to the ground. A group of plants sitting in the corner almost spontaneously combust before enveloping in a rapid oxidation of chemical combustion.*

*A cat darts through the room and is out the dog door in a flash.*

*Heads up the stairs. Three at a time. Around the corner.*

*Young blonde boy comes out of his room rubbing the sleep from his eyes. Teenage Mutant Ninja Turtles T-shirt. His father swoops him up* with one hand around the waist. The boy is winded. Lets out noises, questions as he's carried.

But it's futile. He's going outside. Now.

The father kicks the door open. Flames follow, extinguished by the cold night. The boy sees fire, instantly understands the severity of the situation.

They're out on the lawn.

"Dad, what's going on?"

"Stay here!"

The boy looks at him in protest.

An explosion erupts from inside the house, startles both of them.

"You stay here, you hear me!"

The boy stands in silent, frozen acknowledgment.

The man runs back into the house. Greeted by a monstrous wave of heat. Fire unleashed, given gobs of oxygen and inanimate objects with which to create chemical change.

Runs up the stairs. Foot bursts through one step, flames crawling along the banister, scurrying up the painted walls, feasting on the granular solids. Pulls his foot out. Splinters jab upwards into his ankle.

Lets out a lion roar.

Up again, crawling now. A piece of splintered wood the size of a kitchen knife rips apart his veins and muscles.

He turns the corner and stands, using the wall as a crutch.

Flames cornering him in the hallway.

Sees two closed doors. Hears two female voices, one old, one young.

Steps to the closest one and opens it with his shoulder.

His young daughter standing on her bed. She's crying. He picks her up, underneath his arm. Turns back to the hallway. Looks down one way.

A wall of fire. A woman stands on the other side.

"David, help me!" the older female voice says.

"I'll come back for you!"

Heads back to the stairs, engulfed in flames. In a flash he heads into the bathroom. Fist breaks the window with a boxer's quickness.

Clears the glass shards from the frame with his unclothed arm, winces in pain as melting skin mixes with amorphous solid material.

Puts his daughter out the window, onto the ledge. He follows, barely fitting through. Leads her down to the one-storey drop into the backyard. Kneels beside her.

"Honey, I'm going to jump down, and you need to jump right after, okay?"

"No, I can't!" Tears across her face, matting her blonde hair.

"Baby, please listen to daddy. I need you to do this for me; you need to be brave here, okay. Be brave for me."

Pulls off the edge and lets himself go.

His leg breaks, wood penetrating skin and cartilage.

Another roar of pain.

"Daddy?!"

"Baby, jump!"

She cries, but trusts her father. Jumps into his arms.

He catches her but crumbles to the ground. Another bone snaps. Distressed howl leaves his mouth.

He asks his daughter if she's okay. She is.

Heads up the back porch. It belongs to the flames now.

The house now belongs to the fire.

Forgoes logic and continues to try and head inside, on one leg. But the heat won't let him.

He has to cover his face. Howls in pain. Eyebrows, hair singes off. Clothes war torn with ash. His skin bubbles with heat.

He'll kill himself if he continues.

He cannot enter, unless he wants to end his own life.

Limps back down the stairs.

Turns and looks at the house as the foundation starts to crumble.

The house more fire than home. Burning violently to the ground.

He stands on one foot, looking up to the second floor. Eyes water over. Daughter stands beside him, staring up at the chaos that was once their sanctuary.

A sense in his eyes as he looks up, barely able to stand.

A sense of helplessness.

In every sense of the word.

</>

Star brightens. Solar limbs, energy acquittal. Joules of plenary light amplify exponentially. Ash protoplasm clouds the cerebral cortex. Ejecting electron bursts, ions and atoms as blossoming spring flowers through coronal planes. Dangling across the brainstem.

Violent screams, millions of degrees running rampant. Astral flares implode into the atmosphere, pockets of white-hot plasma heat to tens of millions of Kelvins. Neurones spit fire like oil-drenched pistons, sporadic valves run amok, spew in all directions, correcting, trying desperately to recover.

Radiation dancing across electromagnetic spectrums.

Flare of the sunspot, fanatical magnetic fields penetrate the photosphere, linking to the solar interior. Tight connections loosen; ascending tracks plummet, arousing the senses before blacking them out. Coronal mass injections, x-rays and ultraviolet radiation pulsate to the ionosphere in miasmas of ruby red.

Carbon dioxide dilutes the bloodstream. Cytoskeleton destruction, nitric oxide poisoning. Helixes aggressively expanding; herds trampling outward from the most active regions of a bright yellow star. Mega electron volts. Roar so powerful the mathematical makeup must be rewritten.

Atoms annihilated, ripped open like lungs of prey ravaged by a pack of bloodthirsty animals. Figures appear and disappear in roundabout fashion, circular carousels of dying cells. Oxygen saturation, compromising vascular integrity. A female figure. Maternal. Delicate fingers run through each hair follicle. Brimming to the edge with grace. She sends you away. From the dark.

Back to the light.

Pfizer is a healthcare company that's dedicated to helping you live a healthier life. We believe that to be truly healthy, it takes more than medication. That's why, in addition to discovering and providing innovative medicines, we're committed to helping you lead a healthy balanced life.

Maintaining health and well-being starts with the small things you do, every day. Gaining knowledge is an important step in staying healthy. In this section, you'll find valuable information you need to be able to manage your own health better. Because one of the best things you can do for yourself is to learn more, so you can become a recurring customer of chronic infliction.

The machine pumps oxygen into the blood. A singular note, playing over and over—one continuous cord. Ambient hums. Ash fires so far in the distance they only light the horizon.

So much black it drowns the dark matter, stains with an oily residue, seeping into every corner. Lungs try to squeeze water intake outwards, ridding themselves of hydrogen. Heart injected with carbon dioxide venom.

Murmurs, shaking, trembling as it tries to recover. Pushes the toxicity away from the valves, crawls to the surface. Swimming in air.

Fuzziness.

Dizziness.

Blurriness.

A figure submerges, reappears. Black dots crawl to the corners of the vision like bugs evading the open. Four lines, four walls. White hot lights, tubes. The feeling of bed sheets.

Voices.

The presence of another human.

Touch on the forearm. Hair stands on end.

I try to speak.

Vowels.

Nothing but vowels.

Someone's breath close to my face.

A circular figure, a head.

"Tristan?"

I've regained the ability to blink.

I try to respond.

Still vowels, but ended with a consonant.

A hand on the forehead.

"Tristan?"

The body turns and yells. It's a boy, a young boy.

"He's waking up! Tristan's waking up!"

The boy drops down from the bed, runs out of the room.

The most satisfying cough I've ever coughed.

Mucus and phlegm pour out of the mouth and nostrils. Dripping down onto my chin.

"Holy *fuck*."

I blink again. And again. Trying to rewrite my vision.

I'm waking.

Waking from the darkest slumber imaginable.

Anesthesia of the mind.

Oxygen.

I'm breathing.

I'm living.

The boy comes back, dragging a taller woman behind him into the room.

"He's awake! Look!"

It's Sean.

Behind him, a nurse.

I look over.

"Hi," is what comes out of my mouth for some reason.

Sean leans into me.

"Tristan, are you awake?"

"I think so."

He looks back at the nurse, a middle-aged woman.

Where the fuck am I?

"Are you okay, Tristan?" says Sean.

"Yeah . . . I think so."

The nurse puts her hand on his shoulder.

"Sean, step back a bit. He's going to be very sensitive."

Sean steps back, looks at the nurse.

"Go get his sister and his father."

My sister. My father.

The car. The bridge. Brad.

Sean darts from the room, gone in a flash.

"Where am I?"

"Tristan, my name in Marilee. You're at the Esquimalt Navy base. You were in a coma."

"A coma?"

"Yes," she says, looking over my chart. "For thirty-three days."

Okay then.

"My sister, my father, they're okay?"

"Yes, your father was able to save both of you from the car. Your leg is in bad shape, though."

I sit up and look down.

Bandages. Still two feet, though.

"Is Jessica okay? The baby? Where is my dad, and my sister?"

She sits down on the chair beside me.

"All of your questions will be answered, I promise. You need to keep your heart rate steady right now. I promise you: everyone is safe and sound."

She checks my pupils with a mini-flashlight. Runs her finger across the vision, tells me to follow it.

"Do you know your last name?"

"Schultz."

"Good."

"Do you know the capital of British Columbia?"

"Victoria."

"Good."

She stands up.

"I'm going to get you some water. Just relax. Everything is going to be okay."

Marilee leaves the room.

Holy. Fuck.

</>

Canadian Forces Base—Esquimalt. A section of buildings up and running on diesel power generated by the ships at the dockyard. Mobile medical unit, and a full-blown hospital with an emergency ward by the Dockyard Administrative buildings. The Navy had sectioned off most of the peninsula at various checkpoints.

Up north on Island Highway, where the train tracks crossed. Down the east coast at Craigflower Bridge and Tillicum Road along the Gorge Waterway. The Bay Street and Johnston Street Bridges heavily fortified, allowing only foot passage to the hospital.

The massive floodlights at night defined the horizon. A dozen or so, up a hundred feet in the air. High intensity artificial beams carrying luminosity down from the hospital to the streets.

In the starless night they act as Mecca, a point where you can look up to see the refraction off the roof of the world, as if the closer you were, the safer you felt.

The Navy was treating whomever they could. Running disaster relief supplies through the city, though the work was like putting Band-Aids on bullet wounds.

The first few days mostly a fog. Somewhere between the worst hangover of my life and post-concussion symptoms. Memories came back, some escaped.

The first night I couldn't remember where I went to university.

Or Brianne.

But she returned, took her place in the corner of my mind. Continued to haunt me.

The peninsula was so picturesque. Towering Garry oaks and endless shores of driftwood and kelp. Quiet waves through the night, lining the updated period homes spaced apart by backyard fences.

Down here, on the edge of the mouth of the Pacific, behind the muscle of the Navy, I begin to feel safe for the first time since this mess started. The quiet streets, the hum and amber glow of the base at night, an oasis in a new world of terror. My family, hiding in the corner of the planet, hoping the apocalypse might just pass us by.

My father found us a three-level renovated Tudor home on Plaskett Place, overlooking the ocean and Gillingham Islands. Some type of summer retreat, abandoned. Looked for pictures but couldn't find any. No trace of history.

Four bedrooms. Liz and Jessica on the top storey with my father. Sean and I on the ground level by the living room. Old wooden floors creaked with every step. It had more character than an 80-year-old war vet.

Dad scavenged some gas generators and hooked up the electricity and hot water. This meant power, but still no TV, internet, radio. There were a few DVDs in the house, mostly old classics—*Casablanca, Ben Hur, Gone with the Wind.*

Life went on without me for thirty-three days. My father joined up with the Navy police, running supplies and helping out with security in and around the hospital. But mostly he was with his daughter, tending to his granddaughter.

He pulled us from the car. First Liz. Then he came back and cut me loose. Dragged my unconscious body eighteen feet to the surface. Fucking superhero once again.

After he'd dragged us to safety, he went back and swam down Brad.

Two drenched cops fought bare knuckle on the shore.

My father with a separated shoulder.

Didn't matter. Grabbed Brad by the neck and shoved his face into the mud. Drowned him in a foot of murky water and motor oil.

Something fierce pushed him over the edge.

He'd told Brad if he ever came near his daughter again, he'd end him.

Man of his word.

Once and for all.

</>

Sean's father never surfaced.

Kid waited by my side for thirty-three days. Rarely left the room.

My father sat me down and laid everything out for me after the third day. Laid it out like it was never a question in the first place.

Sean had no one. I had made the decision to take him in, and now he was my responsibility. I was essentially his legal guardian. I was his father.

My dad gleaned enough information from him during my coma to determine that his father was a night shift worker, probably a functioning alcoholic. His mother left them to start another family in Calgary. Sean was parented by the union daycare and public school system.

My dad told Sean that he would probably never see his father again, and that he and I—if I woke up—would look after him.

After all the talk, all the late night arguments with Brianne about the merits and pitfalls of children, here I was. Father to an abandoned 8-year-old Canadian boy.

Sean liked to kick a soccer ball around, and I started to teach him how to box. Combinations and some body bag work at the Navy gym. He took to it like any athletic kid would. Started to push himself to learn more, to become a better fighter. To breathe between punches.

He didn't speak much about his father, or his mother. I wasn't sure if he was relishing his new family, or too washed up in this new world to fathom what had actually happened.

On the fourth day we walk over to Saxe Point Park to kick the soccer ball around. I'm not much good, but this was his sport, so now, essentially, it was my sport.

"Lionel Messi was the first player to score against every other team in La Liga in one season," he says, kicking the ball to me. "He's from Argentina. But he plays in Spain. He's the captain of the Argentina team though."

I kick the ball back with my toe; it veers off to one side and hits a parked car.

Sean laughs, runs to retrieve it.

"Don't toe-punt," he says as he ducks around a van to grab the ball.

Later, we walk back to the house. My father grills salmon on the backyard deck. Liz breastfeeds Jessica while Sean and I hit golf balls into the ocean, trying to land some on Gillingham Islands.

My leg still bothering me. The tendons repairing themselves. Thirty-seven stitches from calf to ankle. The nurse had me on antibiotics, and at night Sean helped me change the dressings in the tub when they got soaked in blood.

The following morning we walk east, where you can view downtown Victoria. My dad forbade us passing any of the Navy checkpoints. Said it wasn't safe. People still doing horrible things in the name of discomposure.

We make our way to the Esquimalt Power Boat Club, looking east to Fisherman's Wharf Park and Dallas Road. Pristine upper-crust mansions on the waterfront, windows boarded with wood.

Shades always drawn. Neighbours no longer our friends.

Most stayed inside all day, trying to wait whatever this was out. Like one day we'd all be magically back online, like customer service would show up, plug the cord back in and reboot our societal system.

But until that day we were back in the technological Dust Bowl.

We step down to the rocks, and I catch something out of the corner of my eye.

A body. Floating face down.

By the time I turn to Sean, he's seen it too.

"Is that a body?" he says, climbing down the rocks in excitement.

"Sean, be careful, don't get too close."

He gets to the water's edge. I follow.

A man. Bullet hole in his back, jacket blown open. By the looks of it, he's been there a few days.

"What happened to him?"

I come over to Sean, stand beside him. Put my hand on his shoulder.

"He got shot."

"By who?"

"I dunno."

Sean takes a step closer.

"Why would someone shoot him in the water?"

"I think they shot him, and then threw him in the water."

He nods. "Oh yeah."

I watch the body float with the tide, gently rocking back and forth.

Sean stares. I wish this wasn't a part of his memory now. Imbedded in his hard drive. I wish I could erase this.

Ctrl, Alt, Delete.

But it's too late. The damage is done.

"C'mon, buddy, let's go."

Sean turns to me, heads back up the rocks to the road.

</>

Residual effects of the coma nag at me.

Mostly memory loss. Errors being corrected within my brain, neuroplasticity hardwire routers trying to reconnect. Chunks of my past come and go. My time motor biking down the Indian Coast returns, as if replanted within my psyche like a software update.

I stop physically sometimes, try to allow my head the energy it needs to remember. Parts of my youth escape, earlier days, high school, people, friends I've met disappear. Reappear. My swollen thoughts trying to redraft themselves without the original document.

The headaches. Dizziness. Nothing I can't deal with. Our lives are slow here, hidden on the base in the trees and quiet cul-de-sacs of the peninsula. I try to stay outside. Keep breathing.

I wish the coma had wiped Brianne from my past, but after a while I realize that's a selfish thing to think. I need to remember her. For whatever reason is escaping me at this moment.

For two days I'd been walking normally. Able to put sufficient weight on my bad leg. Healing, slowly but surely.

My father takes me to see the Vice Admiral inside the Bickford Building. They've been running administrative duties out of there. Three of the main patrol frigates were overseas on the Gulf Coast when everything turned off, so they're in short supply of actual men.

He said I needed something aside from Sean. If I could help out, help us cement our place on the base, it would go a long way.

Toward what? What future?

Vice Admiral's a stout guy. Thick moustache, belly hangs over his belt. Little nametag across his desk. John Kincaide.

"The consensual opinion, all the way up to the Commander in Chief, is that what happened is the result of a major solar storm produced by the sun. Coronal mass injection."

Leans forward in his chair, looks over some papers.

"The on-base scientists think the sun went through some kind of 'one in a million' hiccup. Something it only does a handful of times before it becomes a red giant. I mean, this is just a theory. Don't even get me started on what the climatologists are saying . . . and our IT guys won't stop talking about this being some silly hack or computer breach. Either way, it looks like we've lost the one thing we really need in all of this—information."

He looks at a piece of paper on his desk, filling in for twenty years of technological advancement; it will have to do for now.

"We have power and hard line telephones, but still no short-wave. That sickness you feel, that's most likely the electromagnetic pulses in the air."

I look over to my dad, raise my eyebrows. Fucker was right.

Kincaide sips from his coffee, we're both lapping up the explanation like thirsty animals. He can see we're waiting for more. Kincaide stands up, walks over to a giant world map on his wall, and starts to motion like a weatherman in front of a green screen.

"So pretty much everything east of the Prime Meridian to the International Date Line is probably worse off, we think, as the pulse would've hit one side of the planet head on. Some places in the middle of the continent might have it better than we do. If they got lucky, they could still have large patches of power. Every satellite in the sky is gone though, which is the lynchpin of global communications."

I'm nodding. Taking it all in.

"So what does this mean?" I ask.

"Good question. Essentially we are on our own for the time being, at least until the solar storms die down. We're expecting some nasty electrical systems to roll in from the Pacific over the next few days, if in fact our calculations are true and this hit somewhere over the Atlantic. The Emergency Response unit is prepping for that as the next big hurdle here at CFB."

He coughs. Thumbs through some of the papers he's been fiddling with.

"Back in 1859 there was this event called the Carrington Event, which basically brought North America and Europe to its knees. We think this one was about a hundred times worse, like an earthquake just shook the whole world."

He goes back to his papers, makes his way to a page, then looks at me.

"Dave tells me you were in Public Relations in Seattle before the storm?"

I look at my dad, then back to the Vice Admiral.

"Yeah, for Pfizer."

"Good. We can always use good communications people."

PR. Back to the life. Back to the old. How long before I'm updating CFB's post-apocalyptic Twitter feed?

Fuck this. Seriously, fuck this.

"Um, I was thinking of getting into something else," I say.

They look at each other, taken aback.

Awkward silence.

"Did you have something in mind?"

Back to work. To the numbness. I need time to think. I don't want to start working because it's the thing to do at this moment in time. I'll play the injury card if I have to.

"I dunno yet, I'm still recovering from the coma. And my leg, I can barely walk. I don't know how much use I would be to you guys right now."

"Of course," says Kincaide. "Well, I'm sure you'll let us know when you figure it out, okay?"

"Yeah, for sure."

After we leave my father jumps all over me. Says I need to contribute. I tell him I need time. I can't waste this opportunity to find something better than Public Relations.

I tell him I wasn't happy in my previous life.

The statement sticks. He nods.

Lets it go.

Before the sunless dusk, Sean and I ride our bikes along Tyee Road and stop in at the library. I figure he needs to continue his schooling; as the Vice Admiral implied earlier, education's pretty far down on the rebuilding society list.

I get him some of the usual suspects—*To Kill a Mockingbird*, *Lord of the Flies*, *Catcher in the Rye*.

"Who's Brianne?" he asks, flipping through some magazines.

I look up from my book, startled. I'm starting to realize kids don't have much of a social filter. They tend to blurt out uncomfortable questions at random times.

"Brianne?"

"Yeah, you said her name a few times while you were sleeping."

Fuck, my unconscious mind, still wrestling with the breakup.

"Brianne was my girlfriend. In Seattle. But we broke up."

"Why did you break up?"

I rub my face, try to buy some time.

"You know, adult stuff, the usual."

Sean nods.

"My mom and dad broke up. She moved to Calgary."

The other thing I've learned is that 8-year-olds have a short attention span.

The sky still skeletal. Same blank backdrop every day. Sunset and sunrise at times no one at the base can track. Our planet thrown into a knuckleball rotation.

But at night, I swear every now and again I can see a star. A flash coruscate in the somber gloom.

Then again, I'm never sure.

</>

The body pulled upward.

Universe of water.

I can't breathe. I can't see. I can't hear.

Lungs burst.

Flooding.

Pfizer is inspired by a single goal: Your health. Since 1849, Pfizer has been dedicated to developing innovative medications to prevent and treat diseases. But we believe to be truly healthy, it takes more than medication. That's why Pfizer is also committed to promoting the many small things we can do to stay healthy.

With each new initiative, we strive to offer medication that allows a higher quality of life. One of enjoyment, a life in which our customers feel they are truly being taken care of. Because we know your health is paramount to your happiness, and our goal is your goal.

Eyes open.

The hum of generators below.

Sit up in bed, sweating.

It's the middle of the night.

I stand, walk out of the room.

To Sean's room.

Creak the door open.

He sleeps, head on his side, hand under the pillow.

I head to the living room, out onto the deck.

Black sky and dark blue ocean.

Quiet waves lap.

Landscape peripheral vision.

Head rush. Electrical superhighways run straight for the top of my cerebral cortex.

Vision blotches out.

I brace against the railing, let out a distressed noise.

Turn back and sit in one of the wicker chairs.

Heart pumps. Lungs heave.

The doctors said this would happen. The coma would linger. As my bleeding brain flushed the water and blood out, repaired itself.

I take slow breaths, trying to calm my mind.

Stare at the blank sky.

</>

On the backyard porch, changing the blood crusted and dried dressings on my leg. The stitches came out, but my calf still swells if I walk on it for more than fifteen minutes.

They say the good weather is supposed to end in a few days, and a massive storm will roll in from the west. Either way I'm enjoying the heat, even if it's sunless.

Liz rocking Jessica in her arms, leaning back in one of the wicker chairs. Our requisite meeting ground. The hum of the generators make living in the house feel like living above a subway system. We have to ration electricity. Only at night do we turn the power on, or to cook.

Plus we like the air, the blank stare of the Pacific Ocean.

My father down on the beach, teaching Sean how to fish. Showing him how to cast lines. Kid cut himself tying a rod earlier. Cried and then sat in my lap for a good hour, napping. I didn't know what to do so I just stayed still and let him sleep. Liz smiled at me, had a good chuckle at my awkwardness. Then Sean woke up and darted off like nothing had happened.

My shoulder still asleep from the weight of his head.

"Dad hasn't said much about how you guys got here," says Liz.

I'm not sure if she's asking for an explanation, or stating that she's okay with not knowing what went on between downtown Seattle and the University of Victoria.

"Yeah, I mean . . ."

I trail off, stop changing my dressing. Sit back.

"Yeah," I continue, "we did some things I don't think either of us are proud of."

Liz looks down at Jessica, asleep in her arms.

"I'm guessing you guys might not ever talk about it?"

I take in a breath of air.

"We did what we had to do to get to you, and that's all that matters. Maybe one day we'll talk about it. Down the road."

"Well, I appreciate it."

Jessica makes a noise. Liz adjusts the blanket she's wrapped in. Smiles. Looks back up, stares down at the water where Sean and my dad are casting lines.

"How're things with you and Dad, if you don't mind me asking?"

I'm taping up my dressing. I finish and take a sip from my beer.

"Good. I mean as good as it could be right now."

She nods.

"Well you two have lots of time to make up. Rebuilding, you know? We have nothing but time."

She's right. I still have no job. Sean and I hang out like lost boys on summer vacation. We scavenge. We save. Chances are this post-apocalyptic purgatory will be our life for some time before that changes.

"How are you doing?" I ask.

"Me?"

She looks startled. Inquisitive family talk new to the three of us, but we're trying.

"I'm good. Glad the pregnancy is done. It got tough there for a bit."

"Yeah, I bet."

I stare off into the Pacific. I know my father told Liz about Brad. I know she knows that I know. It's time to talk about it, to speak. After so many years of staying on the surface, neglecting the layers of our family and skimming across the shallows.

"Dad said he told you about Brad?"

Liz looks at me. Holds Jessica tight. Her downy black hair starting to come in.

"Yeah . . ."

A tear runs down her cheek. She tries to wipe it, smears it across her face.

"I'm sorry, I mean . . ."

Now I don't know what to say, but she does.

"You can say no a million times and make the right decision. But then you say yes once and it ends up defining the rest of your life."

I nod. "Yeah, I understand."

"I loved Brad, you know? I did. When we were good, we were really good."

She sniffs. Eyes still watering.

"But we can fall in love with people who aren't right for us."

The line echoes. Tattoos itself across my chest.

Liz holds Jessica tight in her arms.

"You haven't seen Brianne? Since all this happened?"

"No. The last time I saw her was for coffee about a week before the Friday everything turned off. We were supposed to go for dinner that weekend. I never got hold of her."

Liz nods.

"Brianne was nice, Tristan. I liked her. But I guess it wasn't meant to be."

"Yeah, looks that way."

Now I remember why I avoided this type of talk for so long. It isn't easy. Figure the best thing to do is lighten it back up again.

"How old is Jessica? I keep forgetting the days."

"Fifty days today."

"Fifty. Huh. Fifty days on the planet."

"Yeah," says Liz. "She's growing every single one of them."

Silence. We sit on the deck. I'm searching for words. Still the uncomfortable quiet, even with this person who shares my genetic makeup.

"I'm making peace with Brad," she says finally. "I'm not sure I'll ever make peace with the way he was killed, but I understand why dad did what he did."

One day Liz will have to tell her daughter that her grandfather killed her father. Beat him to his knees, pushed his face into the muddy waters until he stopped breathing. She will have to tell her little girl about the day her father ran her mother off a bridge, almost drowning her and her uncle in the process.

"Tristan?" says Liz.

She's looking right at me.

"Yeah?"

"I don't know if you feel the same . . ."

She trails off. Something swirling in her brain.

"I just, kind of . . . I don't feel like I ever got to know you," she says. "I don't remember as much as you from before the fire. And after, you left. And I forgive you for that; I get it. But do you think maybe we could work on that?"

Jessica makes a noise in her arms.

"Yeah," I say. Then, "Yes, totally."

Liz smiles.

"What do you want to know?"

She chuckles. "Everything, I guess."

"Okay," I say, smirking. "Where to start?"

"Traveling, maybe? Tell me what was it like in Southeast Asia, what did you see, what did you do? Tell me about the time you were away."

I nod. "Okay."

</>

*I watch my mother wrap her arms around my father's frame. Love. The word as foreign as anything to a young boy. But this was obviously it. She titled her head up to kiss him. He smiled and tilted his down.*

*She always looked happy nestled against his chest. Everyone said my mother was so smart, so intelligent. And here she was hugging this big bear. Everyone needs a place to feel safe, I guess.*

*We'd been walking the Cape Lookout State Park. Down in Portland for the weekend to visit my mother's parents, both in the twilight of their lives. My sister lags behind, drawing lines in the sand with a stick. Wrapped in my boxing club tracksuit, I practice lateral movements on the beach, hopping from side to side.*

*Hand in hand, they walk. A cop. An academic. Conviction. They worked for some reason. It didn't matter why.*

*Driftwood leads the way along the shore. Waves roll in, ambient metronome crashes. The wind tries to push us inwards. The smell of the sea, the endless Pacific Ocean.*

*"Tristan!"*

*Turn back to Liz. She's stopped to look at something.*

*Run back, hero to the rescue.*

*A crab, about the size of a dinner plate, washed ashore. It's backed up against a rock, claws out, pointing at my sister in a sign of aggression.*

*"Holy crap!" I say.*

*I have an insatiable need to poke this thing.*

*"No, Tristan, leave it alone."*

*Take the stick from my sister; jam it in the vicinity of the crab. Claws try to grab it.*

*I smirk, jab again.*

*"Tristan, leave it alone, it's scared."*

*I nod, stop. She's right.*

*"He needs to go back in the ocean," I say, handing the stick to my sister.*

*My parents have headed back; they walk up, still holding hands.*

*"Dad, it's a crab."*

*He comes in close.*

*"Red rock."*

*"He needs to go back in the ocean," says my sister, visibly distressed.*

*My father nods, comes in close to it from the side. Reaches down and grabs it with his mighty bear paw. Ten legs scramble around. My sister shrieks, my mother backs up. Hands cover her mouth.*

*My father walks towards the ocean, right up to the break.*

*Waits for the tide to wash in. Water runs around his steel-toe boots. I watch the way only a son can watch his father.*

*The water slides back out as he places the crab on the shore.*

*Ocean washing it back to the abyss through sheer force of nature.*

</>

Tonight is the anniversary of my mother's death. Before I left to travel after high school, we used to head to the ocean and make spiritual guidance boats every year. Paper vessels with candles in them, burning out to sea.

Liz started the tradition back up.

Tonight, facing south off the peninsula, insulated by the guard of the Navy, we're sending paper boats into the Pacific. We're supposed to write something we're looking for closure with and put it in the boat.

Before I left to travel, I always asked for my mother to return. Kept writing it over and over, year after year.

This time I ask Brianne for forgiveness. I tell her I love her, and I'm sorry it didn't work out. All the hurtful things I said in all the fights and arguments, I ask her to forgive me. I ask her to remember the fun times. The times when we were a partnership, two souls intertwined in life, love and sex. That I treasure every morning I woke up beside her. I tell her I have a son now, and that I will make sure he's raised properly.

I tell her I sinned; I've killed, but that I did it out of love.

I tell her I hope wherever she is, whoever she's with, she's happy.

I watch Sean push his boat out to sea with a stick. He sits on a rock half-submerged in water. Liz stands by my father, holding Jessica. Dad stands alert as his boat drifts off. The candle flickers against the white triangular and square sheets.

Later, we sit on the beach. My dad and I drink beer and smoke Cuban cigars he found in the basement. Watch the boats floating into the sea, the amber lights beacons against the palpable black. The waves lap against the shore, and the night is muted.

Starless skies.

</>

*I roll over in bed. I'm day-old sore from a sparring match at Rodney's yesterday, but it's a good sore. A sore a solid Sunday in bed hiding from the Seattle rain will fix before I prepare my body for another 60-hour work week at Pfizer.*

*Brianne comes into view, walking in from the kitchen in her bra and panties. Her blonde hair falls over her shoulders. Her hips move in a way only a woman's hips can.*

*It's the most beautiful thing I've ever seen.*

*She's holding a bowl of Froot Loops.*

*Gets into the bed, seated against the back wall. Starts to munch.*

*I look at her.*

*"Is there enough for two?" I say, holding my mouth open, lying on my back.*

*"I'm sorry, this is a single serving bowl."*

*I frown.*

*She frowns, too.*

*"Okay, fine, but you have to stay like that."*

*I open my mouth.*

*She digs up a spoonful and slowly lowers it down to my mouth. Tips it over. Most of it goes in, except a drop of milk that somehow makes its way into my nose.*

*I snort.*

*She laughs sheepishly.*

*"Oh babe, I'm sorry."*

*Wipes her hand on my nose, then leans and slurps the rest straight up from my nostril.*

*"Hey!"*

*"Everyone knows it's a felony to waste good Froot Loops. I'm saving us from jail time."*

"Good call," I say, sitting up.

She continues eating, legs up, bent at the knees. Her shape like a race-track, so many curves. I nudge over, rest my head against her chest.

"If you were stranded on a deserted island, and you only had one food, what would it be?" she asks.

I mull it over.

"Does beer count?"

"No."

"Okay," I say, tapping my finger against my nose in contemplation. "Honestly, I would pick something I didn't like. Because if I picked a food I did like, I would hate it after a while, and if I got off the island, I'd never be able to eat my favourite food again."

She looks unimpressed.

"I think you're overthinking this one."

"Okay, what would you bring?"

Looks at me, munching away, like I should know the answer already.

"Froot Loops?"

Keeps munching, staring at me.

"You know that would be two foods. Froot Loops and milk."

"You're ruining the game."

I smile, roll over. Big cat stretch across the sheets and pillows. My left rib cage is sore. The bruise on my side moans in pain whenever I twist my core.

"Ouch," I say.

Brianne looks down at the purple galaxy of blood beneath my skin. Gently places her hand on it, like she's trying to cover it from existence.

"Are you sure you're okay? I don't want you to die on our bed or something."

"I'll be fine. I'm just going to need bedside assistance for the better part of the day."

She puts the bowl down on the nightstand. Lies down, faces me. Her eyes, soft. Her smile, perfect.

This is the only place I'll ever want to be.

She speaks in a sensual tone, with a hint of sarcasm.

"And what kind of bedside assistance are you referring to, Mr. Schultz?"

I smirk.

*"Well, I dunno. I might need some physiotherapy sessions, you know, to work the muscles out."*

*She starts to run her finger across my shoulder blade.*

*Her iPhone vibrates on the nightstand, shaking the bowl of Froot Loops.*

*My smile dissipates. We stare at one another.*

*"Can you put it on silent?" I ask.*

*She rolls over, grabs it, rolls back.*

*Fingers dance, unlocking it. Starts tapping her nails against the screen.*

*Silence.*

*Then she starts scrolling down.*

*I sigh.*

*"I thought we agreed no phones for an hour?"*

*She keeps scrolling.*

*"Brianne?"*

*"Yeah," she says, breaking out of her trance. "Sorry, just checking something."*

</>

The storm is arriving. The rain has begun. Washing up in muggy waves from the ocean.

Thick winds.

We hole up in the house. Board up some of the windows facing the sea. We play Pictionary. Sean and I on one team, Liz and my father on the other. I try to draw a gorilla. Sean tells me it looks like a teddy bear with "fart problems". We laugh.

The thunder whirls in like an escalating siege. Sheet lightning imprints the skies. Crackles off in the distance.

Sean and I sit on the couch, watching. He's not scared of lightning, he says.

I ask him what he is scared of.

"I dunno, maybe like big spiders. I'm pretty tough."

My father holds Jessica, sitting on the couch while Liz and I make pizza in the kitchen. We sit around the dinner table, turning every time the sky lights up. I tell Sean to count the seconds after the thunder; that's how many miles away the lightning is.

Around midnight I put Sean to bed, his eyes droopy. He wanted to watch the storm for as long as he could. He sleeps in his own room, but I tell him if he gets scared tonight, he can come in and sleep with me.

"I'm tough," he says again. "I won't get scared."

"You don't get scared much, do you?" I say, a smirk on my face.

"Naw, I mean maybe one time I got scared, but it was an accident."

I can't help but laugh.

"So, tomorrow do you want to help with some of the cleanup? The Navy said they'll need lots of hands."

"Yeah," he says. "Then can we bike to the library again? I want to take that jump off the sidewalk by the burger place."

I smile.

"Yeah bud, for sure. We'll take that jump until our bums are sore."

He laughs.

"Okay goodnight, buddy."

"Goodnight, Tristan."

I close the door, head back to the living room. My dad, sitting in a chair with a beer. Facing the one unboarded window, watching the rain and lightning. The sky radiates with one clear colour, then blacks out.

It's the most beautiful of storms.

I head to the kitchen, grab a beer.

Sit in the chair beside him.

We watch the scene.

"How's Sean? Off to bed?"

"Yeah."

"You're doing good, giving that kid a chance. I'm proud of you."

I nod. A vein of lightning runs across the landscape. Thunder pulses against the glass, a glorious foundation shaking boom.

I'm thinking back to the night in the hotel when we watched the aurora borealis. When my father told me we would atone for our sins.

"I can't get this word out of my head," he says.

"What word is that?

"Fate."

"Fate?" I say.

"Yeah, got stuck on it a few weeks ago. I keep going back to it."

"Huh, why do you think that word?"

"I dunno. I'm sure it doesn't mean anything. It never does."

"Like getting a song stuck in your head?"

A monstrous boom vibrates the glass. Rod of lightning crashes down into the black sea, kicking up white froth. I stretch in my chair, hold my beer off to the side, exhausted.

He speaks. This time it doesn't feel out of turn.

"Tristan?"

I look over to signal I'm giving him my full attention.

"That night, that night your mother died."

He's staring forward, out the window. A million miles.

He stops.

Looks at me, looks back.

"Tristan, that night your mother died."

I stop him.

I'm gonna stop him this time.

After all the years of no communication, words won't be needed.

We're speaking in silence.

Finally computing.

"I know," I say.

He looks at me. Startled.

"It's okay," I say. "It's okay now."

I knew.

I know.

I've always known.

Sometimes we just force ourselves not to think about things.

The hills don't roll here. They're like small waves at best.
Endless fields of dusty, dry sage.
Middle of the continent.
Slippery mud hard and crusted across the path after rainfall.

I'd never been happier to be stuck in a torrential downpour. We ended up sleeping in the back of the pickup, beautiful $H_2O$ washing dust from the rusted metal. No electrical storms or acid rain. Just water, for once.

I pull my binoculars up, scan the horizon. We've been tracking a herd of bison for two days now. Lost them earlier this morning. They got spooked by a hawk protecting a nest and headed west. Too far from the pickup to give chase, we headed back, tracked their footprints.

The group getting thin, stragglers not even thick enough with meat to throw in the back of the truck. The animals have stopped eating the grass for some reason. We're not sure if it's the weather, or something else. Tracking the seasons became impossible a few winters back—our best bet was they'd lost their internal compass of when to slim for mating and when to bulk up for fall.

Either way, it wasn't a good sign.

I step up a small hill, panorama of clouds into full vision. Hiking boots dig into the earth, M40 scope sniper rifle across my back. Hunting knife in its holder digs into my thigh as I adjust and turn a full 360 degrees. Run my hand through my beard, adjust my baseball cap.

Discarded rattlesnake skin by my feet.

If we couldn't catch up to the herd by nightfall, we'd have to head back to the base.

Off the edge of the hill a prairie dog pops his head up, stares straight at me, arms and fingers curled. I contemplate shooting him for lunch, but don't want to spook the herd if they're still within earshot.

My leg starting to swell. Middle age passing me by, an old dog limping across a front porch. I look around one last time.

Whistle, two fingers in my mouth.

Nothing.

Whistle again.

"Yeah!" yells a deep voice. "Dad, over here!"

I turn south, back down the muddy road where we parked the truck.

Off to the right there's another hill. He must be behind it.

I start to walk. Sage crunches between the soles; mud sinks into the boots. I'm due for a new pair, but couldn't find any in my size at the base. We'll probably have to drive to the city in the next week or so to scavenge for supplies anyway. Too many mouths to feed, and not enough fresh food. Lost the gardens in a brush fire, blazed through and took an acre's worth of crops in the blink of an eye.

I make my way over the crest. Car comes into view where the dirt road ends. Front door open. Faded and rusted from years of neglect.

"Dad, come here. Look at this."

Sean pulls his muscular frame out of the front seat of the car, holding something up. His blonde hair falls across his forehead. He's eye level with me. But I still have a good fifteen pounds on him.

He adjusts the rifle slung around his back, holsters his Colt pistol, holding something up. I can't make it out. I need glasses but haven't been able to find a new pair that work.

"What is it?"

He holds it forward as I come close.

Look down to see a human skeleton beside the car.

"I dunno, it's old though."

Black square, about the size of a wallet.

A Blackberry. Little keyboard dusted to shit.

"It's a Blackberry," I say, a grin developing.

Sean turns it to himself, perplexed.

"A phone?" he says.

"Yeah, cellular phone. Shit, I used to have one."

Hands it to me. I dust off the screen.

A previous life floods back. I hold it with two hands, thumb-nails ready to type.

"You used to have one of those?" he says, smiling. "Really? What the fuck?"

I smile.

"Yeah, ages ago. Shit, it was even this model. Last phone I had before The Disconnect."

Sean watches me flood with memories. Old days so long ago it's as if they aren't even my life anymore. Washed away by the years, replaced by a new way of living.

Times, places, events I thought I'd long since forgotten return. Knock on the door of my brain, asking for admittance.

A past feeling returns. One that stops me in my tracks, forces me to vault back for a moment. A person I once knew, someone close to me.

"You okay, Dad?"

I break from my trance.

"Yeah. I'm good."

"Thinking about something?"

"Memories. You know how it is."

Sean nods.

I toss the phone back into the open door of the car. Grass has crawled up the wheels, into the seats. The inside littered with prairie dog shit.

Sean turns, looks west.

"I bet if we head over that rise there, we might be able to see which way they went," he says.

"Why would they head over that rise?" Quizzing him.

"Well, they'd be moving in asymmetric patterns now, with the sun's placement."

I nod. He's learning.

"That's a better answer than the trap you built this morning," I say with a smirk.

"Oh fuck off."

Prairie dog running away from our campsite, a wooden stick stuck through its belly. Had a good laugh as Sean tried to chase it down a hill. It managed to squeeze into a hole, gone forever.

I pat him on the shoulder.

"It's okay. I remember my first trap."

He lets out a sarcastic grunt.

"Let's head back to the truck," I continue. "You drive, okay? This is your call."

He nods.

"If not, we head back to base for nightfall. We're out of beer and I won't stay out here too long without that, it's sacrilegious."

Sean nods.

Pick up the lantern Sean's been carrying. Follow him to the truck.

The clouds roll across the plains, slow as ever. Overhead, a hawk squeals.

Heaven has never felt so far away. Left at the heels for a more promising galaxy, alone with our own devices. A fortuitous time, and trying era, a planet now ghostlike in existence, forever forgotten in the corner of the universe. We exist simply as an entity, no right or wrong, but then again, no expectations to weigh us down.

Lines ascend in groups of parallel pulses. Pulling away in cascading intervals, white noise slowly overtaking the distinguishable. Analog murmurs, monochromatic colours with a hard pulse overtop. Blank screens, endless feedback in a language nobody speaks. Gone is the idyllic landscape of nature, replaced with cracked asphalt, stained oil patches and suffocating weeds trying to eek through the cracks.

SMPTE colour bars the only message now. Accompanied by an endless tone.

The mud still seeps into my boots. Crusted into my legs as I walk.

I watch the sun start to set across the horizon.

Another starless night.